Praise for *Girl Last Seen*

'Every good thriller has a shocking plot twist. *Girl Last Seen*
...ery first page, *Girl Last Seen* jettisons the reader into the life of
a crime victim trying to outrun her past. Fast-paced and hard-
edged, it is a heart-stopping thriller that had me guessing to the
very end.' Heather Gudenkauf, *New York Times* bestselling author

'This debut novel is a gritty thriller with dark twists
you won't see coming. The heartbreaking, heartracing
journey . . . will keep you guessing to the nail-
biting end.' TheSuspenseIsThrillingMe.com

'*Girl Last Seen* gripped me from start to finish. Laine Moreno
is a riveting heroine, a kidnapping survivor who will only
escape her demons if she faces her greatest fears, and Nina
Laurin brings her vividly to life. Psychological suspense doesn't
come much grittier or more packed with satisfying twists
and turns.' Meg Gardiner, Edgar Award–winning author

ALSO BY NINA LAURIN

What My Sister Knew

The Starter Wife

GIRL
LAST
SEEN

NINA LAURIN

MULHOLLAND
BOOKS
HODDER

First published in the United States in 2017 by Grand Central Publishing
An imprint of Hachette Book Group Inc.

First published in Great Britain in 2019 by Mulholland Books
An imprint of Hodder & Stoughton
An Hachette UK company

1

A CIP catalogue record for this title is available from the British Library

Paperback ISBN 978 1 529 35874 2
eBook ISBN 978 1 529 35875 9

Printed and bound in Great Britain by Clays Ltd, Elcograf S.p.A.

Hodder & Stoughton policy is to use papers that are natural, renewable
and recyclable products and made from wood grown in sustainable forests.
The logging and manufacturing processes are expected to conform to the
environmental regulations of the country of origin.

Hodder & Stoughton Ltd
Carmelite House
50 Victoria Embankment
London EC4Y 0DZ

www.hodder.co.uk

GIRL LAST SEEN

PROLOGUE

ELLA

The night is so bright it hurts her eyes. She's used to the dark ceiling, always unchanging and so low she could barely stand up straight, so the night sky is blinding. She's used to the tomb-like silence of the basement, and all the soft sounds of the night assault her eardrums, set her teeth on edge. She fights the urge to shut her eyelids and press her hands over her ears. She stumbles on along the edge of the road, even though tiny bits of gravel sink into the soles of her feet with every step.

She's no longer used to walking. Her weakened muscles tremble with the effort of every step. Every gust of wind chills the scalded skin of her exposed arms and legs, and when a big icy drop lands in the middle of her forehead, she jumps. Other drops pitter-patter all around her as the air grows colder and damper; she shivers. Rain, she remembers, straining to retrieve the word from the foggy recesses of her memory. This is rain. It's nothing to be afraid of, just water from the sky.

The memory of buckets of water being dumped over her head, flooding her nose and mouth as she tries to scream, jolts her nerve endings. As the rain turns from a drizzle to one endless sheet of icy water, her legs buckle. She barely feels the stab of gravel on her knees. She has time to break her fall with her outstretched hands, and she stares at them, bewildered. There's no rope, no chain. Instead, thick bands of scars circle her wrists, still crusted with scabs in some places.

In a stupor, she can't look away from them.

Her hands. Her hands are free.

A whimper escapes from her, lost in the hiss of water on pavement. Even when she hears the car through the noise of the rain, even when the headlights blind her and when the car pulls over and stops next to her, she can't bring herself to look away from her hands.

She has no more strength to fight.

Fighting never did her any good anyway.

Steps crunch across the gravel. Someone leans over her, momentarily shielding her from the downpour. "Girl. Are you all right?"

She wishes she could answer, but she's not sure she has a voice anymore. Maybe it died months ago and she never knew. She'd like to answer, but she's afraid of finding out.

"How did you get out here?"

She hears more steps and another voice. "Sean, dammit. Look at her."

"Yeah, I see."

"No, I mean look at her." A string of curse words. "I'm calling for backup."

"We should bring her into the car," says the first voice. It's different from the other one. Smoother. Soothing. Filled with an emotion she thought she had forgotten a long time ago.

"No," says the other one. "Don't touch her. I'm calling an ambulance."

"Are you out of your mind? It's pouring. Her teeth are clattering. I'm going to get her into the car, and then you can call a dozen ambulances if you want."

"Protocol, Sean," the other voice says. He sounds angry, and a rush of terror makes her curl in on herself, pressing her forehead into her knees. It never helped, but for some reason, she keeps doing it.

"Fuck protocol," the first voice snaps back. "Look at her, dammit. She has no shoes. She's bleeding."

Finally, she raises her head just a little and squints. Red and blue lights are flashing through the curtain of rain. Red, blue, red, blue, red, blue. It's beautiful, she thinks. It's been a while since she's seen that much color. It makes her want to cry, although it could just be rain getting into her eyes.

She tries to remember what a white-and-blue car with red and blue lights means but can't.

There's a rustle, and someone kneels next to her. She quickly presses her forehead back into her knees.

"Sweetheart," says the voice. It's the first voice, the good voice. "Sweetheart, are you all right?"

"Sean," barks the bad voice in the background.

"Fuck off, Murphy. She's just a little girl."

She looks up, blinks away the rain, and sees him for the first time, only for a second before rainwater floods her vision. He has wide, dark, almond-shaped eyes, and they're filled with concern and worry and sadness.

And something inside her just tears, and an eternity's worth of sobs spill out all at once. She collapses, and he has no choice but to catch her before she hits the gravel again, his arms warm and dry and—and safe.

She had long forgotten what it feels like to be safe.

She barely hears the other voice cursing behind them, and she's lost to her pain, to her grief, and to his warm presence, so she nearly misses him saying:

"Dammit, it's that girl. The missing girl. Ella Santos."

CHAPTER ONE

LAINE, PRESENT DAY

Normal is something you can fake really well, if you try hard enough. You have to start by convincing yourself, and everyone else will follow, like sheep over a cliff. You act as normal as possible; you go through the motions. That veneer of normalcy may be tissue-paper thin, but you'll soon find out that no one is in any hurry to scratch the surface, let alone test it for weak spots. You can go through your entire life like this, from one menial action to the next, never breaking the pattern, and no one will be the wiser. At least, that's what I'm counting on.

The day I see Olivia Shaw for the first time, I know it's not going to last much longer.

Usually, I get to the grocery store at seven and leave at two, either to go for a run or to nap until my shift starts at my second job. At least two runs a week, usually three, and when I don't go between shifts, I go in the morning, getting up early. When I told this to another cashier, she said she wished she had my discipline, and I nodded along because what are you supposed to say to that? Since then, I try not to talk to people much about anything I do outside of work. I've had this job for almost six months now, which is a long time for me, and soon it'll become strange that I don't socialize.

That girl isn't here today. I haven't seen her in a while; maybe the manager changed her shift, maybe she got fired—I don't know. The manager is Charlene, and she looks like a Charlene, orthopedic shoes and perm and eternal frosty lipstick in a shade that should have been discontinued back in 1989. I suppose she thinks of herself as some sort of mother hen figure, but I noticed the look she gave me when I came in fifteen minutes late. The air outside is like breathing a swimming pool, and my hair is frizzing, stubbornly curling despite being racked with hot tools only an hour ago. I'm still cold and clammy even though I changed into my uniform, the purple shirt with the store logo over my right boob, my name printed underneath: LAINEY M., the M. because I'm not the only Lainey here; the chubby girl who had so innocently tried to be my friend was Lainey R. Still is, I guess, if maybe not at this store. That was her icebreaker: *Oh look, we have the same name—what are the odds?* I didn't tell her no one calls me Lainey, no one important anyway.

It doesn't matter. I didn't even choose the name for

myself. They picked it at random at the hospital, some soap opera heroine's first name and a generic surname to go with it. As common and unremarkable as possible. Hiding me in plain sight—that was the rationale.

And it worked, the hiding thing, at least until today. Today, Charlene the manager pushes a slim stack of the usual flyers for me to put up beside the double glass doors of the entrance and exit. I'm still a little slow, and I take them, automatically, forgetting that it's not Sunday and I just did that, the specials for the week: ground beef, three ninety-nine a pound; condensed cream of tomato, three for four dollars. Only when my gaze slips down do I see what they are, and my brain grinds to a halt.

It's nothing unusual. Nothing that hasn't happened before, twice, in the time I've worked in this store. One was the six-year-old boy who was found a week later, whose dad skipped town in defiance of shared guardianship, the other the elderly woman who disappeared in the neighborhood and was feared to have killed herself. No one knows what happened to her, least of all me, except one day I came into work and the poster was gone, replaced by more of the weekly specials, by cantaloupes and broccoli and store-brand chips. For all I know, she did kill herself. But she's not the kind of missing person who interests me.

But today, I look down at the stack of papers in my hands and I see her, Olivia Shaw, age ten.

It's a typical Seattle PD missing-person poster, with

the neat columns of stats underneath. The original picture must have been high quality, full color, but the printer was running out of ink, so the colors bleed into one another like one of those Polaroid photos.

Olivia Shaw has been missing since last Tuesday. She was last seen outside the entrance of her elementary school in Hunts Point wearing a white spring jacket and pink boots. My brain registers the information on autopilot, searing every word into my memory, and in the meantime, a part of me is distantly, methodically, checking off the items one by one. Like pieces of a kaleidoscope, they all click together.

If you have any knowledge of Olivia Shaw's whereabouts, or any relevant information, please contact...

Images surface in my mind moments before dissolving into black dust, like a dream I'm trying to remember. I spent a long time in the last ten years peering into the faces of girls on missing-person posters, wondering which one replaced me in the basement. But they were never quite the right age, the right look, the right circumstances. Until Olivia Shaw, age ten, missing for one week tomorrow.

From my many sleepless nights of research, I know that most kidnapping victims are dead within forty-eight hours.

You were lucky, Ella.

I force myself to look at the face in the photo, into her slightly smudged features, and I can't bring myself to move.

Olivia Shaw could be my mirror image, rewound to thirteen years ago. She has a wild halo of dark curls around her head—like mine, when I don't torture them into submission with a hot iron. Dark skin, like mine. Her eyes—I can't distinguish the color from the blurry pixels of the poster, but the description says they're gray.

The sound of my name, my other, new name, takes a while to reach me inside my bubble. It's my boss. It feels like my spine has turned to brittle stone, and my neck might snap if I turn my head too fast. I register confusion on her face.

"The tape," she says, blinking her sparse, mascara-clotted eyelashes.

The tape? Right. The tape. Without realizing I'm doing it, I scratch the inside of my wrist under my sleeve. Charlene holds out the clear Scotch tape, her expression shifting closer and closer to annoyance. It takes five steps to cross the distance between us so I can reach out and take the tape from her hand. Doing this, my sleeve rides up and my wrist bone pops out of the fitted cuff. Her eyes flicker to it for just a fraction of a second, the same way people sneak a glimpse of disfigured faces: staring without staring, looking away with such intensity you wish they'd just glare outright, get their fix of the morbid, and get it over with. I can't wear fingerless gloves here; "accessories" aren't allowed by the dress code. So I've developed a habit of always tugging my sleeves down, a tic that persists outside of this place too.

Probably not the worst habit to have, all things considered.

The sound of tape peeling off the roll raises the hairs on my arms, and I hold the poster in place as I tape its corners to the glass outside the entrance, taking too much care to make sure it's perfectly straight. As if that will help her. I know it's all an excuse for me to reread the text, examine the photo, burn it all into my retinas forever and ever and ever. To add Olivia Shaw to my ever-expanding mental collection of the disappeared. Except a part of me already knows one of these things isn't like the others.

The automatic doors of the entrance hiss open as I pass through, my muscles humming with tension. "Charlene," I hear myself say, "I'm going to go for a smoke."

She says something about opening the store in five minutes, but I won't take longer than that. I'm already on my way out, patting down my pockets before the door has a chance to slide aside and let me out, wondering what I did with my emergency pack of smokes. It might be in the pocket of my jacket, which is in the back of the store, stuffed in the shoe box–sized locker in the employees' lounge. Too bad. I don't think a cigarette will do it for me right now anyway. Instead, I take my phone out of my pocket, stare at the screen until it blurs, key in the code and screw it up three times until it unlocks. Open the browser and start feverishly typing in the search window.

Another thing I know from my late-night Internet forays: kidnappers, rapists, serial killers—they don't just stop one day. They are stopped. Whoever stole me—stole Ella—was never found. But in the last ten years, there hasn't been another girl.

And now there is.

CHAPTER TWO

In the books and movies, the broken girl always dies at the end. Sometimes she's allowed one final heroic act, one last snarky line before she goes out. Maybe she sacrifices herself to save the real hero, or maybe her death is just a meaningless accident, an afterthought. But she always dies, because she's too tarnished to live.

Every time I see her die, I'm jealous. That should have been me, a long time ago.

It would have been better for everybody if I had just died, like they presumed I had—for years before I was found. Especially for me, the nameless, voiceless creature that was born out of Ella Santos's remains, an abomination. A living dead girl.

They had to give this voiceless creature, this Frankenstein's monster covered in scars and stitches, a new name at random because the creature couldn't speak to pick one for herself. The most I ever had the where-withal to do was drop that last *y* from Lainey, turning it into Laine, one syllable. Sounds like something you'd find on a highway.

I will probably never know what exactly glitched in my kidnapper's mind that made him decide to take a risk, to allow me to live. I've never given up wondering, though. And I never could quite let go of the suspicion that some nameless force in the universe was saving me for something even worse.

Now, as my sneakers rhythmically hit the pavement, the shock of impact thudding in my bone marrow, I can't help but wonder if this is it.

I was spared so I could do something, help the next one. And a darker thought: I was spared so that I could watch it all happen again, unable to do anything about it.

I focus on the burning in my lungs, the steady fire kindling in my leg muscles, but it's not enough to keep my thoughts from drifting to the thing burning in my pocket, folded up next to my phone in half, then fourths, then eighths, until the layers of paper refused to bend. Charlene gave me four posters to put up, but only three are still there, next to the flashy yellow flyers advertising a discount on whole chickens. Charlene is of an exacting nature, just like everything about her suggests, and she will probably notice, but hopefully, she won't think it's me. She'll think one of the shoppers decided to snatch it off the wall and keep it for some unknown reason.

I catch myself with my hand in my pocket like a thief, when it's too late. The thick folded edge of the poster brushes the back of my hand, and to distract myself, I take out my phone instead and check the screen. Nobody ever calls me, and I'm not on any social media, unlike pretty much everyone my age. No one expressly told me to stay off it—it's just an ingrained instinct too strong to go against: the instinct to hide.

The first thing I see is the missed call, followed by the new voice mail alert. How did I not hear it? My heart lurches, and it has nothing to do with the exertion wringing my smoker's lungs. Another bit of ingrained knowledge: missed calls, and especially voice mails, are never good news. Fighting the tremor in my hands, I dial my voice mail and groan inwardly as the phone recites the date and time with agonizing slowness. A hiss, a snap of static, and then a familiar voice floods into my ear, heavy with its nasal accent, and a sweet balm of relief spills in my chest even though my heart hasn't gotten the memo yet and keeps hammering. It's my coworker from my second job. I didn't recognize the number because she's calling from the one ancient pay phone at work, the one they keep there for God only knows what reason. I'm so overcome with that feeling of having gotten away with something that I forget to even get mad about what she's asking. They need me to come in early, because so-and-so didn't show up. I hang up without waiting for the message to play to the end.

It means no time to take a nap beforehand, which

is just as well because it's not like I'll be able to sleep now. But I had other plans for these two hours, plans that will have to wait until the end of the night—which, right now, might as well be in a hundred years. Ever since I saw Olivia Shaw looking at me from that poster, time shifted. It's no longer an ephemeral thing that trickles away while I look on with indifference. It feels voluntary, as if I forgot how to breathe and have to consciously pull and push every gulp of oxygen into my lungs if I don't want to suffocate.

Up in my apartment, I lock the door behind me and slide on the chain even though I'll be out again in under an hour, which leaves me just enough time to get ready. This is why I need the second job, sacrificing sleep and sanity, because I need this place. Living with roommates didn't work out so great—surprise, surprise—and it's impossible to get an apartment in this city on a single cashier's pay. Even a shitty apartment like this one, on the worst street in the worst neighborhood. And I don't just have to pay rent. I'm a twenty-three-year-old female who needs makeup and clothes and sometimes even jewelry, though my options are somewhat restricted here.

And other things.

I didn't do such a bad job making this place homey. It may be three hundred square feet, but every inch is mine. I have furniture from Goodwill and the great free market that is the curb on moving day: a narrow desk so old it verges on antique and a chair that almost matches it. The apartment has a built-in counter too small to eat on, so the desk doubles as a dining table. I have a cute little nightstand from IKEA. Well, not *from* IKEA but I think it's IKEA. Someone tossed it out because a corner is chipped, exposing the cheap plywood underneath. I don't have a bed frame but I have a decent mattress on the floor—the bed frame is going to be my next big splurge. Depending on how I'll make it through the next hours-days-weeks. Whether or not I can keep reminding myself to breathe at reliable intervals.

I'm sweaty and consider jumping in the shower but reject the idea. I don't feel like being naked right now. So I run a towel under the tap and rub it in my armpits and across my chest, under my grocery-store sweatshirt. The water hardly makes the cloth less scratchy, and I feel like someone scrubbed me down with steel wool. When I pull the sweatshirt over my head, I realize my chest is covered with little splotches that will hopefully fade by the time I get to work.

The dress code at my second job is fairly simple, no uniforms—they either can't afford them or just don't care. You can wear what you want, but whatever it is it has to be white. The girls complain about the color, so unforgiving of spills and nearly transparent under black lights, but I think it adds an illusion of curves to my streamlined body, which helps with the tips. My two identical work dresses are cheap polyester, twenty dollars after the discount at one of the fast-fashion chains, but they have an appealing plunging neckline and the skirt hits midthigh.

Next, boots, knee-high with thick heels and blunt toes that boost my height by a couple of inches but are still comfortable enough, considering I have to be on my feet all night. I own lots of boots of all shapes, forms, and colors—boots are kind of my thing, although not entirely by choice. The other alternative is high-top sneakers, and I hate those. I never wear stiletto heels, and no sandals either, even in summer. Or ballet flats or those trendy platform Mary Janes with the delicate ankle strap.

Girls with scar rings around their ankles don't have many options. Some asshole I made the mistake of hooking up with still tells everyone I fuck with my boots on.

On my arms, fingerless gloves that go up to the elbow, and on top of that, three bracelets on each arm. Foundation, concealer under my eyes, eyebrow pencil, a touch of highlighter on my brow bones and in the Cupid's bow of my top lip, a beauty routine out of a women's magazine. I have a plain face without makeup, except for my big, brown eyes that some love-struck fool in another life might have called soulful, and I know how to play them up. I line my eyes with heavy strokes of dark-blue kohl, a little silver in the inner corners. Gobs of gloss on my lips, darkening their natural color to that of dried blood. Lastly, I pump the mascara brush in the scuffed tube that I really need to replace, if I can spare the ten bucks. The effect is clumpy, but I doubt anyone will notice in the dark.

Almost ready. I check my phone; I have just enough time, and the traffic usually goes the other way at this hour. The grocery-store sweatshirt is still where I left it on the bathroom floor, a puddle of cheery purple-pink, and I dive after it to get my keys and wallet out of the pocket only for the poster to fall out, landing at my feet.

My heartbeat thuds dully in the back of my throat as I retrieve it, unfold it, and smooth it out on the kitchen counter. With my fingertip, I trace the smooth, round outline of her face, the one ringlet of curls that springs off to the side, escaping from the elastic of her ponytail.

If you have any knowledge of Olivia Shaw's where-abouts, or any relevant information, please contact...

I should call the number, the thought crosses my mind. I even begin to reach for my phone. Call the number and say what? Everything's been said many years ago, and much good it did to anyone.

Before the temptation can become too strong, I grab the poster off the counter and race across the room to my bed by the window. Careful not to look at it, I lift up the mattress and slide the poster underneath, on top of the pile of printouts, folded yellowed newspaper pages, and other posters, weathered by time and faded by rain, that I collected all over the city over the years. Olivia Shaw is part of my collection now. As long as I can keep her there, maybe she'll stay out of my thoughts. Maybe her face won't flash in front of my eyes every time I blink, like it's been tattooed on the inside of my eyelids.

Enough. I'm running late. I put my wallet and my

phone into the pocket of my pleather jacket then remember something and open the drawer of my nightstand. Grab the folding knife that sits there, under a pile of year-old tabloid magazines with frayed covers. Put it in my pocket, next to the phone and wallet.

Every single night I leave my apartment, I secretly hope I'll need it. But I never do.

CHAPTER THREE

The night shift is already starting by the time I get to the Silver Bullet Gentlemen's Club. A few of the day girls shuffle past me, sweatpants tucked into UGG knock-offs, duffels slung over shoulders. The other barmaid, an Eastern European former stripper who goes by Chloe but whose real name is Natalia-something, is already behind the bar, waving to me, and by the somewhat desperate smile that flashes yellow under black lights, I know I'm in trouble with the boss.

Natalia is as close as I have to a friend. We've gone out after work a couple of times, and I've been to her place once or twice—it's nicer than you'd expect, a two-bedroom house she's renting on the outskirts of town. Or maybe she owns it, something to show for her time in the Lucite heels—and it must be a long time, even though I never asked her outright. Her face is smooth as an egg, helped by makeup plus injectables in her lips and already prominent cheekbones, her hair bleached till it glows and stuffed full of keratin extensions, so it's thicker than mine. But that difference of a decade or two is there between us, intangible but present, like the heavy scent of her department-store perfume. She always tells me I'd do much better as a stripper, that I'm wasting my good years breaking my back at a cash register and behind a bar when I should be on the other side of it, making hundreds. I considered it. Flexible schedule, good money, and I could just wear those dominatrix boots to cover my ankle scars, plus some arm bands— like the girls with the drug problems, the kind that require needles. And the belly scar, well, there's much worse here, and I could cover it with makeup if I wanted to. Natalia's own C-section scar is almost as bad, and it's another thing I never brought up—don't ask, don't tell.

I'm not exactly a prude, but I've always told her the job just wasn't for me. It's a line I don't want to cross, for the time being.

Speaking of which, I should probably go kiss up to the boss while I still have a job. But I can't bring myself to care; it seems unreal, like I'm thinking about some show I watch on TV every night, not my own life. What is real, however, is the ghostly face from the photo on that poster. Olivia Shaw. Age ten. Last seen...

A part of me wonders if I'm just imagining things. Latching on to random details and weaving them together with nothing more than desperation. But something about the way she stared at me from that poster sent a shiver through me, like a drop of ice beneath the skin. Like she was the one searching for me, not the other way around.

Great. Maybe I'm coming unglued, finally, like everyone seems to think I will someday. I'm starting to think exactly like those psychos. *It's the way she was looking at me, Mr. Judge, sir. I read it in her eyes and couldn't help myself.*

I'm sure someone, somewhere, has all my Internet searches on file, but I learned all about these things. Deviations, delusions, dehumanization. Whenever a girl goes missing, any age, they always have the relatives on TV, imploring the nameless audience to please help them bring their loved one back. Hoping against hope it'll work.

Search as I might, I couldn't find a single instance when it actually *had* worked. Maybe that's why I don't feel so bad that no one cried on TV when I went missing, because it's not like it ever helped anyone.

No one knows the exact date I disappeared, least of all me. They've established a weeklong window, and even that is approximate.

Just like one of those psychos, my mind won't let it go. Like a child who stubbornly peels away a half-healed scab, I insist on prodding myself in all my tender spots, deliberately pulling every trigger—and I never had any shortage of those. Not for the last ten years anyway. Almost half my life. I roll the details around in my achy brain until it's raw, until my hands are shaky and the beer I'm about to slide across the counter nearly slips from my grip, slick with condensation.

Two more people settle at the bar just as I turn around. They look at me like I've been muttering something out loud without realizing it, and a new rush of paranoia overtakes me. I lean in and ask them what they're drinking.

One looks young and kind of shifty; the other must be in his late thirties, and his weathered skin has a darker cast to it. Not unlike mine. Puerto Rican? I wonder. Cuban? I can't see his face clearly because he's half-hidden in shadow, but something about it, about the angle of his jaw, looks familiar. The two of them seem to be together, except he's dressed a lot nicer than his buddy, who's in a weathered hockey jersey that hangs off his skinny shoulders like a rag. No, this one has a jacket. A nice jacket. Where would I know someone who has a jacket this nice? Must be wool or something, so black that it seems to draw the light in. And his scarf is embarrassingly fashionable. Either he has a wife who picks these things out for him or he swings the other way. Which, since he's sitting in a titty bar, is unlikely, but you never know.

The shifty one orders an alcohol-free beer. Heh, maybe Nice-Jacket-guy does swing the other way, and he's here with his DL lover—either as cover for an illicit meeting or for some kind of twisted thrill. I bare my teeth in a smirk before I realize I'm doing it and tell him we don't have any of that.

Could be just me, but the one in the nice jacket chuckles. Without batting an eyelash, Shifty asks for a Coke. I want to cheekily specify if it's diet—we don't have that either, it's unmanly or something, but Nice Jacket measures me with a glance, and the words die somewhere halfway up my throat. As I turn to get the Coke from the fridge, I can feel him looking.

Enough people stare at me every night, even when I can't motivate myself to doll up. Monday-night patrons aren't picky—they'll ogle anything—but this one skipped right over the part where he undresses me with his eyes, and instead, he seems to be x-raying my skull. The hairs on the back of my neck stand up, and I can't spin around fast enough. I scoop cloudy half-melted ice cubes with a glass and slide it across, along with the damn Coke.

It's Nice Jacket who puts the ten-dollar bill on the counter, holding it down with his fingertips as I reach for it. And I don't want to touch his hand. Creep. Damn creep.

Well, he's about to find out that it takes more than a wool jacket to intimidate me. I make myself meet his gaze and let my professional smile drop from my face. I learned this one from the dancers, and it works miracles. In no uncertain terms, it says pay up, buddy, and stop fucking around.

He takes his hand off the tenner. I'm about to slam

my palm down on the crumpled piece of paper when he says, curtly and simply, "Lainey. Lainey Moreno?"

His voice.

My hand hovers. I look up and meet his electric glare. Already, something within my mind is curling like black smoke, solidifying, taking shape. But before I can put the picture together, he leans in and speaks.

"Lainey, I'm Detective Ortiz with the Seattle PD. I . . ."

Whatever doubt I might still have had evaporates. It's not a lightbulb going off in my mind—unless the lightbulb explodes with a zap and crackle and a burst of tiny, deadly shards. Something alien takes control of my limbs, an animal instinct that's only kicked in once or twice before. I don't think. I just turn around and flee through the narrow staff door at the other end of the bar.

The shifty guy yells *holy shit*. A girl shrieks. Without glancing over my shoulder, I hear the clatter of a barstool and know that Nice Jacket is leaping right over the bar, going after me.

The door swings shut behind me. I wish there were a latch, but even if there had been, my hands are shaking too much. The storage room is blindingly dark, boxes and crates tower on all sides, and for a moment, I think I might be able to hide—to curl up in some corner and be still and quiet until it's over.

Then the door clangs open and the dim reddish light from the club pours in. I spin around and keep going, maneuvering through the maze of boxes. I hear him on my trail, surprisingly light footfalls that drown in the sound of my blood rushing in my ears. He trips over something, curses under his breath. Seizing the moment's chance, I dive for the door, for the delivery entrance that leads outside into the alley behind the club.

Cool air envelops me, coating my overheated skin with a mucky, polluted dew. My breath rises up in billows of steam so thick they obscure my vision. Overhead lights blur and pixelate as I draw humidity into my lungs and run, splashing through the puddles.

My boots are dead weights at my ankles. Within seconds, I'm out of breath, and at the same time, I feel as much as hear him behind me, getting closer.

All the while, even as he inevitably catches up to me, as he grabs the back of my dress, I wonder why the hell I ran.

I have nothing to hide. I didn't do anything wrong.

A cry bursts from my lips as he pulls me backward. My feet slip on the wet pavement, and I topple, twist, and land on my side. Mud splashes the side of my face and the impact knocks the breath out of me.

He twists my arm behind me until I howl.

"Lainey," he says. I can't see his face. At this angle, all I can see is an expanse of cracked, shiny-wet asphalt level with my eyes and looming brick walls above. But his voice. His voice cuts deep. I remember it, and right now it's brimming with reproach.

He loosens his grip but doesn't let go—at least my

shoulder is no longer screaming in pain—and the weight lifts off me so I can raise my head and breathe.

"Let go of me," I choke out. I've daydreamed of this moment so many times, back in the hospital, then in the psych ward, in the lonely, dark, scary moments, alone late at night. It was like a warm blanket over my shoulders: his face, his eyes, his voice. What I remembered of it anyway.

Not how I pictured our first—second—meeting. Not what I hoped my first words would be.

To my surprise, he lets go. I get up, pushing the asphalt away with my palms. My arms strain, threatening to snap like a couple of matchsticks. He clears his throat, and I realize he's holding out his hand. I look at my own palm, cold and clammy and coated in mud, and scramble to my feet by myself. My dress is a Rorschach pattern of mud splashes where I rolled on the asphalt, and snagged threads crisscross the fabric—fit for the garbage can.

"Why did you run?" He doesn't flinch from my gaze. He's gotten older, I realize with confusion. Of course he has. He's not some immortal angel. He's a human being of flesh and blood. Except to me, he was always so much more than that.

His hair—there are hints of gray around his temples. Maybe they were there ten years ago, and I was just too out of it to notice. His skin looks different, and there's scruff on his chin and jaw that I don't remember from last time. But his eyes are exactly as they were on the day he found me. I still have to tilt my head up to look into them.

"I'm a cop, Lainey. You shouldn't have run."

"I know who you are," I say.

"You do?"

It's a struggle not to let my emotions seep into my voice. "I remember you." I gulp. "Am I under arrest?"

"I don't know. Why did you run?"

I lower my head. My hair tumbles into my face.

"Do you know what this is about?"

"No," I lie.

"Look at me, Lainey."

"Laine," I say curtly.

"What?"

"Laine. No one calls me Lainey except my shrink."

I have no idea why I told him that. He's not the person I remember, not the person I imagined, and he's not here for me—this much I know. But he nods, like he gets it.

"Laine." Somehow it sounds better on his lips, softer. "Can you talk to me like a normal person now? I don't want to have to handcuff you."

His gaze drops to my hands before he can stop himself. I stare down at them too, twisting one of the bracelets around my right wrist. We look up at the same time, and his gaze locks on mine. I can't read it no matter how much I try; it's like staring into opaque, murky water.

"Depends," I say.

"Promise me you're not going to bolt."

I swallow the lump in my throat so I can speak. "If I get arrested, I could be in trouble. But you already knew that."

He exhales noisily. "I'm not going to arrest you. If, and only if, you talk to me. Hear me out and answer all my questions. For now, it's off the record. Let's keep it that way."

I let him assume my silence is a yes.

"Laine—" He catches himself at the last second. "This is about a missing-girl case."

I give a curt nod.

He says Olivia's name, slowly, his heavy, wary gaze not leaving my face. He's waiting for me to give myself away somehow.

"What about her?" My voice is thin and brittle.

"She's been missing for a week now. She's ten years old." He keeps watching me for a reaction, and I'm not about to give him one.

"Don't you care?"

"It has nothing to do with me," I choke out.

"Olivia Shaw was adopted."

I squeeze my eyes shut. My breathing is ragged, too fast, and the thundering of my own heartbeat fills my ears. I barely realize I'm grinding my jaw. "You're wasting your time. Why should I know anything?"

"Laine—she's your daughter."

CHAPTER FOUR

"She's not my daughter. She's Jacqueline Shaw's daughter."

I realize my slipup, too late to bite it back. Now he knows that I know. He knows I looked her up.

"You feel nothing for her? No sense of—"

Tears burn my eyes. I don't know how much time passes before I can speak again.

"What the fuck do you think I'm supposed to feel for her?"

The words are ugly, violent, and cruel. He winces, and I wish I could take them back, but at the same time, anger brims in my chest, suffocating. Crowding out the pain. What am I supposed to feel for the girl? For the child whose father kept me in a basement for three years, who—

A girl I haven't even held, not for a minute. I was

out, floating on a sea of anesthetic drugs, and when I woke up, she was already gone. She could have been adopted by the people next door or shipped away across the country or stillborn—I never would have known.

"I had nothing to do with it," I snarl. "So stop wasting your time."

I half expect him to do something, to say something. Or to slap me, maybe—I deserve it. But to my frustration and fury, he just patiently waits for me to finish.

"Well, I hate to disappoint you but the one and only time I ever saw her was on a missing-girl poster. Now will you please let me go?"

"I'm sorry," he says. "But I can't do that."

"I didn't try to steal her back," I say hoarsely. "If that's what you're wondering."

"I never said any such thing."

"What is it you think, then? Why are you here?" A part of me must already know the answer or at least guess at it, deep down. "What do you really want from me? Why did *you* show up, when it could have been anyone else? Why am I so important?"

"First, I'm the detective on this case. I wasn't going to send anyone else. Second . . . I wanted to talk to you off the record. I know about your situation. I didn't want to cause you trouble."

"Well, you already did. I'm probably going to lose my job now."

The silence in the alley is so intense that it crackles and hums like electricity. Even the soft thud of bass inside the club, separated from us only by a graffiti-covered brick wall, is nothing but white noise.

"I'm trying to tell you that the man who did this to you might have your biological daughter. And you don't care?"

Everything reels before my eyes. Shiny asphalt, brick, deep slate-gray sky almost indistinguishable from the rooftops. Blurry lights.

"How dare you say that to me." My tinny voice betrays the tears before they have a chance to spill out.

"I just want to know. Genuine curiosity."

I don't know what comes over me. My fist flies up, racing toward his face. In the back of my mind, I already know how badly I fucked up, but it's too late to stop.

Instead of blocking my arm or catching my wrist, he barely tilts his head. My knuckles just graze his jaw before my arm falls limply back at my side.

We stare at each other, me with terror and him with a strange glint in his dark eyes—almost like interest. The thin skin on my knuckles still burns from scraping against his stubble, the only sign that this really just happened. I don't try to run, just lower my head and hold out my hands, wrists up.

"Arrest me if you want to," I whisper.

"I'm not going to arrest you, Laine."

"Why not? I attacked you. I was uncooperative." The tears dry on my cheeks.

"I'm not here to screw up your life. All I want is to save Olivia's."

Something in my chest clenches as he holds out a card with something printed on it, an address, a phone number. Another number is written in blue ink below it.

"Come to the station tomorrow. We'll need you to make a statement about where you were the day she went missing." He must see me tense with mistrust, because he adds, "You're not under arrest, and no one's accusing you of anything. It's just routine stuff."

"And what if I don't?"

Only a puff of steam betrays his patient sigh. "You can reach me off the record on my cell," he says. "If you think of anything. Or if you just need to talk."

I take the card with my fingertips. "I will."

He walks away, never once looking back, and I realize he's absolutely certain I'll show up.

And, I suppose, so am I.

CHAPTER FIVE

Here's the thing about Sean Ortiz.

He was the first person I saw after three years in captivity. That was the first and last time I saw him until ten minutes ago. Sean Ortiz was a traffic cop back then. I wasn't his problem. It was sheer chance that he decided to pull over when he saw something strange through Seattle's eternal curtain of rain. All he had to do was call someone else, someone who could take me off his hands and deal with me.

He did, and they did. Some strange people in pale-green masks put me on a gurney, and the last thing I remember is an ambulance technician sticking a needle in my arm, cooing something reassuring like I was a dog he was putting to sleep.

I never saw Sean Ortiz after that. Not that I was surprised. I was certain he never even thought about me much.

But, boy, did I think about him.

I guess this is what my well-meaning shrink calls a coping mechanism—displaced affection, as she'd put it. But what I know is, when other girls my age were crushing on sparkly vampires and shaggy-haired musicians, I crushed on Sean Ortiz. Or at least the mental photograph I had of him, those few brief moments of pouring rain and flashing lights, the photograph that grew blurrier every year, like fading newsprint, until what I had left was closer to fantasy than reality.

It mattered little to me. Where my memory failed, my imagination filled in.

I wander back to the club, barely feeling my legs. It's like I'm floating aboveground. I don't feel much of anything, not the cold, not the pitter-patter of icy raindrops on my bare arms. I'm a shell of skin filled with heartbeat as I make my way to the storage area and slide down to a crouch behind a stack of boxes.

Rusted hinges screech, the door clatters open, and thundering steps grow closer. It's Dom, my boss. His giant shadow falls over me, but when I look up, he seems more concerned than angry. Although he has every right to be angry.

I bleat a useless apology.

"Forget it," he says, waving his tattooed arm. "Just tell me, honestly, are we about to get raided?"

I manage to make my head swivel on my neck, side

to side, feeling like one of those dashboard dogs. He slumps with a sigh of relief.

"Well then, what the fuck was that all about?"

"Nothing." I make a weak attempt at a smile but he doesn't look convinced. "Just tell me Sugar is around."

He scoffs. "Yeah, right. Sugar hauled ass as soon as he so much as heard the word *police*."

I curse under my breath. My teeth are starting to clatter.

"Go back to the bar," Dom says, frowning.

"In a minute."

He shrugs but leaves me alone.

Huddled between two cases of empty bottles in the freezing storage room, I reopen the tabs on my phone, every scrap of information on Olivia Shaw that I painstakingly bookmarked, every news article on every major news website. My hands shake so much I can barely manage the tiny touch-screen buttons.

This is what I already knew: Olivia Shaw, ten years old, vanished on her way home from school. Her parents are a rich couple, Tom and Jacqueline Shaw, nee Velasquez. They have a house in the chic neighborhood of Hunts Point, and Olivia went—goes, Olivia goes; don't think about her in the past tense—to the local school. No one knows how she could have slipped away.

It doesn't mention anywhere that she was adopted.

But the moment I saw Sean Ortiz at the bar . . . I just knew.

I knew it was her. She was mine.

That's bullshit—she was never mine. She has nothing to do with me. We belong to different worlds; our paths never crossed and never will.

Unless.

I squeeze my temples with the heels of my hands. I want to scream but can't find the sound within me. I think of Sean Ortiz, the first face I saw after years in captivity. The first person to speak to me. The first person to show me kindness in my whole miserable life.

The look in his eyes, back in the alley—I can't get it out of my head. The pity and dismay. The disappointment. He saw what a fucking mess I've become. He saw how broken I am.

I bite down on the inside of my lip and taste copper. Lots of copper, a handful of pennies, and I never felt a thing.

Shit. Tonguing the jagged tear in the lining of my mouth, I race to the employees' bathroom, a tiny cubicle of a room where I can barely stand up to my full height. The door is locked. I pull on the handle in disbelief, pound on the door, and give it a kick for good measure. Finally, Natalia's muffled voice curses and yells out for me to cool my fucking jets in that familiar accent. It's not the first time I see this happen; she didn't just get a sudden urge to pee the moment the police showed up, I'm sure. The toilet flushes, and Natalia emerges, pupils like inky saucers that become even bigger when she sees my face. She gets out of my way without a word.

I close the door behind me. My soles stick to the floor, and the stink of sewer mixed with industrial-strength cleaner fills my head. Leaning over the rusty sink, I run the tap, gargle with cold water, and then dab at my lip with some rolled-up toilet paper.

My hands shoot to my stomach, under the waist of my skirt and my underwear, and settle over the horizontal scar on my belly where they cut her out.

CHAPTER SIX

What do kidnappers, child molesters, serial killers, and other scum of the earth have in common?

I have many saved links on my phone, but it all boils down to this: they're like a puzzle missing a crucial piece. They may not all be psychopaths in the proper sense of the word, but there's some kind of glitch in their minds. It allows them to view their victims as something other than human, incapable of feeling and suffering. That, and they were usually abused as children as well—like some sick game of tag. Another thing my shrink would call a coping mechanism: one surefire way to get rid of pent-up anger and pain and torment is to inflict it on someone else.

At least that's the theory.

Whoever writes these Internet articles must have been

lucky never to find themselves in the same room with one of these people. Because I may not have any fancy letters tacked to my name—I may not even have finished high school—but I did spend three years studying one of them up close. And my theory is they do know I feel fear, and pain, and the same range of emotion everyone else does. They know it, or else why bother? Just make some kind of voodoo dummy; buy a blow-up doll if it's all the same. But no. It has to be a real person who lives, who breathes, who preferably screams and begs for her life.

And now Sean thinks I did it. Or at least that I had something to do with it, and who can blame him?

Paranoia fizzing in my veins, I'm distracted and clumsy, and after a drunk trucker nearly starts a fight because he thinks I shorted him on his change on purpose, Dom takes me aside and gives me the rest of the night off.

The first thing I do when I get home, before I even take off my boots, is grab my laptop and climb onto my bed. I log into a forum where I used to be a regular, ConspiracyTalk. It's not what you'd call a healthy and sane environment, and a few of the regular members might actually be even more messed up than I am, but I did spend a good five years there, on and off, posting as lostgirl14. The thread about my case—the case of Ella Santos, that is—runs about twenty pages and mostly consists of speculation. There are theories ranging from the disturbing—that I didn't identify my kidnapper on purpose because of Stockholm syndrome or some such thing—to the downright deranged. Lately, it's been buried under other, fresher stories with more readily available sordid details, but the first thing I see when I log on is a new thread titled *OLIVIA SHAW: Rich Girl Vanishes Without a Trace*. The members are posting at alarming rates, speculating their hearts out, but as I feverishly skim through the posts, I don't see anyone get close to the truly disturbing truth.

Roswell82: I bet it's something really simple. Maybe they killed her themselves by accident. Like JonBenet.

Mike6669: My guess is a ransom thing. Rich parents. Like sickeningly rich. I bet dirty money too, so someone was understandably pissed off…

Roswell82: Nah. I bet you anything the parents did it. Did u see that woman's pic in the Tribune article? Blouse was halfway open. Who puts her tits out when her damn child is missing?

Mike6669: Yeah I'd tap that.

It doesn't take long to find the article in question. The text itself is only two scant paragraphs, but the photo is huge, taking up half the screen. Her blouse isn't halfway open, of course. It's a white button-down shirt that barely shows her collarbone—or what could just be a shadow. She's one of those women who could be anywhere between twenty and forty, although I know it's closer to the latter. I zoom in on her face, studying it in as much detail as the low-resolution screen of my old laptop will allow. Definitely closer to forty, and no tacky surgery-a-minute like some of the girls from the club. If she's had work done, it's all tasteful and discreet. She has the look of, if not a natural beauty, a once reasonably attractive girl polished and preserved by vast amounts of money and never having to do a goddamn thing for a living. As I peer closer, I see the look of resolve on her face, lips pressed together like she's biting their insides, firm chin and jaw set tight.

I expected a rush of antipathy toward her, and I'm a little surprised that I feel none. However, I seem to be alone in that sentiment. The comments don't spare a thing.

> Surgeried rich bitch. That's what you get for letting nannies raise your children instead of doing your damn job.

Nowhere in the article does it mention a nanny.

> She doesn't even look worried. Does she look like she's been crying?

Re: She doesn't even... Must be the Botox. Ha!

Where is your daughter, Jackie? What did you do with your daughter?

That's it. Enough for today. I close the laptop with a click and push it away with such violence that it lands on the floor with a thud. I have to pick it up again and check that it's working before I take it to the charger. I can't afford another one.

Once I crawl into my bed, the nightmares pull me under almost immediately, so intense that my sleeping pills do nothing for them. All the pills accomplish is keeping me under, not letting me escape the sticky grasp of dreams, no matter how bad it gets.

When I sit up, panting, I have no idea if I was asleep for five hours or five minutes or five days. Weak light filters in through the blanket over the window. Dawn in this city looks the same as a rainy afternoon, and when most afternoons are rainy... well.

Damp bedsheets cling to my sweaty skin. Blindly pawing for my cell phone, I squint at the dim screen: six a.m.

I can't stop shivering so I amble to the shower and turn on the hot water. The bathroom in my apartment is the size of a Kleenex, or as one hookup or another put it with a smirk, you can shit while you brush your teeth. It has no bathtub, only a plastic shower stall, very much like those at the loony bin. There, everything was blunt and plastic so I couldn't do something dumb like inten-tionally crack my head open on a tile or a sharp corner.

Here it's because the slumlord is a cheapskate. But at least there's no nurse on the other side of the clear cur-tain, watching me like a hawk.

The memory still makes me shudder. I remember cry-ing into the stream of hot water because I couldn't look down without seeing my distended stomach. I ended up staring at the ceiling the whole time.

I push the memory away, into some far recess of my mind where it can rot until it poisons me. I've barely had time to rinse my hair when the water turns from warm to lukewarm to freezing. With a sigh, I turn off the tap.

When I try to climb back under the blankets, I realize I won't be going back to sleep. The sheets are still soaked with sweat, and while I was showering, they got cold and clammy. So I get dressed in baggy jeans and a T-shirt with the logo of some band I've never heard of, a relic left behind by some guy I don't remember having slept with.

It's nearing seven a.m. when I lace my boots and shrug on my jacket, pause on the threshold of the apart-ment, thinking, then go back and refill the hole in the lining of my pocket with a new lump of foil. Normally, I'd never be dumb enough to bring pills to a police station—but these were prescribed in my name. Techni-cally. I ran out of my monthly prescription two weeks ago, but no one has to know that.

I'm ready to face Ortiz. As ready as I'm going to be.

It's not quite light enough when I venture out, and the street is deserted, shadows still clinging to every crevice, reluctant to leave. The glow of the streetlights— whichever ones are working, that is—is muted, diffused in the light fog that shows no intention of lifting. Everything about it clearly rings unsafe, a tinny trill of alarm in the back of my mind: you, of all people, should know better. I put my headphones on and crank up my music to the loudest setting. Like I'm really asking for it.

* * *

As I push open the heavy glass door with the Seattle PD logo and go into the station, no one pays much attention to me. Men and women in cop uniforms go back and forth, phones ring, a din of general chaos hangs over the place like a cloud of smog despite the early hour. Only when I get to the nearest counter and tell the woman behind bulletproof glass that I'm Lainey Moreno does she cut herself off midword, cover the receiver of the phone she's been yammering into, and look at me like I actually exist.

"This way."

I half expected to find myself in one of those ominous rooms like on *CSI*, with gray walls and a two-way mirror, but this looks more like the cluttered office of a middle-school principal. The shifty, skinny guy from the other night gives me a tepid hello and motions for me to sit. I don't shake the hand he proffers. He looks like one of those people whose palm would be cold and clammy to the touch, although without the hockey jersey, he's almost handsome.

I look around. He'd closed the door behind me, and the noise outside is reduced to a soft din. More than anything, I feel trapped.

"Where's . . . Detective Ortiz?" I ask in guise of hello.

"He's busy. I'll be interviewing you, Lainey. If that's all right." Judging by his close-lipped smile, it doesn't really matter if it's all right or not.

At the same time, I'm furious with Sean . . . with Detective Ortiz. He's busy? What does he think he's playing at? My teeth are gnashing, and my jaw starts to ache. I really, really should have slept longer.

"I'm Detective Morris, Lainey."

Morris. A name fit for a guy who wears a fedora with his black trench. I half expect him to call me a dame. The thought makes me crack up, and I catch the neurotic chuckle between my clenched teeth before it can escape.

His pale-orange brows knit. He has that blotchy redhead skin, thin like papyrus. It's already starting to crease in myriad microlines and folds.

"Is something wrong?"

I shake my head. He gives me a last lingering look and then on to the questions, without warning. *What did you do on this day at this hour?*

What did I do? "I was at work."

"At eight in the morning?" A rise of his brows again. He communicates his entire range of emotions through them, like a dog, and his mouth is set in a firm line the whole time when he's not talking.

It takes me a moment to get his meaning. My other job, I explain hoarsely, although it's supposed to be the other way around. The grocery store job is my real job, the one I put on my lease and credit card applications. The night shift is my other job.

"There's nothing to be embarrassed about," he says evenly, with a note of condescension. "You're not doing anything illegal at that club, are you?" Chuckle, chuckle. This is supposed to be the punch line to some joke that went over my head.

"No, I'm not." I answer even if I'm not sure he wants me to, just in case. Nothing illegal; I don't even take my clothes off—but I don't say that part out loud.

"So for how long were you at the grocery store?"

I tell him. "From seven to two, like every day."

"*Every* day?"

"Well, uh, except," I stammer, stumbling over my own thoughts. "I get my schedule every week. I had Thursday and Friday off. I think." I curse myself—who the hell doesn't remember when she had a day off just the week before? But he moves on without skipping a beat.

"What time did you get off work?"

I have to repeat myself. "Two o'clock, at the end of my shift."

He doesn't have a notebook or a tablet or a keyboard, because he's recording the whole thing with his phone. Is this it? Doesn't strike me as very...professional.

"What did you do after work?"

"I went running," I say. Not because of any kind of malice or ill intent, it just rolls smoothly off my tongue, and I don't have time to catch it. Too late. My armpits get clammy, and I swear his nose twitches like he can sense it through my layers of T-shirt and jacket.

I can lie to myself all I want, but lying to the police has consequences.

"And then?"

"I went home."

"Straight home?"

"Yeah."

"Did anybody see you? Running?"

"What? . . ."

"It's not very safe in your neighborhood. Is it?"

I shrug.

"Let's move to yesterday," he says smoothly, too smoothly, and just like that, I know he knows, and he's aware of it, and we sit here in the middle of the knot of my lies that tightens with every word I say.

"Yesterday, where did you go after work?"

When he sees that I'm not answering, he adds, "Did you go straight home?"

Opening the door for me to lie. Waiting for me to lie. Expecting it.

I dip my chin. Saying yes, but not vocalizing it so it doesn't end up inside that scuffed little phone of his.

"Did you stop anywhere?"

Of course I had. Sugar hightailed it out of the Silver

Bullet and never came back, so I made a detour to pick up my stuff. Took all of fifteen minutes, and most of them a blur, this part as much a fabric of my day as brushing my teeth. I mostly remember sitting in my car, idling at a traffic light that was taking forever. Red light from it spilled down the rain-slicked asphalt, brighter than fresh blood, and I drummed my fingertips on the steering wheel, picking away bits of fake leather as I wondered if I could just blow past it. The street was empty on all sides—no one to see. No one to know. But I didn't, in case of traffic cameras.

Shit. Traffic cameras. I've watched enough *CSI* to know how these things work.

"I did." I try my best to keep my voice even. "I made a detour. Stopped at a . . . an acquaintance's house. But—"

He cuts me off before I have a chance to explain—to lie—further.

"Acquaintance? What acquaintance?"

"This guy I was sort of seeing," I stammer. I'm hoping to move on from there, but he latches on to it.

"And who was this acquaintance?"

"Just this guy I met. Su—James." That's Sugar's real first name, isn't it? It's gotta be James, or Jack, or Jon, or something.

"And what kind of acquaintance is James? Does he have a last name?"

"I don't know, all right?" My mouth twists like there's something sour under my tongue. "I only sort of know him."

"Know him how?"

"Through work."

"The grocery store?"

"The club," I say. My voice turns into a hiss. "I thought this much was obvious. You're a detective, aren't you?"

He lets that sail over his head with true professional cool. I, however, am this close to losing mine.

"So he came to the club," he says. "The strip club. Where you work."

"Where I bartend."

"Yeah." He shifts in his chair, a comfy, ergonomic chair with a high back. "Was he a client?"

"What?"

"Well, if he came into the club, that must mean he was a client. Why else would he be there?"

"Maybe he was. So?"

"You have a habit of leaving with customers, Lainey?"

I shoot to my feet without realizing I'm moving. The room falls away, and I loom over him, the air in my lungs pulling me toward the ceiling like a balloon. "You wanna know if I turn tricks? Is that it?"

"I was just asking you a question." As he says this, his face smooths out, his forehead an uncreased plane of thin, freckled skin.

"Yeah, well, the answer is no."

"How long did you stay at James's?"

"I didn't." I swallow. "Ten minutes. Five."

His eyebrows rise. "It only took five minutes?"

"What are you getting at?"

"Nothing. Just trying to figure out what could have been in it for you." And he gives that close-lipped smile again.

"What the fuck does that have to do with Olivia?"

"Let me worry about that. I'm the detective—you said so yourself. You just answer the questions, please."

"Yeah. It only took five fucking minutes." My voice cracks. I realize this is being recorded, but it's too late to backtrack. My ugly words are trapped in the chips and circuits of his old smartphone with its cracked screen, and there's no way to take them back. My control over them is lost forever. People will listen to the words replayed over and over, analyzing, scrutinizing, shaking their heads. My humiliation mingles with rage and powerlessness.

"If you can't behave, we can conduct this interview with you in handcuffs. If you like that better."

I steady my voice. "I have nothing else to say. I went home and went to sleep."

"Do you live alone?"

"Yes. Why?"

"Just wondering if someone can corroborate your story."

My story.

"Fuck you."

Before he can say anything else, I turn around and storm out.

No one stops me; no one calls my name. At least I don't think anyone does. The only sound I can hear clearly is my pulse pounding in my eardrums. I shut my eyes, and an image surfaces: the house where I grew up, so unreal it looks flat like a theater set. The thin wall that separates my bedroom from Val's, and the sounds I always pretend not to hear. The casual insults flung at me by the other neighborhood kids, *s* words and *w* words that always send me into a frenzy of violence. Val's shoes, platform heels scattered by the front door, shoes I put on while she's sleeping and amble around the living room like a baby deer. The prettiest shoes in the world, I thought back then, shiny red or black or clear heels like Cinderella. Knowing full well that if she ever caught me, she'd beat the crap out of me, but I put them on all the same.

The panic attack scratches at the edges of my subconscious, insistent, growing closer with every moment. And when it hits, I don't want to be in this place. I want to be outside, in the cold drizzle of early morning. I want to be home, in my bed, or at least in the driver's seat of my car with the door locked.

Throwing my weight against the door, I topple out into the burnt-rubber and diesel stink of the parking lot. And collide with Sean Ortiz, face-to-face. More like face-to-chest, like in the movies, minus the cute romantic component. The wool of his jacket is scratchy and soft at the same time as it connects with my palms; I reel back with a jolt.

"Here you are," he says. Not surprised, just observing. I'm seeing him in daylight for the first time. His eyes are darker than I thought they were and his hair, lighter. Pale sunlight brings out the grays that hid in the shadow, many more than I'd noted at first glance.

"Yes," I exhale. "I'm here." And you weren't. I needed to see you, and you weren't there. You left me in the care of others, of more people who don't give a shit. Again.

As if he can read my mind, his gaze grows somber. "Yes, I just got a call. I hear it didn't go so well."

My face flares, and I study the cracks in the asphalt at my feet. Ten different brands of cigarette butts soak up the rainwater by the edge of the sidewalk.

"This is important. Couldn't you keep it together just this once? Do you realize how it makes you look?"

"I didn't do anything." My voice cracks.

"I know. But it's them you have to convince, not me."

My fists clench inside my sleeves.

"You're making yourself look guilty. Like you have something to hide. If that's what you were going for, then you did a great job—congratulations. And Morris—"

"Morris," I say, spitting each syllable in a furious staccato, "tried to insinuate I was some kind of two-bit whore."

Sean groans. "Come with me, Laine. We should talk."

"I think I'm done talking for the day."

He throws a grim, squint-eyed glance around, over my head, at the building. "Not here. Somewhere else. Somewhere private."

CHAPTER SEVEN

I keep my head down as I follow Sean to his car. He opens the door and practically shoves me in like I'm being arrested—not that I'm resisting. Empty energy-drink cans litter the floor, and the crumpled wrappers of nicotine patches fill every nook and cranny. In spite of that, the seats kind of smell like smoke.

Sean slams the door on the driver's side. He won't look at me. "Put your seat belt on," he barks.

I sit on my hands. "These don't really work, you know."

"What?"

"The nicotine patches. How long have you been at it?"

He cringes, like I reminded him of something he was trying to put out of his mind. "We're not here to discuss my bad habits."

He peels out of the parking lot, going way above the speed limit, I can tell—as are my thoughts, and all my attempts to slow them down are in vain. They go around in a circle, getting louder with each loop. Until I saw that poster, I didn't even know for sure if Olivia existed, if she had a name. And today, they think I took her, at least this Morris does. But then I'd be in handcuffs, wouldn't I? Why am I here and not in the back of a cop car, separated from Sean by a metal grille?

I steal a sideways glance at him. "Don't you have work to do? Missing people to find?" I manage to keep the bitterness from my voice.

"Yes, I do. I think you're it."

Well, that's reassuring. That's how he sees me, a missing person, even though I haven't been missing for a decade now. But to him, and to the rest of the world, I'll forever be Girl Last Seen. My defining moment.

And now Olivia's defining moment.

Don't think about it, they'll find her—Sean will find her—and everything will be fine. She won't end up broken like me. She has parents who love her, and half the country is looking for her and...and...

I realize I'm grinding my teeth and clench my jaw, which only makes it worse.

Sean takes me to a twenty-four-hour diner near Pioneer Square. If I were him, I wouldn't leave a decent car parked within a mile of the place, but he doesn't seem to give a damn. I understand his motivation when we walk in, because the diner is mostly empty. A few tables are occupied by the last bleary-eyed holdovers from the night activities, a few homeless guys warming their hands on unlimited one-dollar coffees, a table of hookers in high vinyl boots smoking and laughing raucously. He steers us to a booth in the very back. A few of the patrons follow us with bored glances. They probably think he's some rich businessman dude here to buy drugs from me.

Clearly, this isn't going to be a conversation fit for a Starbucks.

I plunk down onto the bench. The blue vinyl is scarred with cigarette burns and torn in places, exposing yellowed stuffing. Sean watches me intently as I pat myself down to retrieve my crushed pack of smokes. The smooth feel of my lighter in my hand is like an old friend. I light up, looking Sean straight in the eye as I take that first, sweet drag.

His eyes narrow a little, and a vein pops on his forehead, but he doesn't tell me to put it out.

I hold out my pack to him. "Want one?"

"Laine."

"I'm asking seriously. You must be twitchy from all that NicoDerm."

"If anyone is twitchy, it's you. Have you slept at all lately?"

A waitress shuffles to our table. She barely passes through the aisle. The tag on the distended chest of her uniform says Patricia. "If you're gonna sit here, you gotta buy something," she says in way of welcome.

I decide that I like this place.

"She'll have the pancakes," Sean says. "And I'll have a coffee, black."

"I'll have a coffee," I snap.

"You'll have the pancakes."

I glower at him, but Patricia is already licking the tip of the pencil and jotting down the order. I watch her amble away, the ash from the tip of my cigarette tumbling right onto the Formica tabletop.

"Thanks, Mom."

"You're practically shaking. When was the last time you ate anything?"

I want to reply with something sarcastic except I genuinely can't remember. Antidepressants really mess with your appetite.

At the hospital, I started throwing up everything I ate to keep my stomach from growing. They force-fed me. And by the way, being fed with a tube through your nose really fucking hurts.

The memory is like a live wire to the back of my neck. My upper lip breaks out in beads of sweat, and more of it slicks my chest and back under my T-shirt.

"You should eat," he says. "You'll need the energy."

I loathe every part of that sentence with a fiery passion. Trying to assess possible escape routes, I throw a glance over my shoulder.

Patricia comes back and plunks down two chipped mugs before sliding a heaping plate of pancakes in front of me. Steam billows above it, and the smell of grease and sugar is overpowering. The coffee is a black oil slick with some kind of thin film floating on top. My stomach clenches even as my mouth reflexively fills with saliva.

I'm too aware of Sean's eyes on me when I grab the fork and start to pick apart the closest pancake, chipping away tiny pieces that soak up the syrup at the bottom of the plate.

If this shit touches my tongue, I'm going to puke.

I notice he doesn't drink his coffee.

"Why did you go by yourself? You should have called me first."

I shrug. "Isn't that what you told me to do?"

"I didn't think you'd go at all, to be honest. Not without being forced to."

"Why not?" I have a good guess why not. Truth is, he had no reason to think I would go, after all the horrible things I said last night.

He gives a solemn nod. "So you do care."

I choke on the tiny bite of pancake I'd tried to force down. "I'm human, Sean. I can regret I gave birth to her, but it doesn't mean..." My throat goes dry. I don't know how I manage to push out the words. "It doesn't mean she deserves...that."

He shakes his head. "No one deserves that." His sad gaze is unflinching on mine.

"I didn't deserve it."

"Of course you didn't. You were a child. And so is she."

We sit in silence. The steam coming off the food gradually fades as the grease starts to congeal at the bottom of the plate.

"Is it him?" I ask. "Just tell me the truth. Do you know something? Is it the same . . . person?"

"We don't know."

"You're full of shit."

"I already told you. We have no leads whatsoever."

"There was never another girl," I blurt. His eyes narrow, and something changes about his posture. The moment I see it, I fervently wish I could take it back, rewind just this one moment. But the words are already out, so I have no choice but to go on and say the rest of it while he sits there and looks at me like I'm about to confess to God knows what.

"There wasn't another girl. In ten years. No one of the right age or . . . type."

"What on earth are you talking about?" He lowers his voice, and the raspy note in it scrapes against my eardrums.

"I've . . . I've looked up all the AMBER Alerts, all the missing girls." I gulp. "For the last . . . ten years or so. I . . . I haven't always been able to keep up to date, but . . ."

"Laine," he exhales. "Jesus."

"She fits the description," I say. Determined, it seems, to slam the last nail in that coffin lid. "She's ten. And she's . . ."

"Don't you think we have professionals working on this?"

"And so far it's doing wonders."

"That's not how it works. It's not the same MO."

"You don't know how he kidnapped me. No one even knows when."

"I'm aware. Your mother got arrested, and only then social services found out you were missing." He rubs his temples, and I notice him eyeing the pack of smokes I'd purposefully left halfway between us.

"You were most likely chosen because you wouldn't be missed for a while, if at all," he says levelly. "Because you were an easy target."

"And Olivia, she was anything but."

He gives a slow nod. "He had to have known there would be a highly publicized search."

"It could have been impulsive. That's how a lot of them tick, isn't it? They just see their type of victim and—" I choke on my own words. She's not a type and not a victim; she's a person. She has a name and parents who miss her.

"Not a chance," Sean says grimly. "The school had security. Olivia didn't just run amok all day. She had a stay-at-home mother, an aunt who watched her, and a nanny. She was never alone for longer than a few minutes. So whoever it was had spent a long time re-searching, scoping her out. He had to have studied the school, the blind spots of the surveillance cameras. Olivia's schedule. He can't not have known who she was or what would inevitably happen if she disappeared."

"So it could have been someone who knew the family."

"That was my first thought. Someone who wanted to cause them harm, or even a ransom situation—but we would have heard from the kidnappers by now. But none of the leads added up to anything substantial. Both parents have solid alibis—the father was in meetings from seven a.m. till late into the evening; the mother had an appointment with a landscape designer for their summer home. The aunt drove straight to the school from her last class at the university, like she always did when she picked up her niece. Except when she got there..."

"But it's not likely," I say hoarsely. "It's not likely that it was...the same man."

"Trust me, this was the last possibility I wanted to consider. But it's been a week and I've ruled out everything else. Besides...it's just too big of a coincidence." He meets my gaze and holds it, waiting for me to flinch away, to betray something—as if I had anything to betray. "Don't you think?"

CHAPTER EIGHT

Silence crackles over our heads. All the sounds of the diner, the drunken giggling at the other table, the hum of heat lamps over immobile rows of French fries, all recede into the background.

"Laine, they're going to reopen your case."

The words are like a slap that knocks all the chaotic thoughts right out of my head. "What?"

"Reexamine all the evidence. Maybe they missed something, something that could lead us to him. Give us a clue, no matter how remote." For the first time, he voluntarily looks away. "I know what you must be thinking."

"Oh, I don't think you do." My mouth stretches in an ugly scowl. "My case has been cold for nearly a decade, and no one gave a shit."

"I know, okay?" He slams his hands down on the table, making the coffee cups jump. "I've been a cop for longer than that. You think I haven't seen enough of this? I've seen it, and I know it, and I'm as frustrated about it as you are but I'm just one person. I can't change anything."

"Frustrated?" I spit. "You're frustrated? They locked me away and forced me to have my rapist's child. And never really bothered to look for the guy, just waited for him to do it to someone else. Because what does another brown girl from a bad neighborhood matter anyway? And you're frustrated. Well, that's a comfort."

I collapse into my seat, utterly drained. Hearing my own words was like tearing off an old scab, almost healed, so I thought I wouldn't feel anything, and now I'm sore and bleeding all over again.

"Laine...I just want you to be ready in case they come to ask you more questions."

"I already told them everything I knew. Ten years ago." I grab for my pack of smokes, shakily light another one, breathe it in till my vision swims with black splotches, let it out. Instead of helping, it only makes me more jittery. It's not a smoke I need. "I haven't remembered anything new since then. And believe me, I tried."

Without a word, he reaches for my pack, takes out a cigarette, and lights it. His eyelids flutter as he inhales. His shoulders droop in relief.

I can't even think of anything snarky to say. I just watch him exhale the smoke, take another drag, and then tap the ashes into the ashtray with a familiar, practiced movement.

"I'll do whatever I can to keep you out of this," he says, "but you have to understand. There's only so much I can do."

"What—"

"I spoke to your former boss, Laine. To Charlene at the Bounty Basket."

My indignant exclamation gets stuck in my throat, and heat floods my face, painful, humiliating. My complexion may hide it from him, but I can't hide it from myself. Like an animal caught in a trap, I tense up, spikes and spines at the ready, no matter how hopeless the situation. The words teem at the tip of my tongue. *What did that bitch tell you? It's all a bunch of lies. She's just petty and jealous. She's always on my case.* Fuck her, seriously, fuck her and her shitty store and her so-called charity operation.

"I know she fired you yesterday morning. After you left your cash register without telling anyone and didn't come back..."

"I did," I interject. "I said I was going for a smoke. I asked the other girl to fill in for me. She must have—"

"For two hours." Sean's gaze doesn't waver from my face. "And when you did come back, you were, as Charlene put it, intoxicated. You smelled like alcohol and couldn't walk straight."

"She just needed an excuse to get rid of me," I mutter. "She always had it out for me, from the start."

"She said it was your third strike. She really wanted to give you a chance, like she does for all her kids..."

"I'm not a kid."

"And she hasn't told your social worker yet. Because she doesn't want you to get in trouble."

I'm the one who drops my gaze. I already know what's coming.

"You know what else she told me? Your strike two was just a week earlier, when you showed up for work late and drunk, at eight in the morning. It looked like you'd been out all night, she said. You know what day that was?"

I say nothing, but I know the answer.

"It was the day Olivia disappeared."

"Have you— "

"I haven't told anyone. Yet. But I'll have to, you realize that, right?"

I start to get out of my seat with the intention to leave, but he grabs my arm right above the wrist and forces me to sit back down.

"I just want you to be ready for when they pick your entire life apart minute by minute. And if it keeps going as it is, they will. Not just the police, the press too. And if you tell me, right now, without lying or fibbing or omitting things, what they're going to find when they do, maybe I can help you."

Looking into his eyes, I can almost believe it.

"They'll try to make you look, and sound, as guilty as possible. They'll try to make you crack, behave as if you have something to hide. And then the truth will matter less and less."

"Thanks," I say. "I already got a preview."

"It'll get much worse than that. So if you have anything to tell me, do it now."

The silence is punctuated only by the hiss of a deep fryer somewhere in the kitchen and the steady rush of running water.

He looks so tired all of a sudden; I almost feel sorry for him, and maybe it's the lighting, but he looks older than his age—very late thirties, early forties maybe. I never asked. With another deep sigh, he crushes his cigarette into the ashtray then does the same with mine that's still idling on the edge, a barely there wisp of smoke rising from the ashen tip. I still haven't said anything.

"I'll do everything I can to keep you out of this. But I can't protect you from it altogether, do you understand?"

"I don't think there's a way to do that." I eye my cigarette, crushed and twisted out of shape, a total loss. "I'm involved, one way or another."

"You don't have to be."

"Yes, I do. It's not because she's . . . she's mine. If she were any other ten-year-old girl, I'd still be involved." I lean across the table and lower my voice. "That man broke me, Sean. He destroyed my life. If he does that to anyone else, I'm involved."

I follow him out of the diner, to his car. The world has a soft, cloudy quality. I barely notice that he's got his arm around my shoulders, helping me keep upright. He holds the door open for me this time, no shoving me in like I'm a criminal. I flop on the seat gracelessly and pull my legs up.

"I'm driving you home," he says as he starts the engine.

"You don't know my address."

"Yeah, I do."

I stare at the ripped knees of my jeans—not fashionably distressed, but regular old worn-out ripped—and pick out little threads that I twist between my fingertips. "Of course you do. You probably have my entire life story in a neat little folder, don't you?"

"I'm a detective. So yeah."

He sounds sad. I look up, but his gaze is on the road.

He pulls up to my building, and it's not ten a.m. yet. My neighborhood is peacefully asleep after another night of debauchery. It's about the safest time of day to be here, but he insists on walking me to my door.

I don't look at him as I fumble with my keys—only to realize the front door lock is broken again. I swing the door open with a creak and look at him quizzically.

"I can walk up two floors by myself," I say.

"Hold on." His hand brushes my upper arm. It only lasts a moment, and I don't know why, but I stop.

"I wanted to say I'm sorry."

"For what?"

"I shouldn't have vanished."

At first I don't understand what he's talking about.

When he meets my blank gaze and I finally clue in, it's like claws across my heart. Heat rises to my face.

"I should have at least visited you. At the hospital. Sent you a teddy bear or something."

"I was too old for teddy bears."

"You know what I mean."

Do I? "It wouldn't have made a difference," I say in a toneless voice. "So don't worry about it."

"Maybe not, but I acted like a coward."

"Doesn't matter. I never thought of you much after that night."

Liar, liar.

"You didn't have anyone. I could have at least—"

"Will you stop?" I snap, tearing the fragile fabric of the moment to shreds. "Please. It's not necessary."

"Ella," he says. My other name, not the one on my IDs or my hospital files or my criminal record. A shudder courses down between my shoulder blades.

"That girl doesn't exist anymore. I'm someone else now."

"Laine."

I manage to smile. "Yeah."

He's disappointed, I can tell. He expected something more from me, but what? I didn't cause this. It's not my fault—the refrain I'd lived my life to for the last ten years, sung by a chorus of social workers and shrinks and cops. I was just a child. It wasn't up to me. Someone else didn't care enough; someone else didn't do their job. And now here we are: me a completely fucked-up shell of a person and my daughter just...gone.

People like my kidnapper don't stop until they're stopped. And I never remembered a damn thing that could stop him. For the last ten years, I knew it was only a matter of time before he did it to someone else, and then, like it or not, it would be on me.

But why? Why did it have to be her? She was supposed to have a good life. And now she's going to turn out like me.

"I'll cooperate," I say. "With the investigation, I mean, if you need me to. I'll repeat everything I already told them, if it helps."

He's so close, close enough to touch. All I'd have to do is reach out.

"I appreciate it." He lowers his head. His eyelashes cast spiky shadows down his cheekbones, like jagged stars. "I know it's such a meaningless, empty thing to say, but it's true. It means a lot. Not just to me."

His eyes are tired and a touch sad, but the corners of his mouth are smiling ever so subtly. "You still have my card, right?"

I do. But I don't nod, don't say a word. My eyes are drinking in all the details, filling the gaps where memory and imagination failed: the pattern of stubble on his chin, the slant of his eyelids, the subtle lines already etched between his dark, full brows. Those lines deepen when he catches my gaze in his.

"Yes," I reply, wincing at the sound of my own voice that grounds this moment in harsh reality. "I have the card."

"Good. Call me if you need anything. I mean anything. Even if it's four thirty a.m. on a Sunday and you just feel like talking." The smile widens a little, without losing its sadness.

With my gaze still lost in the intricacies of his face, I freeze, overcome with an inexplicable feeling. Out of instinct—that instinct normal girls have down to an art form—I lean forward, my chin tilted at just the right angle so his face is level with mine. In a split second, as my lips align with his, I know with absolute certainty that he's about to lean in and kiss me.

Nothing happens. I let my eyelids flutter closed, then open again, and he hasn't moved an inch.

"You sure you don't want me to walk you up?"

"Yeah." My breath escapes in a rush. "I'm fine."

I turn around and race up the stairs. Flee is a better word. By the time I emerge onto the landing, my heart hammers like I just ran up ten floors, not two, and my face is on fire. What the hell was I thinking? Who am I to him anyway?

A part of me is disgusted with myself. Leaning my forehead on the cool, rough surface of my door, I let myself shudder, in no hurry to get my keys. The weight of what I just promised starts to settle onto my shoulders, making itself comfortable there alongside the guilt and confusion and all the other things I carry around unseen.

I try to empty my mind, but instead, I picture Sean going home to his wife-girlfriend-whatever. When she hugs him hello, she's going to smell my tobacco smoke on his coat and in his hair. He'll roll his eyes and tell her it's this crazy witness he had to deal with all day. And when she's not looking, he's probably going to go outside and sneak a cigarette.

I chase the thought away only for another one to pop up in its place. Olivia's parents, who, in spite of all my Internet searches, are still vague, faceless entities, sleepless in their generic soap opera mansion. And like wildfire spreading, jumping from branch to branch, my mind goes straight to Olivia.

I tug at my collar until I manage to get the zipper undone and claw my way out of my jacket. My arms are bone thin and ghostly in the fluorescent light, and the scars look deep purple, slicing across the rivers of veins under the skin like a contradiction. I squeeze my temples between my knees and try to breathe, but the panic attack has me in its clutches and it won't give up without a fight.

I scramble to get the keys out of my pocket, drop them, crouch to pick them up. Momentarily, I lose my balance and catch myself on the door handle.

That's when I finally clue in and realize my apartment door is unlocked.

CHAPTER NINE

The mind fog clears. My vision is clean and sharp when I slowly get up and push the door all the way. It opens without a sound—without the slightest creak of hinges.

Waves of cold and damp wash over me. The apartment looks pitch-black after the neons in the hallway; the navy fleece blanket I've nailed over the window is swaying gently in the breeze.

Before I can think better of it, my hand crawls along the wall and flicks the light switch. In the glow of the ceiling lamp, I can see my entire apartment at once, all four corners. The bathroom door is open, and I can tell the small space is empty. The plastic curtain on the shower stall has been torn down, and it pools on the tile floor, innocent and baby blue. The faucet drips steadily like an IV.

On shaky legs, I cross the room and slam the bathroom door against the wall as if someone might be crouched behind it, waiting for me to drop my vigilance. The sound is sharp and hollow. I race to the window, pull aside the blanket—and curse. There's a hole in the glass, an almost perfect circle with small jagged edges like baby teeth, with cracks radiating out all the way to the frame. Great. A fucking break-in now, of all times.

Frantic, I spin around and take stock of the room. They must have known I have nothing to steal, or if not, they must have figured it out soon enough. Nothing looks like it's been disturbed—not at first glance anyway. My gaze searches for my laptop. I bought it two years ago at a pawnshop, and it's worth nothing. It barely works, but it was enough for my research needs. No one would take it—would they? I throw around the pile of clothes on the bed, dirty and clean jumbled together. Nothing. My nightstand, where I sometimes put it, is empty too. A glance into the corner confirms it. The charger cord is coiled on the floor by the power outlet; the light of the adapter glows faint green, but the laptop itself is nowhere in sight.

The thought is a jolt of lightning down my spine. I rummage around in the drawer of my nightstand, throwing its contents on the floor: underwear, stray socks, hand lotion. My folding knife, which I put in my pocket without thinking. My sleeping pills. My fucking sleeping pills, the orange prescription container with my name on it is gone.

Dizzy, I get up and race to the bathroom. It feels like I'm flying, my toes barely brushing the floor. Electricity tingles in my fingertips. The mirror on the cabinet door has always been cracked, but now a whole chunk of it is missing, exposing the cardboard underneath. I throw open the cabinet door, sweep all my makeup tubes into the sink in one movement, and pick through every last one. My anxiety meds are gone too.

I'm this close to breaking down in tears. I lift up the lid of the toilet tank, and my insides feel hollow with relief when I see my stash still taped securely underneath.

I peel it away and immediately regret it. Did someone tamper with it? Does the tape look different? Is the plastic bag I bundled around the pills the same shape I always roll it into? Too late to tell. I tear the plastic apart, and everything looks exactly as I left it. I count the pills twice to make sure they're all in place.

Two Xanax end up in the back of my throat before I realize I'm doing it. A gulp of tap water and I slide to the floor, my muscles weak with relief.

Now I can start thinking—almost rationally. I should call the cops. Yeah, right. I forgot that I, unlike Olivia, do not live in Hunts Point, and no one will give a shit. There's a break-in here every other day, and they don't think it's worth their time. Even if someone does show up, there's the issue of the plastic-wrapped pills in my pocket. And right now I don't trust myself to act normal.

I take out my phone and thumb through my contact list. Short and sweet: Sugar, work, pizza delivery. My court-appointed shrink. Sean's card is burning a hole in my pocket.

First things first. I find a piece of cardboard to prop up over the broken window and tape it into place; I'll have to call the janitor to have the window fixed. There goes my security deposit...again, not to mention that I'm a little behind on the rent. Tomorrow. I'll do it tomorrow, or the day after, as long as I don't have to think about it right now. I lock the door behind me—even though what's the point?—and hurry downstairs to my car.

My hands shake so much that it takes forever to get the door to open. I clamber in, slam it behind me, and shove the key into the ignition, praying to every major deity that it starts. Maybe someone hears me or maybe the universe is bored with making me its official chew toy, because the engine comes to life with a rumble like the cough of something dying.

On the last fumes of gas in the tank, I drive to Natalia's. Just like I thought, she's home. Her car sits by the curb right across from the entrance of the two-bedroom house. I pound on the door until I hear steps and the door opens a crack, chain still in place. From behind it, Natalia peers out suspiciously then slams it shut again. I almost think she's going to leave me out here on her porch, but a moment later, I hear the chain slide aside, and she lets me in. Her right eye is made up, but not the left, that lid red and raw, fringed with sparse blond eyelashes. She barely looks surprised when I tell her my apartment got robbed.

The place is what she calls open concept, which means the living room has no door and opens right onto the kitchenette and hallway—kind of like the house I grew up in. Val inherited it from my grandmother whom I never got to meet. She passed away before I was born, and Val never had a single nice word to say about her. Since I'd learned to take everything Val said with a cinder block of salt, I have always wondered what she was really like. She must have tried, if she managed to buy and pay off the house. Tried for the sake of her wayward daughter who probably would have sold it for drug money if she could pull herself together long enough to find buyers and sign the papers.

As I climb onto the sofa, Natalia throws a dirty look at my boots, and I start peeling them off self-consciously.

"Just be quiet," she says with a sigh. "Use the key from the back door if you need to go out. And if the phone rings, don't pick up. My boyfriend can't know I'm letting you stay here, okay?"

I reassure her that I'll be out of her hair soon enough.

As soon as I stretch out on the couch, the weight of sleep crushes me, shoving my face into the crackled pleather. My blood is thick and slow with all the chemicals coursing through it.

Maybe it's just as well. I don't have to think about everything that happened. I can just sleep.

In my dream, I'm not in the basement. I'm walking down the fluorescent-lit hallways of the hospital, looking for—I don't know what exactly; all I know is that I can't find it. I reach out to people who pass me by, but I can't get my voice to work, and they hurry past me like they don't see me. There's a trickle down my thigh, and I look down to see blood running down my leg, dripping onto the floor. I open my mouth but I still can't speak or scream. When I clutch at my stomach, there's a gaping maw opening up across my abdomen like a bloody smile, and in the millisecond before I snap awake, I have time to see all my organs spilling out at my feet.

I don't sit up like people do in the movies. I don't dare move my little finger. I lie there, listening to my body's cues for any sign of blood and searing agony. But my body is filled only with the numbing hum of coming down from too many pain pills.

I draw my hand across my stomach, feeling along the slightly raised line of the scar. Closed, stitched, healed a long time ago.

Only then do I let myself sit up. The surroundings are unfamiliar—some living room, a dully gleaming dead TV screen, bare floor. Panic surges, waking me up completely, and then memories trickle back. Natalia's. I'm at Natalia's because my place got robbed and I no longer have my laptop. Or my meds.

I want to fall right back onto the couch and sleep away the entire day.

On the coffee table, my phone is blinking. The battery is half-drained, and it didn't occur to me to grab my charger before I left. I reach for it, frowning as I thumb through the calls: two unfamiliar numbers, but most of the calls are from one. And I have a feeling I've seen that number before.

You have six new messages, the electronic voice informs me. You have room for zero new messages. Please delete the messages you no longer need—

I cut her off and put the phone to my ear, not without a tremor of apprehension. Unfamiliar numbers and voice mails are rarely good news when you're on probation.

First new message:

"Uh, hello," says a woman's voice. It's feminine in that high-pitched way, and timid. Wrong number? "Lainey Moreno? I hope I got the number right. Lainey, please hear me out before you erase this message, okay? This is Mrs. Shaw. Jacqueline Shaw."

The sound of the name jolts me awake better than a hit of speed straight into my vein. I swing my legs over the edge of the couch.

"I was told," the woman's voice says, "about the whole...situation." I can practically hear her squirm on the other end, she sounds so uncomfortable. "My husband and I talked about it." She clears her throat. Only now I recognize that hoarseness in her voice, the nasal note that ruins it: she's been crying, and recently. "We talked to the police and Detective Ortiz, and we would like to meet you."

CHAPTER TEN

Natalia isn't home—probably left for work already. When I peer into her bedroom, I see a bed with red sheets peeking sloppily from underneath the pink bedspread, a pile of clothes on a chair, makeup on the dresser, shoes scattered on the floor.

I feel bad, I really do, but when I sniff the underarms of my shirt, I realize I have no other options. I tiptoe through the mess like a thief, furtively look through her drawers. She doesn't have a simple T-shirt; everything has spaghetti straps or lace or shows massive cleavage. I pick a cheap-looking tank top I hope she won't miss and put it on under my jacket. Her hairbrush is pink, tiny, and clearly made for her limp bleach-blond locks and not my jungle of curls, but I tear it through until my scalp begs for mercy. Her perfume collection takes up half the dresser: expensive stuff, Chanel, Calvin Klein, others I've never heard of. She must have spent a fortune on these tiny bottles. I cautiously take a whiff of one, spritzing a little on my wrist and rubbing it behind my ear. Ashamed of myself, I run to the bathroom and blot the perfumed spots with a wet towel, but the scent is pervasive and stubborn, clinging to my skin and hair.

Glancing at my phone screen, I realize I only have a few minutes left till Sean gets here. He had called me shortly after I woke, irate after leaving three messages following Jacqueline's. I'm still not entirely sure why I said yes.

I throw on my jacket and distribute treats into the secret compartments: don't forget, Percocet in the left pocket, Xanax in the right. Alice in fucking Wonderland. Eat me, drink me.

While I wait outside for Sean to come get me, I keep sniffing the collar of my jacket, which still smells like a Parisian bordello. Who am I doing all this for? To see the grieving parents of a missing girl? For a man who's more than ten years older than me, a cop, and probably married?

What's wrong with me?

Sean's car pulls up, and I practically run out to the curb. He's still dressed in his work clothes, pants and shirt, somber and sober. As soon as I close the car door, his nostrils flare and the frown line between his brows deepens. My face flushes with shame.

"What the hell happened at your place?"

"Some jerks broke the window," I mutter, staring at my knees. "I thought I'd crash at a friend's. She's from work."

"From work," he repeats, and I decidedly don't like the judgmental note in his voice. "Is it safe?"

"As safe as anywhere else," I say peevishly. "I just didn't want to be alone, okay?"

He drives off, and for the next little while, neither of us speaks. It's awkward as hell. He won't put on music or turn on the radio. Who drives without music? Even if it's jazz or classical or some other shit that puts you to sleep.

"Let's go over this beforehand," he says as he drives onto the highway. "You realize this is a very, very difficult time for them."

I gulp. I knew this was coming, and it nearly makes me back out. Take him up on his offer, tell him to just take me back home and let them sort it out without me.

Except I know I can't do that. I might be a serial fuckup and failure, and there's a lot I can forgive myself for—but not this. I can't back away from her, from my— from Olivia. I have to see it through to the end, no matter what end it is. No matter how much it might hurt.

Oblivious to my inner turmoil, Sean goes on.

"I know I have no moral right to ask this of you, but think about how they feel before you say anything. Remember, they didn't know anything about you. It was a closed adoption, so..."

"And they never even asked."

He gives me a cold, heavy look, and I shift in my seat to hide the fact that a shudder courses between my shoulder blades.

"The point is, they didn't know, Laine, okay? They didn't know. They were not out to hurt you or take away your child."

The question that's been gnawing at me materializes on my lips.

"Why do they want to meet me so badly?"

"They think you have the right to be kept up to date on this investigation as much as they do. Jacqueline was extremely...upset when she found out about Olivia's origins. I think she's sort of trying to make it up to you, in her own way."

Sean gives me a look. And I wisely bite back the scathing remark at the tip of my tongue.

"So please, I know exactly what you're thinking, and it crossed my mind too, more than once. Yes, I know it's not fair. I know how terribly you were treated from the very beginning. But please remember, she just lost a child."

"Lost? I thought you were going to bring her back."

I watch his profile intently as he curses through clenched teeth. "I am."

"But?"

"It's not going to be the same afterward, not for anyone. Not for a long time."

"Of course not. That other Olivia is lost forever. The

best you can hope for is to get back her empty, tarnished shell."

"I never said that."

"You thought it."

For a long time, he's silent. Then he takes a too-sharp turn and I nearly go flying out of my seat.

"Are you nuts?" I snarl.

"Should've put your seat belt on."

"Oh, so now you're trying to get back at me? For calling you out on your own bullshit?"

He turns to me and nearly blows past a red light. "Is that what you think you are? Tarnished?"

I collapse back into my seat with a bitter chuckle.

"Laine," he snaps. A car honks at us, and he's forced to turn his gaze back to the road ahead.

"Well, I am."

He throws a curt glance at me. I can't read the look in his eyes.

"No one thinks that. Except you."

The way he says the words, they could almost be true.

We're entering Hunts Point. The houses look like a fairy tale, looming over neatly trimmed hedges. Luxury cars sit in driveways. In every other house, the windows are lit, and I can see the people inside having dinner, watching TV. Couples, families. A life of privilege and luxury that's become so familiar to them that they no longer notice it, like air or light.

I'm some kind of deepwater fish to them, an unknowable, bizarre creature.

We drive the remaining two blocks in heavy silence until the Shaws' house looms over us, dark and forbidding. Only one window is dimly lit behind heavy curtains.

There's no happiness in this house. There might never be happiness here ever again, I realize, and it hits me harder than I expected.

We get out of the car, and I pull my jacket closed against the chill April wind. I stick my hands in my pockets and feel for the barely there lumps of pills in the lining. My chemical salvation. I can do this.

I can do this I can do this I can do this.

Goose bumps race up my arms, down my legs, across my back and my stomach. My scar itches. Sean walks around the car to join me, and unexpectedly his hand alights on my forearm. I let go of the lump of foil with the Xanax inside and pull my hand out of my pocket so he can take it in his. His grip is strong and hot, his palm dry. His fingers intertwine with mine, and the cold in my core slowly starts to dissolve.

"Remember what I promised. I'll take you home any time. Just say the word."

We walk up a neat winding path to the massive front door. Sean rings a bell that I don't hear echoing behind it.

My heart hammers, a bird throwing itself against the bars of its cage over and over. I count the heartbeats, one-two-three-four-five-six. On the seventh beat, there's a soft click, and the door opens. A thin stripe of warm light spills out at our feet.

The face I see in the door is the same face I saw in the news articles. Jacqueline's gaze darts from Sean to me and back, and she hastily swings the door open wide enough for us to pass.

Sean subtly, but firmly, frees his hand from my grasp. Self-conscious, I put my hand back in my pocket.

Jacqueline gestures for us to come in.

Now I have a chance to get a better look at her. She's tiny, only half an inch taller than me, and very thin. Only not thin like me, surviving on pain pills and Twizzlers—elegant thin, like a picture from a magazine. She wears dark pants and a cream-colored sweater, and has a small gold pendant at her throat that I recognize, a tiny icon of Santa María. She plays with it nervously, winding the chain around her manicured fingers. I fixate on her hands, with their slender wrists and pale half moons of nails. Soft hands.

"Detective Ortiz," she says in that quiet, near-childlike voice from the voice mail. She shakes his hand. "Thank you so much. I wanted you to know that my husband and I appreciate it."

I glance over her shoulder, looking for the husband in question, but the hallway is empty.

Finally, she turns to me. "Lainey," she says, hesitant, like she can't pick which tone of voice to use. She holds out an uncertain hand. I shake it, if only because I need to touch it to know if it's as soft as it looks.

She has huge, doe-like brown eyes fringed with full lashes, eyes that peer at me almost pleadingly. She manages to make it seem like she's looking up at me. Her hair is glossy and dark brown, pulled back in a bun like it was in her newspaper picture, but now I can see how long and thick it is.

Olivia's mother, I think, unable to get over the weirdness of it all. We must both be thinking the same thing right now.

"I wanted to apologize. I know this must all have been very abrupt," she says gently. She sounds like she means it, to my astonishment. "Thank you for agreeing to meet me."

"It's all right," I say. My voice sounds hoarse and screechy compared to hers.

"Will you follow me? We can talk in the living room. Would you like something? A drink?"

"Ms. Shaw," Sean starts, and I give him a grateful look. Right now a drink is a bad idea.

"Please. It's the least I can do."

"We'll just have water. If that's all right."

I can't help but stare as we make our way deeper into the house. This is where Olivia grew up. She called this place home. It was all she'd ever known—she was one of the golden people with charmed lives. She couldn't relate to me any more than I could have related to her.

Maybe, if only I'd had a chance to hold her—

I push the thought away for a millionth time. It wouldn't have made a difference, not for the better anyway, for either of us.

The front lobby opens into a massive living room furnished in gleaming glass and shiny dark wood. There are huge paintings on the walls, paintings that look like a bunch of drips and splotches to me, but then again, I live in a place with mold on the ceiling. We find Mr. Thomas Shaw in the next room, one with bookcases lining the walls. He gets up from his chair behind a massive desk, closing the lid of a laptop.

Jacqueline murmurs something disapproving.

I glimpse my reflection in the glass panel of one of the bookcases and I can't really blame him for staying away.

He shakes hands with Sean. "Detective." Turns to me. "You must be Liane."

"Lainey," Jacqueline corrects softly.

He holds out his hand. "Welcome to our home, Lainey."

I force myself to reach out and take it. He looks like he wants to rub down with hand sanitizer. I almost feel sorry for him.

My heart is doing that thing again, the trapped-bird thing. I let my hand drop awkwardly by my side, but to my immense relief, Sean catches it. Squeezes it. *Any time. Just say the word.*

I grit my teeth. I made it this far, and I'm not leaving.

The four of us move to the living room. Jacqueline brings two glasses of water and a tumbler for Tom Shaw filled with something dark amber. Nothing for herself, I notice.

"When I heard your story for the first time," Jacqueline

speaks up, "I was...I don't have words." Her soft voice carries in the silence. "I was horrified. I had no idea. We were told the biological mother wanted a closed adoption, no contact with us before or after. I should have known something untoward was going on. I should have..."

"Jackie," says Tom Shaw, lowering his glass.

"I know. I shouldn't be telling you this. I realize it only dredges up bad memories for you..." She trails off, covering her mouth with her hands. "I'm so sorry. I don't know how I can ever make it up to you."

In my head, I repeat what Sean told me over and over like a mantra. Think of what she's feeling. She just lost a child. But the words dissolve into a bunch of sounds that mean nothing.

How could she make it up to me? Well, for one, she could have looked after her daughter—my goddamn daughter. Not let him get her. I know it's not fair to her, and I can keep from saying it—for Sean's sake if nothing else—but it sure doesn't mean I don't think it.

"I wanted you to know that you'll always be welcome in this house. No matter..." Her voice falters. "No matter what happens."

I understand what she's trying to say, and so does Sean. My thoughts go out to the lumps of foil in my left pocket. Or was it my right?

"And I am immensely, immensely grateful for your sacrifice," she finishes. I don't catch on right away and then realize she's talking about the investigation and my decision to help.

"I didn't have a choice," I say, lowering my head. I let her misinterpret that, and she does.

"They can't force you. Can they?"

Sean intervenes. "It was Laine—Lainey's own decision," he says evenly. "I assure you, she was not coerced."

"She better not be." Jacqueline looks flustered, a mother hen bustling over her baby chicks. "If that's the case, I will not tolerate it, regardless—"

"It's necessary for the investigation," Tom Shaw speaks up. He turns to his wife to speak, but his voice carries like he's talking to all of us. "And I think, even if the chances are slim, as long as it helps us get closer to Olivia..."

He gives me a significant look. He's not like Jacqueline. He makes it very clear who the priority is here: his daughter, and not the weird brown girl who looks like she should be begging for change on the street. "Nonetheless, Lainey, I appreciate it. I know it's not easy for you."

I really wish they'd stop. Is that why they brought me here, to exchange polite, meaningless words? I glance sideways at Sean, who looks as uncomfortable as I'm feeling, and I know he's thinking the same thing.

Jacqueline gets up in a rush, the first ungraceful movement I see her make. "Lainey, would you like me to show you around?"

Sean gives a barely perceptible nod. So I get up, my legs stiff, and follow her softly clacking steps out of the

room. On these gleaming floors, my boots look enormous, muddy, and crude.

"I imagine you'd like to see photos," Jacqueline says
softly as she starts up a huge winding stairway. She glances
quizzically over her shoulder, and I can't bring myself to
speak—I just follow her up the carpeted stairs to the second floor. She stops in front of each framed picture lining
the wall, and launches into stories and explanations—
where this was taken, and when, *and here she has a funny
look because she's mad I made her wear sunscreen.*

But barely any of it registers with me. All I can look
at is Olivia's face. Her light-caramel skin, her crazy curly
hair—like my own, except it's a touch lighter than mine,
with a warm golden tinge to the corkscrew curls spring-
ing in all directions. That didn't come from my side of
the family. And her eyes. She has pale-gray eyes that
look even lighter and bigger in her dark face. Mine are a
carbon copy of my mother's, so dark you can barely tell
the pupils from the irises.

I look at her, and with every second I spend studying
her face, I notice traits that don't belong to me. My palms
turn clammy, sweat breaks out along my spine, and nausea rises steadily in the back of my throat. Thank God I
didn't drink anything.

This is the closest I've ever come to seeing my kidnapper's face, I realize.

Jacqueline misinterprets my distress and makes a big
mistake. She reaches out and pats my back, no doubt
meaning to be reassuring.

I jump like someone jabbed me with a live wire. She lets out a small cry and stumbles back, nearly losing her balance.

"Fuck," I mutter. "I'm sorry. I didn't mean to—"

"No, no." She struggles to compose herself. She pulls on the hem of her sweater and then resumes playing with her necklace, tugging on the thin chain until I think it might snap. "I shouldn't have—I should have known better. I didn't mean to startle you, Lainey."

Startle. I let her have her delusion. Anything else might be more painful than she can handle right now.

"She's beautiful," I choke out. It takes all the effort I can muster, and the nausea rises another notch, but relief floods Jacqueline's face at once. Her eyes fill with tears as she clutches her necklace in her hand.

"She is. She's smart too. She's in advanced math. Her teachers always said she was precocious, even..." She trails off, looks down, and I spy a tear trail down her carefully powdered cheek. She draws a small breath, gathering her courage, and blurts out, "You must have missed her terribly. I'm so sorry; I never meant to do this to you."

"I was very young." It sounds like someone else is talking with my voice. The words are detached from me, emotionless. "I couldn't take care of her. I was a child myself."

Jacqueline throws herself at me and encases me in a hug. It's so unexpected that I freeze up, stiff and awkward. The smell of expensive perfume fills my nose and her scratchy wool sweater brushes against my cheek.

"I'm so sorry." I realize the woman is sobbing. She's crying into my shoulder, like there's something I can do. Like she expects me to comfort her or something. She wipes her eyes, smearing her makeup, and pulls away.

"Will you come with me?" She gestures at the nearest door. "There's something I would like to show you."

Without waiting for my answer, she turns the doorknob, and the door creaks open. It's dark, but she reaches in and flips a switch.

The room is done in light pinks and purples with white doll-like furniture and a fake-crystal chandelier hanging from the ceiling. Somehow it looks too young for a girl of ten.

Olivia's room.

My legs lock, and my stomach clenches. I wipe my palms on my pants.

"Come on in," Jacqueline says softly. "I want you to see where she lived all these years. I think you have the right to know."

Every step is a superhuman effort. I have to pause and hold on to the door frame for a moment before going in.

One look is enough. Olivia lived like a princess. This kind of life I never could have offered her in my wildest dreams—I don't know why Jacqueline feels the need to prove it to me once again. To rub it in my face? Olivia has a canopy bed with pink gauzy curtains, a dressing table with a huge oval mirror and jewelry boxes lined up neatly. A walk-in closet, a desk with a sleek Apple desktop computer, a paper-flat TV on the wall. A huge rhinestoned frame holds three pictures of a grinning Olivia clutching prizes for various math competitions.

No pictures with friends, no celebrity posters that young girls like to plaster their walls with. Everything looks expensive as hell, but besides her face in the photos, I see none of her in this room. This could be anybody's room or a photo from a magazine.

"I love her, Lainey," Jacqueline says. The moment the door closed behind us, it's like someone else took over her vocal cords. Her voice is no longer soft and gentle. It's steel underneath a layer of silk, as if tiny rusty gears turn in the back of her throat every time she speaks. "You have to believe me; I love her more than anything."

Why wouldn't I believe her? This room, the photos, this whole house is one giant expensive testament to that fact.

"And I know you love her too. No matter what her father did to you." She gulps. "I know, or you wouldn't even be here."

I draw a breath to say something but she beats me to it.

"I think my husband underestimates you, and so does Detective Ortiz. You're capable. You're resilient and strong and you have a good heart."

She doesn't know the half of it.

"I know that if you could help us find her . . . get closer to her . . . you would."

NINA LAURIN

94

I'm starting to understand where this is going. Of course. I shouldn't be surprised.

Images flicker in front of my eyes, snapshots from a distant past, and I have to squeeze my eyes shut to get rid of them.

"I already told the police everything I knew." Many times, over and over again while impassive people in uniforms took notes, while nurses waited in the background with syringes full of sedatives in case I started wigging out.

"No," she says with surprising firmness. "Not everything."

"Excuse me?"

She puts her hands on my shoulders and her grip is as steely as her voice. "It's been ten years. You must have remembered something else."

Thirteen. Thirteen years since I was taken. But I don't correct her. "No." My voice is a pitiful squeak. No, I can't help you. No, I don't know anything. No, please don't. No no no no.

"Do you think I haven't tried my goddamn best? Do you think I'm some kind of monster?"

"No, I don't. You're not the monster here, Lainey. But you might be our only chance of finding him."

I want to. I want nothing more with all my heart, but for the life of me, I just don't see how.

"Our only chance is to work together." Jacqueline lowers her voice. "He thinks he's too smart to leave a trace, but we can prove him wrong. We can make him stumble.

Make a mistake—just a small misstep could be enough. And I think you can help."

I weigh her words as moments tick away.

"What do you want me to do?"

"We'll be going on TV again. I want you to come with us. And I want you to say that you are starting to remember."

CHAPTER ELEVEN

It's hard to breathe. More than anything I wish Sean were here.

"Please say yes." Jacqueline's gaze is on mine, un-blinking.

"I—I need a minute," I choke out, and flee into the hallway.

I stumble past door after door until I find the bathroom, dart in and slide the latch into place. Perched on the edge of the tub, I catch my breath. With numb fingers, I feel around the lining of my jacket until I find one of the foil lumps—it doesn't matter which one it is right now, I gulp down its entire contents without so much as a glance.

At first I don't even hear the knocking on the door.

"Lainey?" someone calls. "Is everything all right?"

It's Tom Shaw. I want to tell him I'm fine. I want to tell him to fuck off and die, but my voice refuses to work.

"Laine." This time it's Sean. "Let me in. Right now."

I go to the door and open the latch. He pushes past, ignoring my protests and insults, and slams the door shut. He grabs my shoulders and turns me to face him.

"Don't just barge in here," I mutter through clenched teeth. "I'm fine."

His face grows somber. A tendon pops in his neck as he grits his teeth. "What did she say to you?"

"She wants me to go on TV with them."

His face refocuses, inches away from mine. "TV?"

"Some interview. They want—"

"No." His voice is low but brimming with anger. "Absolutely not."

He grabs a towel from the rack, runs it under cold water, and presses it to my puffy eyes, to my forehead. His every move is so achingly tender that I almost start crying. There are so many things I want to say, but I'm terrified of shattering this fragile moment.

It couldn't last anyway. A second later, someone pounds on the bathroom door.

"Everything okay in there?" Tom's voice. He's trying to sound concerned, but irritation crackles in every word. I can practically hear him thinking on the other side, *Great, now we have to call an ambulance because this little freak can't keep it together.*

"Yes," Sean calls out. "She just needs a break."

"Do you want anything?" Jacqueline calls out. "Some water, some ice?..."

I hear Shaw murmur something disapproving, and I'm not sure if he's displeased with me or with her. As soon as we exit, she starts to fuss over me, her expression betraying guilt. Her smudged mascara gives her raccoon eyes.

"Can I speak with you?" Sean says. "Both of you. Right now."

I sit crouched in the corner of the living room while Sean and Tom Shaw argue in low, angry voices. Jacqueline is pouring coffee into tall mugs, stirring in cream and ungodly amounts of brown sugar. Mutely, she holds out a cup to me, but I shake my head. My hands in my pockets, I play with the empty foil lump I forgot to toss, breaking it down into a thousand pieces that will probably stick to the lining forever.

"We're going to go on TV," Tom Shaw is saying. "I want it to be all three of us this time. If Lainey agrees, of course."

The way he says it, it doesn't sound like I have too many options.

"This is a terrible idea," Sean says. "I will not allow it. It severely compromises—"

"The press has been hounding us for days. Might as well beat them to it." With a creak, Shaw starts to rise from his chair.

"Lainey's safety," Sean finishes without missing a beat.

"I think," Shaw says too loudly, as if he's talking to me

without wanting to address me directly, "it's Lainey's call at this point. We should ask her what she thinks."

I look at my hands—at my fingertips, the only part that can be seen from under my jacket sleeves.

"It's absolutely out of the question," Sean says over my head. "She's not—" He cuts himself off, starts over with as little success. "In her current state..."

"If you think I'm not competent enough to make the decision, just say so," I hear myself say.

In the momentary silence, I feel rather than see all three of their gazes swivel to me. They practically slice apart the air like steel knives.

"I'll do it," I say. "If you think it'll help."

Sean exhales. It sounds like he's been holding his breath this whole time.

"I have to speak to someone about this," he finally says. "I'm going to make a phone call. Don't even think of moving from this room until I'm back."

Mentally I plead with him not to go, not to leave me alone with these two. Then again, I just agreed to go to the press with them.

Tom Shaw gets up and goes to the cabinet, retrieves a half-empty bottle, and pours a good three ounces into his cup of coffee, ignoring Jacqueline's withering glare.

"Hey." He holds out the bottle. "Want some?"

"Tom," Jacqueline snaps.

"She's our guest. And she sure looks like she could use a drink."

Grateful, I get up while he pours no more than one finger of liquor into a tumbler. This much won't even give me a buzz, but I take it anyway and gulp it down.

"There," he says. "We're all under a lot of stress. I know we're asking you for a lot." His weary gaze lingers on my face as if trying to puzzle out what's going on inside my head. "And believe me, I won't forget it."

*   *   *

We will be doing the press conference first thing the next morning, at the police station. I make my way after Sean, down the path leading to his car. The pills amplify the gulp of booze tenfold, and I'm still floating when Sean helps me get into the passenger seat. If he can tell I'm high, he doesn't let on.

I rest my head on the back of the seat and close my eyes. The car sways like a ship even though it's not moving yet. Calmly, Sean closes his door and turns the key in the ignition. Then, as the car purrs to life, he punches the steering wheel until the horn gives a pitiful yelp. "Goddammit. I should never have agreed to take you there."

"It's okay," I say. I'm so cloudy I don't care right now. Just what I needed.

"What were you thinking? Letting them corner you like that. You should have said no."

"I didn't want to say no. I want to help."

"Who do you think this is helping?"

Without opening my eyes, I feel the car drive off. Gravity presses me down in the seat. I let my head loll.

"Laine," Sean says softly. I can't tell how much time has passed—the pills, they do that. When I pry one eye open, diffuse orange lights spin like a kaleidoscope outside the car window. "Wake up. We're here."

"How did it happen?"

The words surprise me as much as they surprise him. Without looking in his direction, I can tell he grows tense. He knows perfectly well what I mean.

"I can't share details with you. You know that."

"I—" I'm about to say I have a right to know, except I don't. And nothing, absolutely nothing, obligates him to tell me a thing.

"She disappeared from school."

"I read that."

In my peripheral vision, he rubs his eyes. "You can't repeat this to anyone, okay?"

"Who do you take me for?" Who indeed.

"No one is sure how it happened. It's like she slipped away sometime between her last class and..." He trails off. "Her aunt was supposed to pick her up that day."

"I know."

"She's Jacqueline's half sister, Jacinta. She's in college. She's been picking her up from school since last year. But that day she showed up and there was no Olivia. She waited fifteen minutes then went inside."

He pauses, letting me figure out the rest. I can only imagine. Their worry collapsing into panic. Into terror.

And from there on, the terror just kept growing, and it still is, a little more with every minute and hour and day that passes. Until terror consumes everything.

I don't know how it feels, of course. Only what it's like from the other side. A little bit the same, as time trickles by and you start to realize no one is going to find you, no one is going to help you. And that's when you stop waiting and time becomes an endless black void that swallows you up.

Except time flows much, much slower when you're a kid.

The car's blue-lit dashboard pixelates before my eyes, and I remember to blink. A stillness has settled over the car, filled only with the white-noise hum of the engine. Snapping out of it, he finally turns the key in the ignition and even that powers down, leaving us alone.

"You can still change your mind," he says. "In fact, I strongly recommend it."

"I don't know. I don't even know if it'll make a difference." When I turn my head, his profile stands out starkly against the window. "But I don't think I can live with myself if I don't try. It might be too late for me, but..."

"Don't say that."

"They must have loved her. I mean, her pictures are all over the house. And I saw her room. She lived like a princess. They gave her everything she could have asked for."

I hope not too much bitterness seeps into my words.

"You're no less important," Sean says. "And you never were. A person's worth isn't determined by how much money their family has."

"Really?" I raise an eyebrow.

"Really. And I know I sound like a walking cliché, but money isn't a magic cure-all. It can't guarantee anything. Not safety—Olivia is living proof of that. Or happiness."

"You don't think she was happy?" A sharp pang in my chest. I feel too much, and the haze of the pills, always so reliable, is of no help. It's like trying to stop a knife with a sheet of tissue paper. I fidget, twisting the hem of my jacket in my hands.

"Who can tell? I went to talk to her teachers first thing. The school psychologist said she had a mean streak. She was a bully, almost got suspended for attacking another kid." He shakes his head. "Sorry, it's not what you want to hear, but it's the truth. Trust me, happy children don't try to stab their classmates in the eye with a pencil."

"She did that?"

"Yeah. And from what I know of public school, you have to screw up pretty damn badly to get suspended."

"Trust me, I know," I say, and instantly regret it. Although I'm sure it's all on my record anyway, in his neat little file. "I feel bad. I know people tried. I was just beyond helping by then."

He says nothing, deep in thought. I glance up at him.

"What is it?" I ask.

"She was in public school. Sure, in the richest neighborhood in the city, but still."

I jolt upright. "If her parents are so rich . . . why wasn't she in a fancy private school somewhere?"

His frown deepens. "Yeah. My point exactly."

Without waiting for me, he gets out of the car. I take my cue and follow. It's near freezing outside, and my skin, spoiled by the wonderful working heater in his car, prickles with gooseflesh.

"What are you going to do?" I say, shoving my hands in my pockets for warmth.

"I'm going to check it out."

He walks me to Natalia's door without another word. The porch light is broken and the window is dark.

"If there's anything I should know, you'll call me," he says in a tone that doesn't bear arguing.

I nod.

"Promise me."

"Promise," I echo. And then, out of nowhere, he pulls me close for a hug, lingering as if he, too, is afraid to let go.

The house is empty, so I use my key to get in through the patio door in the back. It doesn't look like Natalia's been home yet. I throw the tank top I borrowed and my own dirty clothes into her washer, happy to be able to walk around the place in nothing but my bra and underwear with no one to see me. She has an old Apple laptop, and luckily for me there's no password, so I open a browser window and log on to ConspiracyTalk.

There's an alarming number of new posts on the Olivia Shaw thread, and the new message icon is blinking in the corner of the screen. Foreboding creeps over me before I even click on the title. The page loads for a small eternity, and when it's finally done, I find myself staring at my own face.

CHAPTER TWELVE

The image is so filtered and photoshopped that I can't tell when or where it could have been taken. But it's unmistakably me. There's a frown line between my eyebrows, and I'm squinting. It makes my face look harsh and old.

> Roswell82: Hey everybody! New stuff on the Olivia Shaw case! Looks like we have a name for the birth mother: one Lainey Moreno. And this is where it gets really freaky, get ready... it turns out that she's the same person as Ella Santos. Yup, the missing mystery girl who couldn't identify her captor after three years.

Mike6669: Holy shit. This case is starting to seriously give me the heebie-jeebies

Salem_baby: Someone bump the Ella Santos thread

Roswell82: that's like 3 yrs old with no news. Anyone have anything new on Ella Santos? ANYONE?

Salem_baby: Wasn't @lostgirl14 really into that case? R u there @lostgirl14?

Roswell82: @lostgirl14?? Hello?

I close every single window, wipe the history, and slam the laptop shut. I'm reeling with so many questions that it's hard to focus on just one. How? Who? How much do they know? Next is the surge of fear that makes me long to call Scan, tell him I won't be going on TV. Tell him I changed my mind. Tell him to come pick me up and take me somewhere—anywhere—else.

The phone appears in my hand as if by magic, and I know I have no other options now. I'm too numb and too tired to be afraid of what he'll say. I don't even hold my breath while the phone rings.

A click, and a voice. A woman's voice. A melodic, purring hello of someone confident enough to answer someone else's cell phone, and it jabs me under the ribs with a sharp, unexpected pang. I thumb the End Call button and stare at the mute phone, traitor in the palm of my hand, the battery flashing with its alert. Hurt is teeming in the hollow under my ribs and I feel like I'm the one who caught him cheating. I can picture her examining the phone with suspicion, thumbing through contacts, recent calls, texts, voice mails. I hope I didn't get him into too much trouble. No, I'm lying. I hope I got him into a shit-ton of trouble.

Deep down, buried under the protective layer that is Laine Moreno, a small, young girl feels betrayed and alone.

When Natalia comes in, she finds me curled up on the floor at the foot of the couch. I look up to see her locking the door; the clock on the DVD player reads half past midnight. The four-to-midnight shift is never that good, and she looks tired, her makeup cakey under her eyes. "You all right?"

I make myself nod, and this small lie is enough to make the loneliness overflow, spilling out in ugly sobs.

"Hey." She crouches next to me, and a wave of her perfume sweeps over me like a veil. Underneath the synthetic flowers and musk, I pick up all the usual notes: cigarette smoke, a whiff of boozy breath, and that particular strip club smell that clings to you like leeches—yeasty, a touch metallic, with a note of chlorinated stage cleaner. I used to scrub it out of myself every time I came home, even if it meant going to bed with wet hair, but eventually I got used to it. A couple nights off work and I'm starting to notice it again.

I don't have the energy to shake off her arm when she puts it around my shoulders.

"Did something happen? Something you're not telling me?"

Where do I even start?

"Hey, if you want, you can come crash with me. The bed's big enough."

Right now I just don't want to be alone again, so I follow her to the bedroom and let her sit me down on the edge of the pink bedspread like a doll. She reaches around, unclasps my bra, and takes it off, then tucks me under the red sheets, which turn out to be surprisingly soft. The pillow smells like her hair conditioner. I bury my face in it, listening to her get undressed.

The bed creaks and tilts as she climbs in, throwing her arm over me. She's asleep within seconds, her breath a gentle purr on the back of my neck. To avoid waking her, I do my best to lie still, but gradually, the self-consciousness ebbs away as her heat envelops me. She stirs and moves closer; her bare skin brushes against my back, then presses into it. It's velvet soft but her breasts are rigid—she got her implants done a year ago.

I dip in and out of sleep, wishing there were a way to get up and go get a pill from the stash I'd rescued from my apartment. But I don't want to risk waking her, breaking this frail human contact. I can't remember the last time I felt comfortable with someone—and the few brief moments of closeness between me and Sean hardly count. So I let myself skim the surface, hoping at least my body will rest even if my mind keeps reeling.

Next time I wake up, it's because of a touch, butterfly-soft fingertips crawling across my side, counting their way up my xylophone ribs—one-two-three. I hold my breath halfway through an exhale. She must not realize I've woken, because the fingertips continue down the curve of my waist. A soft but assured palm cups my breast then slips down the hollow where the two parts of my rib cage meet. I don't know what to do, how to react—or if she expects me to react at all. I never had the slightest inkling she was into girls—not if her 'roided-out boyfriend was any indication.

The hand continues its downward journey, inching down to my belly button, and my muscles tense as she nears the line of my scar. This time she feels it.

"Shh." Her whisper tickles the hairs on the back of my neck, followed by the touch of lips as her hand dives between my clenched thighs.

"Natalia," I say, rolling over. In the near darkness, I can see her face, the hurt look in her eyes. "I'm just tired. I want to sleep, okay?"

"Sure." Sheets rustle as she sits up. She sleeps naked, and I glimpse the curve of her back as she gets up and walks to her dresser. She looks for something for a few moments then tiptoes back to bed.

When she holds out her open palm, a pill sits nestled in its center. I can't tell what kind.

"Open." She taps my cheek with her fingertips, and I

obey so she can put the pill on my tongue. She gently closes my jaw, gripping my chin. Her acrylic nails are done in long, sharp points, as always.

My hospital-honed instinct kicks in, and I gulp the pill before I realize it. Back at the children's psychiatric, it was better not to argue or ask questions.

"Good." She holds me close and pats my head, the gesture weirdly caring—it would be motherly if my face weren't pressed to her bare chest. She stays there until my head grows heavy and my chin starts to dip. Wrapped in warm silk and perfume scent, I sink into sleep.

The last thing I remember is her gently lowering my head onto the pillow.

CHAPTER THIRTEEN

I'm slathered in cheap foundation that makes my face itch, ready for my close-up.

I woke up late, way late. Natalia was gone, and Sean was pounding on the door—must have been for quite a while before I woke. Light poured into the room through half-open curtains, pitilessly exposing the cracks and dust all over everything. When I sat up, I was naked except for my socks, my underwear hanging on the bedpost.

Whatever that pill was, it sure as hell kicked my little prescription meds' ass. I'd have to ask Natalia to get me more.

If Sean was mad, he didn't let on. He was oddly quiet all the way to the station, lost in his own thoughts.

And now here I am. Ready to do what I agreed to, and my resolve is fading with every passing moment.

It'll make it harder for him to dehumanize her—at least that's what I was told, and that's what I read in my many hours of late-night research, squinting at the computer screen in the dead of night after work. We're supposed to call her by name, all the time, and talk about her likes and dislikes, how smart and sweet she is, and so on. Then she'll become a person to him instead of an object.

That's what the textbooks say. My personal theory, however, is that sick fucks like him actually enjoy it. They get off on it, and I don't doubt that seeing my face on a TV screen is going to be the cherry on the damn sundae.

Jacqueline brought clothes for me. There's something touching in the way she lays out the sweaters and skirts for me to choose from, three of each, and even a pair of shoes. Everything is very proper, pastels, expensive fabrics, and they all kind of look exactly the same to me. I barely glance at the selection, picking up a sweater and skirt at random before heading to the tiny restroom to change.

There's one of those UV lights overhead so you can't shoot up. They turn everything a Twilight Zone shade of purple, and your skin looks like a corpse made of wax so you can't find your veins. This is the last place I'd be shooting up anyway, if I were into that sort of thing, if only because the door has no lock and anyone can come in whenever.

Jacqueline's sweater is only a little too big for me, and the sleeves, paradoxically, are too short. I keep pulling them down nervously, digging into the cuffs with my fingernails. You still can't see my wrists, but some habits are hard to let go.

Just as I start to struggle out of my jeans, there's a delicate knock on the door. Nonetheless, it makes me jump like I was caught doing something dirty.

"Lainey?" Jacqueline's voice. "You all right in there?"

The polite way of saying hurry the fuck up. "Yeah," I yell. "Just a minute."

"Does everything fit?"

I don't know yet because I'm still pulling my jeans down my calves and only now realizing that I forgot to unlace my boots. With a sigh, I sit on the toilet lid and start to tug off the right one. I take out my knife, which had been sitting snug at my ankle, and tuck it in the waistband of my underwear. It's warm from being close to my skin, and its smooth handle fits into the small of my lower back like a lover's hand.

Just in time, because the door opens and Jacqueline slips in. Without a trace of self-consciousness, she kneels next to me and helps me unlace my other boot so I can wiggle out of my jeans.

She unzips the side of the skirt—naturally, she's one of those women who wears skirts that zip up the side—and holds it out, as if dressing a small child. I have no choice but to step into it, one foot, then the other. When she pulls the skirt up to my waist and buttons the top button, I squirm a little, but she doesn't notice the knife behind my waistband.

"A bit loose," she says. "But no one will see under the sweater." She gives a soft laugh. "Enjoy it while you can. When you're my age, you won't be so effortlessly skinny."

I give her a look like she's some kind of alien.

She covers her awkwardness with an even more uneasy laugh. "Shoes," she says, and holds out the beige low-heel pumps in an almost supplicating gesture.

I take a look at them and slowly shake my head. My neck creaks like a wooden puppet's. No way.

"You can't really wear boots with this," she says.

I force my mouth to form a syllable. No.

"Come on," she says and, to my horror, reaches for my right sock and starts to roll it down.

I just about kick her in the face. Not exactly kick—but my leg twitches like she hit the nerve in my knee, an ingrained instinct that has become as close to a reflex as it gets. She shrieks in surprise and topples back, goes sprawling on her ass on the filthy floor. Her eyes are dark, shiny pools—filled with anger, pain, or tears, I can't exactly tell. Her lips form my name but I don't hear the sound over the rush of blood in my ears.

"I—I'm sorry," I choke out.

Her gaze travels from my face down to my exposed ankle. The bluish overhead light tints her skin a shade closer to ash, but I don't need to be able to see color to know her face drains of blood. She clasps her hand over her mouth—a gesture, I once read, of people who have a hard time expressing their feelings.

I tug my sock back into place to cover the scar and reach for my boot, all without looking at her.

"Lainey," she says in a muffled voice, "oh my God."

I resume putting on my boots.

"It's—it's okay," she stammers. "No one will see your feet anyway. You can put your jeans back on...if you want to."

Her voice shakes, and when I look up, there are unmistakable wet trails down her cheeks.

"I'm sorry," she whimpers as she tries to cover her eyes without smearing her makeup. In an unprecedented moment of compassion, I grab a handful of toilet paper and press it into her hand. She dabs under her eyes, trying to hide the fact that she's full-on crying now.

I realize she's not spilling those tears for me—she's just terrified for Olivia, and with good reason. The very thought makes me queasy, and the hollow hum Natalia's pill left in my veins isn't helping.

We come out minutes later, after she's powdered under her eyes and I've finished lacing my boots. "Remember what we talked about," Jacqueline says, her voice soft but intent, and before I have a chance to answer, she takes my hand and squeezes it.

I keep sneaking glances at Sean, trying to see some spark of acknowledgment, but his gaze slips indifferently across my face and away. I notice Shaw side-eyeing my worn, grimy boots, which look even more worn and grimy in contrast with his wife's neat, pretty things.

The actual press conference is a bad acid trip. I try

not to flinch at camera flashes while Jacqueline gives another shaky-voiced speech, all words I know by heart already from watching others in clips and on TV: *I beg you to help us bring our girl back home safely*. Overhead lights are too bright, and my eyes must disappear in my face, because I'm squinting the whole time. Sean isn't in the crowd; he's standing on the sidelines, grim faced. I'm aching to glance over, but it won't look good. I have to look present. Invested, as they'd say.

Jacqueline and Tom Shaw are done, and I'm silently praying for the whole thing to be over when some journalist chick pushes her way to the front of the crowd. Her aggressive red lipstick makes her mouth look like two slabs of raw meat someone slapped across her face.

"Lainey." She makes an ugly emphasis on my name. At least she doesn't call me Ella, but I can hear it lurking under the syllables—like this is supposed to be some secret code only the two of us share. Wink-wink, nudge. "Lainey, do you believe this was the same man who held you captive? How did you feel when you found out?"

All the downers in the world would be no help to me now. In the back of my mind, I already know this is taking a turn for absolute disaster but I can't stop it—like a passenger in a car skidding across deadly, rain-slicked highway, I'm nothing but a passive observer, unable to make any difference, and all my pathetic attempts will only make the situation worse.

Which doesn't stop me from trying.

At the edge of my vision, Jacqueline grows tense, her

spine an arrow. Shaw draws a noisy breath, a bull ready for a fight, and Sean starts to move toward me.

"I don't know," I hear myself say. "And to be honest, I don't think it matters."

There's a murmur in the crowd, and my heart starts to thunder against my sternum.

"You're saying you don't care?" the red-mouthed woman asks. Her painted eyebrow arches. Behind her a photographer clicks away and away and away, and with every click, I feel myself sink. The last time I felt this raw, vulnerable, exposed, I was on a cold metal table with my feet in stirrups while a gray-haired woman curiously peered between my thirteen-year-old thighs.

"I'm saying..." My voice thins and rises in pitch. It shatters in my throat and fills it with broken glass. "I'm remembering things. An awful lot of things." My hand goes for my waistband. I don't think—the blade thinks for me, jumping into my hand, still warm from my skin, and clicks open. "And when I find him, I'll make him hurt in ways he can't even imagine."

Photo flashes glance off it.

And I have no regrets.

CHAPTER FOURTEEN

Sean erupts onto the narrow podium, physically block-ing me from the reporters. He's saying something in his loud, authoritative voice, something expected, *We're finished here, nothing to see, everybody please leave in an orderly fashion.* He half turns and catches my wrist in his grasp—holy shit, he's strong. I suspected that strength in him, but as he squeezes my wrist like a vise, I realize I had no clue. His grip is crushing and pitiless, and he twists my hand until I'm this close to screaming. My fingers unclench, and my knife clatters to the floor.

He never lets go of my hand, pulling me after him off the podium, back into the waiting room. After all the camera flashes, the yellow glow of the overhead light-bulb might as well be pitch darkness. I blink as my eyes try to adjust, and as if someone flipped a switch, the rest of the world flickers back to normal. And I'm starting to realize what I've just done. It feels like something I heard about or saw on TV. I couldn't have done it. I couldn't have.

Sean's face is a mask of cold rage that makes me wilt inside. He looks like he's going to slap me, and knowing that I deserve it doesn't make it better.

"What the hell was that? What were you thinking?"

I swallow.

"Are you out of your mind? Do you realize that I trusted you—a lot of people did, the Shaws did—and you just fucked up massively?"

"I realize," I say softly. I put my hand on his arm, but it only seems to enrage him more. He throws it off, more aggressively than he had to, and I stumble back. "And every word is true."

He runs his hands over his face. "Jesus," he exhales. "Laine . . ."

"You should be happy," I say, unable to keep the bitterness from my voice. "At least it proves that you were right all along. I do care."

He's silent. It scares me in a way.

"Good to know," he says as he composes himself. "Good to know, and much use it is now."

Jacqueline and Tom come rushing through the door and stop, hovering on the periphery of my vision. Tom Shaw is fuming; Jacqueline looks nonexistent, faded.

"I'll see what I can do for damage control," Sean says,

bowing his head. It pains me to see him grovel in front
of this rich asshole—because of me. "Something can be
worked out, I'm sure."

"It's okay," Jacqueline says. "Lainey."

Isn't that what you wanted me to do? I almost ask. And
telling Sean the truth would probably save my ass, but
I can't bring myself to betray her. I'd rather face Sean's
anger on my own.

She meets my gaze, and the corners of her lips turn up
ever so slightly. "I completely understand. God knows
I've felt like saying the same thing a couple of times." I
read it in her eyes: thank you.

I follow Sean without another word of argument.
Thankfully, there's no one in the parking lot behind the
station. No journalists or their vans. "Can I have my knife
back?"

"You've got to be kidding me."

I'm not. Not that I thought he'd actually give me back
my knife, but I felt like I should say something.

"I'm sorry."

Thinking I heard wrong, I look up.

"I'm sorry I got you dragged into this. It doesn't mean
I'm not angry, but for what it's worth, I never should
have let you do this in the first place."

I was ready to be yelled at, to be threatened with arrest or the psych ward. I wasn't ready for his sympathy,
and the worst part is that it seems real. That sets my
teeth on edge more than anything else.

"You realize you've put yourself in danger, right?"

I suppose he's right. But as long as it helps them get closer to Olivia, I really don't care.

"And you know you'll have to revisit your testimony now. The sergeant detective will want to know all these new things you've remembered." He measures me with a look. "There aren't any. Are there?"

Silently, I shake my head.

"Jesus. What the hell were you thinking?"

In any other situation, I'd backpedal, tell him all about that conversation back in Olivia's room, blame everything on Jacqueline, embellish for all it's worth. Tell him she cornered me, coerced me, make everyone look like the bad guy except for me. Make myself out to be just a pawn, a victim of circumstance—isn't that what I am, what I've always been? The girl in the wrong place at the wrong time, the girl with the wrong memories who *just wanted to do what's right*.

Except right now, I need him to get angry with me. Furious. I want him to yell.

"Are you doing this on purpose? Undermining what little credibility—" He cuts himself off, realizing what he just said.

"Yeah. The little credibility I already have. I get it." I grimace. "Not exactly your dream witness, I know."

"That's not the point," he snaps. "I'm worried about your safety in all this. You want to end up in protective custody? 'Cause I can make it happen."

I'm not even sure if he's sarcastic.

"I'll see about setting you up someplace else. I don't

want you staying with some stripper in West Seattle, you hear me?"

"She's not a stripper," I murmur. "And I'm fine where I am. I just want to—"

I just want to go home. Not to my old apartment, although it would be a good start—I want to go back in time to the world I lived in before this week. When I had a life, just barely, but I was holding on. But then I found and lost Olivia at the same time, all in the span of one day. The moment I saw her on that poster, my whole sad, little existence turned out to be like I always suspected—borrowed time, unraveling right before my eyes.

And now I'm in free fall, and I can't tell how much longer before I hit the ground.

Sean leaves me on the doorstep of Natalia's with instructions to stay inside, not open the door to anyone, and for the love of God, not talk to the press. Oh, and not answer the phone unless it's him. Well, he doesn't have to worry about that. The battery is dying, and Natalia's iPhone charger doesn't fit my mastodon of a phone anyway.

As soon as I'm inside, I watch through the blinds until his car disappears into the distance. Now the only cars on the street are a rusty pickup and a Toyota, both there since yesterday—and my own Neon, of course, with a blue-and-white parking ticket clinging to the windshield.

As the afternoon wears on, I grow restless, as if the plaster walls are closing in on me, the house shrinking like something from a storybook. I try turning on the TV, stumble on a news program almost immediately, and can't thumb the Off button quickly enough. The thought of going online makes me nauseous. I can only imagine what they must be saying about me.

Only now I notice that I'm still wearing Jacqueline's things and peel them off me like they're poisoned, making a hollow promise to myself that I'll give them back. If she even wants them back, after what I did—if she can bring herself to think about cashmere at a time like this in the first place. My own baggy clothes are still stuffed in my backpack, wrinkled, smelling of damp and sweat when I shake them out. I feel gross putting them on, but right now it's what I need. Pristine sweaters will only attract undue attention.

The sun is setting when I pull up to the curb a block from my building, and I almost miss it. I'm already backing into an empty spot between two cars when I notice the van across the street, inconspicuous at first glance, but only when you don't know what to look for. It's blank white except for the telltale antenna. At this distance, the windshield is like a black one-way mirror, and I can't tell if there's anyone in the driver's seat, but I'd bet the last penny in my bank account that there is.

Alarm prickles down my spine. I twist my hair and tuck it under my collar, shove my hands in my pockets, and slouch. Incognito, I slip into the alley between my building and the next one over.

Behind the building is a small gravel lot blocked off

by a rusted, bent chain-link fence. It's broken in several places, so it's not hard for someone my size to slip through without so much as snagging my sleeve on rusted metal. A fire escape spirals along the back, and it takes me a few seconds to scale it. As my hands grip the bars, I notice they're starting to tremble. There's a hollow feeling deep inside, a kind of anxious tremor at my very core. A void needing to be filled.

And when the void makes its presence known, it doesn't like to be ignored. My foot slips, and for a terrifying moment, I swing on my arms until my chest connects with the ladder. The clang is deafening. I cringe from it as much as from the pain echoing in my ribs. Rust and chipped paint scrape against my palms, burning, and more of it rains into my face and eyes.

I feel around the emptiness with my foot until I steady it on one of the horizontal bars. My heart hammers, and now it's not just my hands but my whole body that's shaking as I cling to the ladder for dear life.

The longer I hang here, the more likely I am to attract attention. Even if it's only some well-intentioned jackass from the building who might mistake me for a thief and call the cops, which is just what I need right now. After another minute or two of silently pleading for my body to get its shit together and stop shaking, I climb the rest of the way, swing my legs one after another over the railing of the balcony, and hop down. The impact travels through my soles, making my teeth clack together.

I crouch so no one can see me from the windows.

Most people here keep their curtains and blinds drawn tightly all day long. Either they're hiding something or they just don't want potential thugs to see their stuff, cheap flat-screen TVs, faux-leather armchairs, whatever their prized possessions happen to be.

Still, in my state, I don't trust myself not to make noise, so without wasting time, I creep forward. All the balconies are really one long one, separated by metal sheets or plywood panels. I climb over one, then another, clambering over all the crap people feel bad about throwing out so they leave it to soak up the oily Seattle rain.

When I get to my window, I glance around, and having made sure I'm still alone, unobserved as far as I can see, I push the piece of cardboard inward. It falls to the floor on the other side. I freeze like a baby deer, listening, but there's still no sound. My blanket is in place over the window, and it rustles softly in the damp breeze.

I reach in through the hole in the glass—it's big enough that I don't risk cutting myself on the edges. Carefully, I find the latch and slide it aside without a shadow of resistance, without so much as a creak or a squeak. The window opens just as silently.

This isn't the work of some tween thug wannabes from the neighborhood. Unless they felt like oiling the hinges and the latch on my window out of sheer generosity.

I throw one leg over the windowsill, then the other, and hop onto the floor. Broken glass crunches under my

soles with every step, and I can't shake the feeling I'm
in enemy territory. In the dim light of the fading sunset,
everything takes on a new, sinister quality. I step amidst
my own things that, without warning, became danger-
ous relics. In a rush of paranoia, I examine everything,
struggling to remember: Did I leave these clothes on my
bed like that? Was the shapeless mound of dirty laun-
dry overflowing from the plastic basket the same when I
left yesterday? I kick a pair of dirty underwear under the
bed, trying hard not to think of how it got there.

Clothes. I need clothes. That's what I came here for—
right? Drawer after drawer of my rickety dresser flies
open, and I rummage through my possessions. Jeans,
shirts, a sequined top I bought with Natalia in a moment
of craziness. Bras and panties are tangled together in
one wash-faded ball. I feel a tide of nausea and drop everything I'm holding to the floor in a heap.

I don't realize I'm hyperventilating until the room
starts to spin. I sit on top of the pile of clothes and
cradle my head in my hands. It didn't seem important
before, with everything else that was going on, but now
the realization looms, overwhelming: someone was going through my things, and I have no way to tell what
he touched. In a cold sweat, I get up and start to stuff
random clothes into my backpack. No way am I wearing
these until they've been through at least three wash cy-
cles.

Too bewildered to think about what I'm doing, I wander down two flights of stairs as if on autopilot, like

I've done a million times before. The perpetual overhead hum of neon lights, which I'd learned to ignore over the years, sets my teeth on edge. I think of knocking on the janitor's door to ask if he'd seen something, or someone, but change my mind. He's drunk two-thirds of the time, and by now he's probably passed out.

Down in the lobby, I blink like an owl in the bright light. The thought of going outside, into the dark, which I hadn't thought twice about just an hour earlier, suddenly makes me break out in a cold sweat. I take out my phone and look at it, gnawing on my lip; the battery is flashing red.

Then realization hits me. I'm never coming back. I can't keep living there. The place that used to be my home now isn't.

I could call Sean, like I should have called him from the beginning. I thumb through my short contact list and my eyes mist over. Holding my breath, I turn off the phone. Patting myself down, I find a pack with one last cigarette, along with a set of matches from the club, with that tacky phallic bullet logo in peeling silver. The first match crumples when I try to light it. The second bursts into flame with a hiss, consumed in its entirety in seconds, singeing my fingertips. On the third try, I light up. Holding the door open, I step into the humid embrace of fresh air.

I don't even realize what I've done until it's too late. They swarm me. First only one, then three, four others, cameras clicking away, capturing the horror that

must dawn on my face frame by frame. I yell something, swat at them, shield myself with my hands.
Desperate, I toss the cigarette at the most insistent
one, a dark-haired woman with aggressively crimson
lips. I recognize her from the conference—she was the
one who asked me how I felt when I found out, and
in that split second, I fervently wish I could crush that
still-burning cigarette into her eye, pushing in, twisting. But she only flinches as the cherry of the cigarette
traces an arc and goes out on the damp pavement
without ever touching her or singeing so much as a
hair.

But it's enough to startle her, so I turn away and
break into a sprint. The wind whips my hair around my
face, blinding and deafening me. My backpack thumps
against my lower back in a rhythm, something sharp at
the bottom—a shoe, probably—digging into the small of
my back. I can't tell if they're still on my trail, and I don't
dare glance over my shoulder—I just run, pushing my
tired and terrified muscles beyond full capacity.

My car comes into view, and I grab the keys from my
pocket. I've never been so damn happy to see this thing.

Before the reporters catch up to me, I slam my foot
down on the gas pedal and take off with a screech. I
blow past a stop sign, turn, turn again, and come to a
shuddering halt at a traffic light.

I'm alone. At least I think so. I'm seeing shadows
everywhere, encroaching from all sides. Tears blanket
my vision and refuse to clear; the traffic light bleeds

candy-apple red then emerald green. Clumsily wiping my eyes with my sleeve, I twist the steering wheel. The car zigzags on the damp pavement, the tires screech and spin through emptiness. I feel their vibration through the seat and in the steering wheel that I grip for dear life. While in front of me, the world reels, lights leaving long multicolored trails in their wake.

The car steadies too late. It thuds as the wheels jump over the curb onto the sidewalk and, with a dull, bone-rattling thump that makes my jaw clack painfully, hits something and grinds to a stop.

CHAPTER FIFTEEN

The car's not totaled—thank God; I don't know what I'd do if I lost my car now. The bumper has a deep dent and the hood looks misshapen, like a soda can someone squeezed too hard. Nonetheless, a tow truck is here, and just thinking of having to pay a fine and to go retrieve my car from God knows where makes me nauseous with anxiety. Before Sean showed up, they made me pass a Breathalyzer test, and I know I can only thank my lucky stars it's not more serious, that someone else wasn't involved—just a fucking mailbox that has barely a scratch to show for it.

Once Sean arrived, I had no choice but to tell him the truth. I thought I was being chased. I reacted badly. The road was wet. The usual plethora of excuses I should have probably saved for the insurance company.

In the passenger seat of his car, I watch the proceedings with detachment, a silent show of lights and people talking. Sean exchanges a few words with the traffic police, with the tow truck guy. Taking care of my problems for me, again. The police lights flash blue and red, a comforting lullaby, and the tow truck's lights are orange, solid orange, on and off like a strobe. The Xanax I took before the police got here is the only thing that keeps me from freaking out, and I let myself rest my head on the comfortable leather of the back of the car seat, my eyelids tugging down.

Next thing I know, Sean is in the driver's seat but the car is still. The lights are gone, all of them. When did they disappear? God, how long have I been sitting here? My bones feel achy and hollow, my head pounds, and when I crane my neck, there's no trace of the police car, of the tow truck, of my Neon. We're not even on the same street.

Sean is on the phone. He's talking in a hushed and angry voice.

I try to speak but my words come out smudged; the consonants bleed like wet paint in the rain. His gaze shoots to me, and he presses his finger to his lips.

"I don't care. No, I don't know if her life is in danger, but I'm not taking a chance."

A muffled voice drones inside the phone. I push the seat away and sit up straight.

"Then I'll do it myself. I'll pay for it. I don't mind."

"What's going on?" I finally manage to ask.

Sean glares at me to keep quiet. Disoriented, I crane my neck to peer out the window, but I still have no idea where we are. All I see is a low orange-tiled building surrounded by a vast half-empty parking lot.

Sean hangs up the phone.

"You're going to stay here for a while. Not the Ritz, but I prefer you someplace with lots of people and surveillance cameras. And anyway . . . you can't keep living in that awful apartment building."

"Excuse me?" He can't just make the decision for me like that. I have a say. And who is he to decide what's good enough?

"Trust me. You'll be comfortable here." His tone is verging on supplication. "And if you wanted stuff from your apartment, you should have asked me. I would have gone and gotten whatever you needed."

The idea of him going through the mess in my apartment fills me with panic. Besides, I don't have any "stuff." Everything I have is with me, in my backpack, and I tell him so, no longer caring if he's judging me. But he only looks relieved.

"Why are you doing this?" I ask as we cross the parking lot. "I mean, really."

He half turns to me, but I can't see his eyes through the inky shadow that falls over them. "Maybe I'm just trying to make it up to you. However I can."

"You don't have to do that. You never did anything—"

"That's precisely the problem."

I'm still unsteady on my feet, but I follow him into

the lobby. He's right, the place isn't exactly luxurious, a cheap hotel, a generic version of a Best Western. It reminds me of the loony bin, except everything is beige instead of mint green. The wall-to-wall carpeting muffles our steps, and through the haze of the pills, it's like I'm walking on clouds. Like I might fall through any moment.

Sean checks me in. I note that he takes two key cards, hands me one and puts the other in his jacket pocket. A part of me is ruffled, another part is ashamed.

He walks me up to the room and lets me swipe the card in the slot. Behind the door is a small suite, only one room opening into a small kitchen. A flower-print bedspread is smoothed over the modest double bed. I bounce on it—the sheets have a faint antiseptic smell about them.

It makes me think of powder-blue gowns and needles and loneliness.

"You'll be safer here," Sean says softly.

I don't think I'll be safer here. Maybe from some nameless, faceless intruder, sure. Except the things I need to be safe from are inside my own head. But after all the shitty things I've already said and done, I don't want to add to them, so I strain to smile. "Thank you. It's nice."

I try not to think of the inevitable. That he's going to go now and leave me here. Alone. As he starts toward the door, I reach out and catch the sleeve of his jacket. My fingertips brush against the wool, soft and smooth, but I drop my hand at my side. We both freeze, startled by the unexpected physical contact.

"If anything is wrong...or if you just need to talk to someone, you know you can always call me, right?"

His eyes soften, and I try to memorize that look, the rare glimpse of the way he probably is outside of work. The him I will most likely never know.

"Can't you not go? Just for a little while."

"I have to."

"It's late."

"I'm afraid finding missing people is a twenty-four-hour kind of gig." But the hint of a smile in the corner of his lips is warm. I can't help myself: I get up and take a step toward him, self-conscious and aware, like I'm inching closer and closer to a precipice and the vertigo is setting in, but the morbid curiosity is stronger. What will I see if I peer over the edge? How much can I handle without being overwhelmed and succumbing to the pull of emptiness?

"I wish there was something more I could do," I say, aware that my words fall flat. Isn't that what everyone says? Isn't that what you're supposed to say? And in the movies, it's always the bad guy who says that sort of thing. My face warms. "Listen," I say, dismayed at the hoarseness in my voice, "I'm sorry. About what happened at the press conference, and everything else. You just have to believe me. I'm not a bad person. I just never had a chance."

"I know that. I never thought you were a bad person.

I think you have a good heart, or we wouldn't even be here."

If it weren't for me, we wouldn't be here for sure. If I'd remembered—something—anything, then . . .

"I don't mean it like that." He takes hold of my chin with just his fingertips and tilts my face up so I look into his eyes. I feel small and fully at his mercy, but somehow it's not bad. "You can't help but leave a mark on people's lives. We all do."

Sometimes more than their lives, I think, and my mind goes to my wrists, covered safely by my long sleeves. I think about Olivia, and then about my mother, about blood filling my hand and making my grip slick and sticky at the same time. The thought doesn't last more than a fraction of a second, but it's enough to make me shiver, and he notices. He notices everything.

"I've barely been able to leave a mark on my own life," I say. He's so close it's dizzying. "Let alone anyone else's. I've never felt like I was in control of anything. Not before and not after. Never. Like it just wasn't in the cards for me, you know?"

"That's not true," he says, and that, too, is the kind of thing you're supposed to say.

"It is true. For my captor, I was just a fulfilment of some sick fantasy, and then for the Shaws, the source of a baby they could adopt and pass for their own. I couldn't even die when I was supposed to," I blurt, and wish I could take it back because the look on his face is that of heartbreak. But it's too late—the words can't be stopped. "Sometimes I think that's why I live like this. I've never even decorated any place I lived in because I can't shake the feeling that it's all just a temporary layover. Until the next bad thing happens, or until I die."

"There will be no next bad thing," he says. "And you're not going to die. Not until you're old and decrepit anyway."

I can't help it—a little giggle escapes me. And that's when he leans in and his lips touch mine, careful but not hesitant, almost chaste. It lasts for less than a second, but when he pulls away, the wind has been knocked out of me, like I forgot to breathe for a full hour.

He traces my jaw, from earlobe to the tip of my chin, in a gesture that could be friendly, or tender, or even loving, if that's how I chose to see it.

"I have to go," he's saying. "You'll call me if you need anything, right?"

I make myself nod, not trusting myself to speak. Only when he's in the doorway do I spontaneously step forward. "I'll do it," I blurt. "I'll revisit my testimony. I'll do anything you need."

As the door closes behind him, I wonder if I just gave him exactly what he was aiming for.

CHAPTER SIXTEEN

"So you don't know where you were held?"

"No."

"If you had to guess?"

"I have no idea. There were no windows. It was a basement, concrete."

"What else was in the basement?"

"Pipes. Rusted metal pipes under the ceiling. And by the wall. There was a heater but it never worked."

"That's where he tied you."

"Yes."

I blink my dry eyes. I've swallowed a handful of Dilaudid in the precinct's bathroom, and it's making me drowsy as fuck.

It might also be the only thing that keeps me from

keeling over and puking my guts out all over this man's shiny shoes.

"He used rope?"

"Yes."

"No chains? No handcuffs?"

"No. Rope. Always the same rope." Rust-colored stains seeped into the fibers, even before the rope rubbed my wrists and ankles bloody. It never occurred to me then to wonder who wore it before me.

Now I wonder who's looking at my decade-old blood-stains right now, without knowing.

And I didn't take nearly enough Dilaudid for that.

"Did you see what he looked like?"

A shake of my head.

"Ms. Moreno."

It's Santos. Ella Santos.

"No. He wore a mask." My lips shape themselves around the words more than ten years old. Not a syllable has changed. But here we are again.

"A mask."

"Leather. Black. I couldn't see his face. A net where his eyes were supposed to be, and over his mouth."

"Did you see anything? What was his hair like?"

"I didn't see it. The mask covered his whole head."

"Could you pick him out of a lineup?"

"I just said I never saw his face."

"Never once."

"Never once." I feel a rush of vindictiveness and push myself halfway up from my ugly plastic chair. "He usually made me lie facedown on the floor. You know, when he raped me."

I watch his expression hungrily for a grimace, for any trace of a reaction. But his gaze remains steely. He's in his sixties, one of those men with a hairless scalp that became shiny with the years. The lights bounce off it.

I bet he's seen worse than me.

I throw a glance at the two-way mirror, as if I just now remembered that Sean is behind it and he can see and hear every word too. I gnaw on the lining of my lower lip. Shit.

"What about his voice. He never spoke to you." He has that way of asking questions, no intonation. Statements of fact. Which they are. I repeated them often enough.

"Rarely. Only at first. When I still tried to fight back."

"Could you describe his voice?"

"The mask distorted it."

"It can't have distorted it that much." Tension rises in his voice. He shifts, making his chair creak. "Gravelly? Deep? Nasal? Describe what pops into your head."

What pops into my head?

The concrete scrapes my cheek. He's shoving my face into the floor like he's trying to crush my head. I hear as much as feel him fumbling, the hiss of a zipper. There are fingers, shoving, pushing. Something tears, and I scream into the cloth he stuffed into my mouth. Pressure, more pain. I think I'm going to die; I pray to God or whatever is out there to just make my heart stop.

Please.

Please let me die.

"I don't know."

The detective's face comes into focus. I blink, trying to figure out what the hell just happened. Did I black out from all the Dilaudid? Did he figure out I'm high as a kite? Oh shit oh shit oh shit.

The door bursts open, and Sean storms in. He pauses between me and the man, shielding me with his body. "I think that's enough."

"She hasn't told me anything I don't already have in here." The man taps the black screen of a tablet with a bony finger.

That's because there's nothing to tell, asshole.

"That's it. We're done here." Instinctively, Sean reaches out and takes my hand to help me get up. We both realize it simultaneously, but he doesn't let go.

"I'm going to take her home now."

Home never sounded like a better idea. My eyelids are lead heavy and my tongue scrapes against my palate like sandpaper. All I can think of is how soon I can lie down and sleep off those pills.

I follow Sean out without another word. Outside, I gulp air as I pat down my pockets in search of my cigarette pack. My hands are numb like I fell asleep on them, my fingers slow and useless lumps of meat and bone.

Sean sighs, reaches into his coat, and takes out a pack of Peter Jacksons. Holds it out to me.

I look up at him quizzically.

"I know, I know, all right? I think we both need it, so just take one."

Somehow I manage to take a cigarette without spilling the entire pack on the wet asphalt under our feet. He takes out a cheap BIC lighter and lights mine first. The nicotine jump-starts my brain—as much as possible anyway.

"I'm sorry you had to go through that." Sean avoids meeting my gaze.

"It was kind of my own fault though, wasn't it?"

I draw smoke into my lungs, breathe it out, letting it billow in front of my face. Sweet, smoky death.

"Is it still..." When he speaks, his voice is hoarse. He's looking for the right words—I can tell by the anguish on his face—except there are no right words, not for this. "Do you still remember it all? Every minute? Even after ten years?"

"Thirteen." I exhale another cloud. "Yes. Every minute."

"Shit."

"I didn't have rich parents to pay my shrink bills. At the children's psych ward, they were happy enough to pump us full of drugs till we were docile, and that was it."

"Fuck, Laine. I'm—"

"Don't say you're sorry. Please. They're all sorry in there." I nod at the building behind us. "So terribly sorry. If they all stopped saying sorry and used the energy to actually find the guy, maybe they would have by now."

For a few moments, he stays silent. Then he crushes the cigarette into the pavement with his shoe.

"Everything?" he asks softly.

I see it on his face, the real questions he wants to ask but doesn't dare. How do you live like this? How do you get through the days? How are you still alive?

I don't have answers to those either. Or if I do, he wouldn't like them.

"The first thing I remember is waking up there. Maybe he drugged me or chloroformed me or whatever, or maybe I just blacked out. But I remember waking up in the basement. My foot was tied to the heater and my hands were tied together and he'd stuffed some kind of cloth in my mouth till I could barely breathe."

I see him flinch as he struggles to keep facing me, to not let his gaze leave mine.

"And you don't remember what happened before that? Not a thing?"

"Shit, is that what this is about? Unofficial interview?" I toss my unfinished cigarette away from me like it's burning my fingers.

"No. Nothing like that." He rests his hand on my forearm, but I throw it off. "Sean," I say, no longer trying to hide the exhaustion in my voice, "I'm finished here."

He lowers his head. "Of course."

We head for the car in silence. When the car beeps in greeting, Sean suddenly speaks.

"I checked out Olivia's school records, like I told you."

The sound of her name jolts me awake much better than the cigarette did. I look up.

"And you were right. She did go to a private school two years ago. Except her parents pulled her halfway through the year and enrolled her at the public school."

"Why?" I climb into the passenger seat. Restlessness sets in, and I pick at a hangnail until it comes off, leaving behind a bloody stripe. Without thinking about it, I stick my finger in my mouth and taste copper.

"That's what I'm going to find out. I left a message with Tom Shaw and called the school this morning. I'm going to see the principal."

"Do you think..." I look at my finger. Bright-red blood keeps welling up no matter how many times I lick it off. It gushes in little bursts. A red crescent spreads over my cuticle and under my nail like a smile. "Do you think there's anything new they can tell you?"

"I don't know." He starts the engine then glances sideways at me, and his eyes widen. "Whoa, what happened? You okay?"

I glance down and realize he's talking about my finger. Blood has dripped onto my jeans. Good thing they're black and you almost can't see it.

"N-nothing. I just ripped off a hangnail. Nerves."

"It's bleeding all over the place. Did you peel your whole finger by accident?"

"I was—distracted."

He reaches into the glove compartment and throws a small first-aid kit into my lap. I fumble with the clasp, trying not to bleed all over it, then clean the cut with a disinfecting wipe. It's half an inch long and deep. It does look like I was trying to peel my finger.

Except I couldn't feel a damn thing. Thanks to the fucking Dilaudid.

I curse under my breath and wrap gauze around my finger, securing it with a piece of tape. Blood is already seeping into the fibers, tinting the gauze a deep crimson. I wrap my other hand around it and try to put it out of my mind. But when I glance up at Sean, the frown line between his eyebrows only deepens.

"Do you even own a first-aid kit?"

"I have some Band-Aids," I say with a shrug. "It's fine."

"Do you want me to stop by a drugstore on the way?"

"No."

"Are you sure?"

I draw in a breath and blurt out, "I want to go with you."

He frowns, uncomprehending. "What?"

"I want to go with you. To the school."

"I can't bring you with me, Laine."

"Why not?"

"For one, it's against every rule in the book. Second, it's just unethical. A breach of privacy, both yours and—"

"Privacy? You're not seriously going to lecture me about respecting privacy." I glance over my shoulder, at the precinct building looming behind us.

He heaves a sigh. He knows I'm right, and I know I

hit a sore spot. He feels bad. And that means he'll give me what I want.

"Just, for the love of God, no stupid stuff this time. Think you can manage that?"

I don't know. But for Olivia's sake, I can try.

Before I can answer, he's driving onto the highway.

Looks like I won.

*   *   *

The school is how I pictured the kind of place Olivia would go to: an enormous building with marble stairs, some kind of crest over the entrance and a designation like "academy," even though it's meant for ages five to twelve. It's facing a large park with neat rows of trees and clean-swept lanes. Every step I take across the property, I'm less and less convinced this was a good idea. Apprehensive, I follow Sean up the stairs and through the front door.

We must have arrived in the middle of class—the hallways are empty and pristine. The front lobby has high ceilings with skylights. Shelves full of trophies and photographs line the walls. I look them over: winner of this, first runner-up of that. All with pictures of different smiling children behind them. Aren't you supposed to play with blocks at that age, not compete for trophies? Seems like it's not just the poor kids who have to grow up too fast. A grim chuckle escapes from me, echoing in the empty space. Sean turns to me, frowning.

"Nothing," I say. "I was just seeing if I could find Olivia. Jacqueline said she was a math whiz, didn't she?"

He follows me down the wall of awards to the mathematics section. The dates on the trophies go back a couple years, but no Olivia anywhere.

Hurried steps echo through the lobby, and I turn to see a woman in a tailored suit hurrying toward us. When she gets close enough, I see the school's crest-logo thing emblazoned on her lapel. I wonder if even the teachers have to wear a uniform here.

She calls out a hello. She can't be older than Sean, and when she sees him, a smile blossoms on her face. She has really white, straight teeth. Her dark hair is tied back in a simple low ponytail, and her skin is a touch darker than mine. And flawless.

Behind my back, I squeeze my injured finger until I feel something.

"You must be Detective Ortiz," she says, beaming. She's wearing a lot of mascara, I notice. At least it *has* to be mascara. Except there are no clumps and no smudged line on her lower eyelids. "Principal Chaney told me to expect you. I'm Eva Marquez, his assistant." She holds out her hand.

He takes it. "Could you please show us in right away? This is a time-sensitive matter."

She nods. Her smile dampens a little—like Ms. Flirty Lashes finally clues in that this is about a missing ten-year-old girl. I hate her already.

"Of course. Absolutely."

Sean follows her, and I follow in his steps. She has yet to acknowledge that I exist.

We walk up a giant stairwell to the third floor, then turn into a hallway. I crane my neck, but the doors on either side of us are closed. I hear someone's voice, loud and clear—a teacher, dictating a text in slow, measured syllables.

I wonder if I could spell any of these words without a hundred mistakes. Probably not.

The principal of the Academy for Rich Young Geniuses resides in an office that wouldn't be out of place in the White House. What I originally thought was the office is just the antechamber, with Flirty Lashes Marquez's desk in the corner. With a picture of her cat. Aww.

She says a few words into the speaker on her desk then leads us to the double doors across the room. Only when I'm on the threshold does she seem to take notice.

"Excuse me, but Mr. Chaney has an appointment with Detective Ortiz only," she says in a carefully measured voice, gazing down at me with a look of serene superiority.

"Ms. Moreno is my assistant," Sean says without missing a beat. She looks thrown, like she's trying to figure out if he's messing with her or detectives really have assistants.

Well, I guess they need someone to bring them coffee too. I give her my widest, most insincere smile.

She leaves me be. I follow Sean into the principal's office, and the woman closes the doors behind us with a clang.

This is starting well.

Principal Chaney looks like he belongs in a TV commercial. For toothpaste. Or Viagra. One of those wiry older men who still has all his hair, neatly cropped and completely white. And a smile. As wide, white, and straight as Ms. Marquez's. Do they all go to the same dentist here? Or the same lobotomist.

His gaze travels from Sean to me and back, confused. I hope Sean gives him the same assistant line. I want to see if he buys it. But luckily for all of us, Chaney decides not to ask questions.

"I've been following the story," he says. He gets up and shakes hands with Sean, acknowledging me with a nod before settling back into his chair. Better than nothing. "It's a terrible tragedy. Olivia was one of our more promising students, and we miss her greatly."

Talking about her like she's dead already. I realize I'm clenching my jaw when my facial muscles start to ache.

Calm down. Don't wig out. Sean won't like it.

"According to my information, Olivia was enrolled here—"

"From first grade to third," he says. "That's exact."

"I understand she only did half of third grade at this school though."

Chaney nods, solemn. "Only the first semester, yes."

"Is it common?"

I study the office. There are pictures of graduating

classes, a good decade's worth. More trophies, award certificates, except these are for the school and not the students. Award for General Excellence in Teaching and such. The window takes up half a wall, and the rest are bookcases piled with heavy leather tomes.

"Is what common?"

"For a student to leave halfway through the year."

I glance from Chaney to Sean. Chaney has that wide-eyed look, *ask me whatever you want*, but something about it is just too forced. He never relaxes into the office chair, as if points of rusted nails were hiding right beneath the cushioned leather. I'm sure Sean notices too.

"It was Olivia's parents' decision, and it's not up to me to argue."

"And they didn't give you any reasons? Didn't say what wasn't up to their expectations?"

"We exceed expectations, Mr. Ortiz. It's our job here, and we pride ourselves on it."

This was meant to shut Sean up, I can tell. Well, he doesn't know who he's dealing with.

"Mr. Chaney—"

"Doctor," Chaney cuts in. "Dr. Chaney." He regards Sean with an air of well-concealed condescension.

"Dr. Chaney." Sean doesn't bat an eyelash. "Just out of curiosity, what's the cost of a year's tuition at this school?"

Calmly, Chaney folds his hands in front of him and names a sum that's more than I'll ever see in one place and probably half of what Sean makes in a year. "That's standard. Extracurricular activities and equipment are calculated separately. Why? Are you considering it for your child?"

"No, not exactly. How do the methods of payment work?"

"Payment must be made before the start of the school year, in full."

"And in case the child decides to leave?"

"The child doesn't decide to leave, Mr. Ortiz."

Sean ever so subtly rolls his eyes. "I mean if her parents decide to pull her. Are they given a refund?"

"I see what you're getting at. Well, it might seem like a large sum of money to some people"—his sly glance darts from Sean to me, and it's abundantly clear he means people like us—"but trust me, for the kind of head start our education will provide, it's worth every penny."

"Well, did the Shaws ever try to get a refund?"

He gives a single, sharp laugh. "We screen all our applicants, and with an income like that of the Shaw family, such a sum hardly registers."

I have no trouble believing that. I've seen their house.

"Still. That seems like a wasteful thing to do for no reason at all. And as far as I know, Tom Shaw is hardly wasteful. His companies—"

"I'm aware. Like I said, we screen our applicants. But I'm sorry, I don't know any more about this than you do. I wasn't told. Maybe you should ask Mr. Shaw himself."

"I intend to."

Chaney nods. A self-satisfied smile floats on his thin lips. I glance sideways at Sean.

"Feel free to contact me if you have any more questions, Detective Ortiz." Chaney leans back in his chair. "Ms. Marquez will give you my contact number."

This is supposed to mean, unequivocally, that the interview is over. A surge of panic wells up in me. "Sean—" I start in a low hiss.

He shushes me with a gesture and shakes hands with Chaney. "I appreciate your help. You realize how important this is. A ten-year-old girl's life may be at stake."

"It's nothing," says Chaney with a wide grin.

I want to punch him in his perfect set of veneers.

"Come on," Sean says quietly to me over his shoulder. "Let's go."

I follow him out through the large doors, through Ms. Marquez's office. She gives Sean a card with Chaney's number next to an embossed logo of the academy. I'm surprised she didn't scribble her own number on the back, with *xoxoxo* and a heart.

We walk downstairs by ourselves, our steps echoing down the staircase.

"Well?" I snap. I feel like I'm in church. My words resonate under the high ceiling. "What was that? Did you see his smug expression the whole time? Old perv."

"Laine," he says, but underneath the fatigue and irritation, I hear an amused note.

"What now? I mean, you're not going to leave it like this."

"No. Of course not. Don't worry about it."

We don't make it to the front door when I hear the familiar clacking of hurried steps. Ms. Flirty Lashes Marquez. When she catches up with us, she's panting, her smile is gone, and her perfect hair is disheveled, strands escaping from her ponytail in a halo around her head.

"I'm sorry," she gasps. "Detective Ortiz."

Great, I think. Here comes the phone number.

"I left the intercom on. By accident." She clears her throat, lowering those clumpless eyelashes. "I over-heard."

Sean patiently waits. My heart starts to hammer, and my upper lip is sweaty. Oh hell, the meds must be wearing off.

They sure know their timing.

"Well, I . . ." She twists her hands. "I don't know, maybe it's wrong of me; I mean, it was so long ago, and I don't really believe it has anything to do with . . . with . . ." She stops for a breath. "I just thought I should tell you."

"Tell me?" He sounds genuinely caring, curious. He reaches out and puts his hand on her arm. I feel a pang, but predictably enough, her face softens.

"I mean, I remember Olivia; she was such a sweet girl. This whole thing is a horror." She gulps nervously.

"Sweet girl?" he echoes. "At her new school, she had behavior problems."

Ms. Marquez sighs. "She did here too. I mean, nothing

too bad. Even if they expect them to act like PhD students in this place, they're still just kids. So she got into a couple of fights. She was a smart girl."

Is, I correct mentally. The back of my head is starting to hurt.

"But there's a reason her parents pulled her," she finally blurts.

"Because she attacked someone."

"No. Yes. Not exactly." She throws a glance around like someone might be eavesdropping.

"Maybe we can talk outside," Sean suggests casually. She gives me a look brimming with mistrust.

"I'll only talk to you."

Sean heaves a patient sigh. "Look, Eva—is it okay if I call you Eva? If you're willing to talk to me even though your boss won't, I appreciate your honesty, and I owe you as much. This is Lainey Moreno. She's Olivia's biological mother."

Eva Marquez gapes at me in stunned silence.

"You knew she was adopted, right? It would have been in the school records?"

"It wasn't," Eva finally says. "But I did know. Everyone knew."

The bell goes off, and seconds later the din of children's voices fills the building like the hum of bees in a giant marble hive. Without a word, she leads us outside, down the paved path to the entrance, and out the gate and into the empty park.

Eva hurries down the main lane, to a small fountain

walled off with a spiked grille. I have to break into a jog to keep up with her and Sean.

"I'm supposed to be on lunch break," she says with a neurotic little laugh. "So I hope he doesn't find out."

"If you get into trouble, I'll assume full responsibility," Sean assures her. But she's hardly listening. She's still staring at me like I'm about to bite her.

"Oh my God," she murmurs, not so much to me or to him but to herself. "So you're really her. You're Ella Santos."

I sputter. Sean reaches for my hand but I pull it away, out of his reach.

"What?" I choke out. "How—"

"Oh God." She collapses on one of the narrow benches circling the fountain. "I'm so sorry. That was so tactless of me."

Inside my sleeves, my fists clench and unclench, a near-involuntary movement I can't seem to stop. And if she doesn't start talking sense, and soon, I don't know what else I might do by sheer accident.

Eva gnaws on her lower lip then makes up her mind and draws a breath of resolve. "There was an incident," she says at last. "Two years ago. With Olivia. And a teacher."

CHAPTER SEVENTEEN

A cold kind of abyss opens up beneath my ribs, threatening to swallow me up. Ringing fills my ears, but I don't move a muscle. I barely see Sean in my peripheral vision but I can tell he tenses.

"What kind of incident?" he asks in a carefully measured voice. "I checked and triple-checked. There wasn't anything—"

"It never got as far as the police. The Shaws settled it outside." Eva Marquez presses her lips together until they turn pale.

"Eva, you have to tell me what happened. Everything that happened."

"There was a teacher who used to work at the school. Art teacher. Jakes, Lynden Jakes. And now...he doesn't."

I can't keep silent. "What did he do to her?" I burst out. Eva's eyes fly wide open, frightened. "What did the bastard do?"

"That's just it," Eva sighs. "We don't know for sure what happened."

"Well, *you* seem to know," I scowl. Eva looks hurt.

"Just let her talk," Sean mutters.

"What happened was . . . Olivia . . . I know this is going to sound completely crazy, and I know you will probably hate me." She turns her supplicating gaze to me. I kind of want to tell her that yes, she's probably right. "But . . . I saw the whole thing, all right? We have a policy at the school, no student is ever left alone in a room with only one teacher—we've had incidents in the past, you understand?"

"Just tell me what happened," I growl. Sean gives me a look, and I return it. Even he seems to shrink away. There must be murder in my eyes.

"I was a teacher's assistant back then. I'd just started at the school too, like him. His art class was the last of the day, and I was going to stay behind to help him put away the materials, clean up the spilled paint and stuff. Kids—they always make such a mess." She gives a watery smile and collects herself. "All the students were leaving, the third-grade class, Olivia's class. She was the last one. She loved the art classes so much. Everyone said she was a math whiz, but what she truly loved was drawing and painting. I could see it in her face every class. She would pick up her brush or her stick of charcoal, and she just lit up. She was always so serious, but in his class, she became happy and serene. It was the only time I saw her happy, really. Ever."

"And that son of a bitch took advantage," I mutter. Sean puts his hand on my shoulder—a big mistake. I throw him off violently. I can't be distracted. I need to hear every word. Every horrible goddamn word.

Eva dabs under her eyes. "No! He would never do something like that. I know him. I—" She cuts herself off and lowers her gaze. "Look, I'm not just saying this because we went on a couple of dates. Nothing serious ever happened anyway..."

"I don't care about your love life," I snap. "Just tell me what the bastard did."

It's obvious Eva already regrets agreeing to talk to Sean with me around, but there's no going back at this point.

"Olivia was the last one to leave. Unlike the other kids who threw down their brushes and ran out as soon as they heard the bell, she would always help clean up, wash and dry all her brushes, rinse the water dish. So it was the three of us. They were at the sinks, and I was at the other end of the room, hanging up the paintings to dry on the line. I reached for the next one and that's when I saw it happen."

She pauses and closes her eyes. My breath catches. "What happened? What did you see?"

"They were talking about something softly. I didn't hear what they were saying because the water was running. And then she turned and she—well . . . she grabbed him. Between the legs. Just went for it, like it was nothing special."

The air I'm holding in my lungs turns to molten lead. It burns but I can't seem to let it go.

"He freaked out, of course. Then I ran over and he tried to pull himself together, as much as he could. We sat her down—she looked a little confused, nothing else, like she didn't understand what the fuss was all about. He tried to explain to her that this isn't something that you do. And she just got more and more upset. Her face, the look in her eyes—it was just . . . heartbreaking. She started to cry and to mumble things I couldn't quite make out, but I think she said she loved him and it was okay when you loved someone. She just wanted him to love her back. And the more she talked, the more she cried. We tried to explain to her that he's too old and it's not right, but she became hysterical. I tried to hold her back, but she broke away and ran through the hallway.

"I told Lynden to go home, and went to get her. She was hiding behind some lockers, and she was a mess. I tried to talk to her, to explain, and I thought I was getting through. In any event, she stopped crying and seemed to calm down. I took her to the bathroom to help her wash her face, and then I took her downstairs where that girl, Jacinta, the one who used to pick her up, was already waiting. She asked what took so long, and I just told her we were cleaning up after art class. I think she didn't believe me, even though that's what Olivia did every Wednesday. Anyway." Eva heaves a sigh. Her shoulders droop in exhaustion.

My spine is a rigid arrow, the only thing holding me up. Rage boils beneath my skin but not a drop of it reaches the surface. I stand there like a toy soldier, and I listen.

"And the day after, she doesn't show up at school. Next thing we know, we get an infuriated call from the Shaws. They grilled her, and she said that Lynden had touched her. Dr. Chaney told them what I just told you, that we have a policy, a student is never alone with a teacher, all that. And the Shaws descended on the school the very same day. The wife's pale as a bedsheet; he's all fire and brimstone. They brought me in to testify. And I told them the truth."

Sean's frown deepens. "What makes you think he didn't touch her, on another occasion, and only pretended because you happened to be there?"

"He didn't," she repeats obstinately. "He's not like that."

"No one wants to think people can be like that," Sean says, trying to sound neutral.

"She's the one who did it. I saw."

"You think an eight-year-old girl was to blame?" I say, managing to keep my voice down to a whisper. "What's wrong with you?"

"I never said she was to blame." Eva's gaze flees mine. "I'm just telling you what I saw."

"So why did it never get to the police?" Sean speaks up. "Why did the Shaws decide to settle?"

"I don't know," she snaps with sudden bitterness. "Maybe because they realized they'd be ruining an innocent man's life?"

"From what I know of Tom Shaw, he's not the type to care."

Her nostrils flare, and her chest rises and falls rapidly. "Or maybe they didn't want the matter to get more attention. Dr. Chaney told them that much. If they pursued action against Lynden, despite the school policy and the testimony that he was not to blame, it would also be against the school, by default. And such a scandal would be incredibly damaging to the academy's reputation. So if that was the case, he wouldn't hesitate to do the same to them."

"What do you mean?" Sean asks calmly.

She looks him in the eye, suddenly composed. "They'd go to the press with the case. So that at least the public has both sides of the story, Dr. Chaney said. And that means reporters would dig into the family's affairs. It would all be anonymous, but everyone knows who's involved in things like this, especially in a small school and community. So that pretty much meant they'd tell the world Olivia was adopted. They'd make it known she was a child of a pedophile and his victim."

I think I'm going to be sick.

"Olivia didn't know she was adopted," Eva says flatly. "Her parents never told her."

"Then how the hell did the principal know?" Sean can't keep the disgust from his voice. Eva lowers her chin.

"Like he told you." She studiously avoids meeting his gaze. "We do a very thorough screening of our applicants."

He mutters a few unrepeatable words in Spanish, but by the look on her face I see she gets them. She sniffles and stares down at the square toes of her shoes.

"And?" Sean asks.

"They made an arrangement. Lynden got dismissed. The Shaws pulled Olivia from the school."

"And you?"

"Me? What was I supposed to do?" There's an edge of hysteria in her voice.

"I don't know, Ms. Marquez. You've followed the news, since you're standing here now. What do you think? Are you still sure he was innocent?"

She raises her tear-filled eyes at Sean then turns her gaze to me. When she speaks, her voice is brimming with hatred. "Maybe," she snarls, "something was rotten about her from the start. Have you considered that? Bad genes. Has it occurred to you that maybe she simply ran away?"

Sean's eyes narrow.

"Bullshit." My voice rings loud and clear, and both of them turn at once like they forgot I was there. I back away slowly, my hands curled at my sides. "This is all such fucking bullshit," I say through clenched teeth.

And then I turn around and run.

CHAPTER EIGHTEEN

All I feel are the soles of my feet pounding rhythmically against the path. Gravel absorbs the impact of my steps, slowing me down. It's like running through sand, but I don't stop. I keep running and running, deep into the park, until my thighs burn in agony through the fading haze of the pills.

I zigzag from one path to another until I don't know where I am anymore, until my legs give out, until my knees buckle and hit soggy ground. The earth rushes toward my face, and I rest my forehead on a mound of limp grass.

I breathe in the smell of mud and damp, the smell of rain.

I try not to feel. As usual, I fail.

Unlacing my right boot, I reach into my sock, my icy

fingers crawling down my shin to the scar on my ankle. The pills are there, by my toes, cocooned in some cling wrap. I swallow the three mismatched lumps, white and hospital blue and mint green, without checking what they are. My throat is so dry that they get stuck halfway down, a hard and bitter lump.

I don't know how much later I hear the muffled steps. Can't be that long.

"Laine." Cloth rustles as Sean crouches next to me. "Laine, talk to me."

"Where is she?" I choke out. "Where is that bitch, so I can knock the fake teeth out of her fucking head?"

"I told her to go back to work," he says softly. "It's not like she can disappear on us. I have all her info. She's an elementary school teacher, not an international spy."

"So it was him, then."

"We don't know for sure."

"What is there not to fucking know?"

He takes hold of my shoulders. I'm shaking from head to toe, and I just don't have the energy to push his hands away, so I let him pull me to my feet. His arm goes around my waist, and I lean on him with my full weight.

"Let's get you back to the car, okay?"

"No."

"Don't be an idiot, Laine. I'm going to drive you home. And you're going to take it easy and rest."

"I don't want to rest. We have to find that guy. That Lynden guy."

"I'll find him. He's not going anywhere, trust me."

"She could have called him already. Warned him."

"I already made a call too." His arm around my waist holds me up gently like he's afraid I'll break in half. The tenderness of it makes my eyes sting. "He's not getting away."

Maybe the pills manage to dissolve in my gullet or maybe it's just Sean's presence by my side, but I manage to make it back to the fountain—no trace of Eva Marquez—and past the school gate, to Sean's car waiting in the parking lot. I get into the passenger seat by myself, without needing to be hauled in, and don't argue when he makes me put on my seat belt.

I rest my head on the back of the seat and stare at the car's beige ceiling. My eyelids grow heavy, and I don't fight the pull. The nightmares that I know will plague my sleep are far less terrifying than facing reality.

Lynden Jakes. His name was Lynden Jakes. He was a freaking art teacher in a school full of little girls.

I don't want to live in this world.

Please take me away.

Please let me die.

I close my eyes then open them, and it's like someone flipped a switch. The sky grew three shades darker, with a spill of orange above the black outline of a building. I blink, disoriented, trying to figure out where the hell I am until I recognize the hotel.

"I don't think you should be alone right now," Sean says as he locks the car. I'm shuffling along like a zombie and can barely bring myself to look up. It's what I've been hoping he'd say from the beginning, and now that he has, it no longer matters.

"I'm going to call someone to keep an eye on you," he says. He's not asking me.

"No. I want to be by myself."

He gives me a gloomy look.

"I'm tired. I just want to take a bath and crash, and I'm not sure I want some uniformed guy watching me sleep right now. Thanks for understanding."

"Are you sure?"

"No one knows I'm here," I say. "And there's security out front, and cameras everywhere. It's a hotel."

"I want you to stay put until I get in touch."

"I will. Where do you think I'm going to go?"

He gives me a look like he doesn't really want an answer. That makes two of us.

"Promise me you won't go anywhere. Not even for five minutes."

"Promise."

He's not the only one who's good at making promises he knows he can't keep.

* * *

In the hotel lobby, there's a lone desk with a computer monitor. I see it from across the hall because it's one of the prehistoric, white, boxy ones. Doesn't matter—I don't need the latest tech for what I'm about to do. I ask at the front desk, where the receptionist gives me an odd look but informs me that I can use the computer for free for up to ten minutes.

Ten minutes will have to be enough. I plunk down into the worn chair and open a browser window.

Lynden Jakes. If it's you, fucker, I swear I'll take the next bus to wherever the hell you moved away to and modify your anatomy with some rusted gardening shears. My hands shake so much it's hard to type, even though I know it has more to do with the comedown than my righteous outrage. But my comedown will have to wait.

It takes me a while to find him. I'm guessing I'm over my ten minutes because the receptionist is giving me the evil eye. But I find a link on a Classmates-type site that takes me to a social media site where he has a profile. L. Ethan Jakes, as he calls himself now, is a smarmy blond who must have been into sports once but has since let himself go, with a paunch the flattering angles of his photos don't hide. I can be reasonably sure it's him. He lives in Connecticut, has been there for two years now, and the profile says he used to teach high school but now works for some company. He has a lovely fiancée with a weak chin and earnest eyes.

He also updates obsessively. It takes a while to scroll through all the minutiae of his days, updates about going running, pictures of food, the fiancée's smiling mug, and a bored-looking dog, until I find the right dates. On the day Olivia went missing, he posted four times. He checked in at some Mexican place with the fiancée and friends; underneath the crappy picture of a half-drunk Mr. Jakes surrounded by bros, there are several likes. The other statuses show location. A thousand miles away from here. From Olivia.

I know as well as the next person that these things can be faked. I know Sean will run a real check, but a part of me knows exactly what he'll find. Jakes was where he was supposed to be. And I was just grasping at a straw, because deep down, I already know it could never have been Jakes. It could only be one person.

I'm the only one who has ever seen that person. And I'm of absolutely no help.

CHAPTER NINETEEN

Even though I've long ago used up my ten minutes, I open a new window and log into ConspiracyTalk. Sure enough, the Olivia Shaw thread has exploded.

> Donttreadonme: hey guys, check this out. News from our favorite baby mama.

It's a YouTube clip of the ill-fated press conference. My cursor hovers over the Play button for a moment, but then I glimpse something that makes me forget all about it.

In the next post, there's a link to some tabloid. The headline reads *SHOCKING TRUTH ABOUT ELLA SANTOS: The Kidnap Victim Whose Case Baffled the Nation.* And in smaller letters: *Ella's Roommate and Lover Speaks Up.*

My insides turn to ice as I click on the link: the source, who's being referred to as Naomi, tells about "Ella's" forays into sex work, her multiple partners.

> Many times after she'd come over I'd notice things went missing, intimate things, like my lingerie, clothes. One time she took a bottle of my favorite perfume and sprayed it all over her things. I've always had nothing but compassion for her, as I know how hard her circumstances are, and I didn't want her to get into trouble—

If I read any more, I'm going to throw up or do something I'll regret, so I close the window, struggling to contain the rage bubbling in my chest. Natalia, that bitch.

The forum members, on the other hand, are having a ball.

> Roswell82: Did some digging, she has quite the arrest record.

> Salem_baby: Why did they even take her on TV? For all you know she really did it lol

> Roswell82: well she's def a little unhinged.

> Mike6669: Heck I'd still hit that lol lol

OliviaShawsDaddy: :P :P

Donttreadonme: dude

OliviaShawsDaddy: hey you guys I have a theory. I bet she's been working with her supposed kidnapper all along. Probably helped him get the girl. I read about it, some kind of Stockholm syndrome thing, it's messed up.

Donttreadonme: That's crazy but plausible in a way

OliviaShawsDaddy: isn't it obvious that's why she never turned him in? Bet they were still hooking up on the dl this whole time

Roswell82: sicko

OliviaShawsDaddy: hey bro

Roswell82: I meant her :P

Roswell82: So anyone heard from @lostgirl14? She must have theories. Good ones not perverted shit like you @OliviaShawsDaddy.

Donttreadonme: her green light is on, shes online just not talking

Donttreadonme: hey stop lurking @lostgirl14

Roswell82: I bet its really something super simple and lame like the parents killed her themselves by accident.

Donttreadonme: yeah but where does Moreno come in? or should I say santos lol I still say she did it. or at least had something to do with it

OliviaShawsDaddy: maybe she's helping them cover it up

Roswell82: That doesn't even make sense.

Roswell82: She couldn't have done it and not left a single trace anywhere.

My private messages icon flashes 10+. Numbly, I click on it.

The first two or three are from other forum members, messaging me about the Ella Santos thread. But the fourth one dates from two days ago, and there's no text in the subject line. It's from a username I haven't seen before. Against my better judgment, I open the message.

It's my photo, the same one that was posted in the main thread about Olivia, except unphotoshopped, and I can clearly tell where I am: leaving my building, and the way I squint in the daylight suggests it's early morning.

Before my apartment got robbed. Or even before that?

All the following messages are from different dummy usernames, and every single one has a photo of me. Outside Natalia's. Smoking with Sean outside the police station. Getting into his car.

My head snaps up, and I look around. The receptionist looks sleepy behind her desk, but apart from her, the lobby is empty.

Shit.

The chair nearly goes toppling when I shoot to my feet and race upstairs. The room feels like a pastel-toned cage in which I pace, nervous energy coursing through my arms and legs. My supplies are running low so I make a beeline for the minibar instead. One tiny bottle upends into my mouth, then another, then another. I don't really look at the labels. On the third, some of the liquid goes the wrong way and I double over coughing, liquor searing the inside of my nose. Tears pour freely down my face, but once I can breathe, I notice I have a nice buzz going. The booze is kicking in fast. I down one last bottle—cloyingly sweet liqueur of some kind that makes me grimace. It's cheap, malt-based booze and it won't last long. By the time my guy gets here, I'll be sober again and able to think.

Right. For that I'd have to call him first. I pick up my phone and thumb the contact marked Running Buddy.

As usual, Sugar picks up immediately. "Princess. What can I do you for?"

He knows damn well. I tell him where I'm staying,

realizing belatedly what a not-great idea this is, but he's already hanging up.

For a drug dealer, Sugar is reliable as fuck and surprisingly punctual. You could set your watch by him. He's knocking on my room door within twenty minutes. He whistles when he sees the place over my shoulder.

"Wow. Nice digs. What happened, find a sugar daddy, finally?" He's making fun of me. Even scum of the earth like Sugar know I'm damaged goods.

"Problems with my landlord," I lie artlessly. I don't give a shit what he thinks—I just want my stuff.

"Hey." His pointy-toothed grin widens. "If you need a place to stay—"

"As if."

Sugar lives in a slummy top-floor apartment that he has the audacity to call a penthouse.

"What? I'm always happy to share my space with royalty," he says with a smirk.

"Do you have the stuff or not?"

He glances over his shoulder, subtly, and the goofy grin vanishes without a trace. There's a time for fucking around and a time for business. "Not in the hallway."

I don't want him inside my room, inside my living space. But he gives a slight nod at the security camera at the end of the hall and I don't have a choice.

Once he steps inside the doorway, I block his way so he doesn't get any farther into the room. He's pushy, craning his neck, trying to see around. This unwelcome proximity makes the tiny hairs along my spine stand on end.

He reaches into the bottomless pockets of his baggy pants and produces the goods. I count out the pills: OxyContin, Adderall, Xanax. The unholy trinity for anything life might throw at you. No Ambien, but I should still have a refill on my prescription.

He tells me the price, and as usual he's inflated it way beyond what those pills are actually worth, but right now I don't give a shit. While I waited for him, I'd made a trip downstairs to the ATM where I withdrew everything I had in my account, the last dregs of my Silver Bullet paycheck. I tried not to think about how the bills in my hand were all I had to my name. I tried not to think that I might need a new job now and no one in their right mind will hire me.

I count out the twenties. He tips his baseball hat at me and—finally!—heads for the door.

"If you need anything, you know where to find me."

"Don't I always." I return his crooked smile. Relief pools in my chest when I close the door behind him. Although the pellets of pills in my pocket might also have something to do with it.

First thing I do is head to the bathroom to find a new hiding place. I don't have time to get creative but I don't trust the staff in this place not to snoop around. A vitamin bottle is inconspicuous enough, hiding in plain sight, so I put it on the shelf behind the mirror, next to the array of scuffed makeup tubes I fish out of the bottom of my backpack. Just a girl keeping pretty, making sure I get my As, Bs, and Cs.

I pick out an Adderall and take it. Then I think about it and take another one. Any more than that and I get the shakes, or I'd just gulp down my entire supply.

For what I'm about to do, I need to be all I can be.

*   *   *

After thirty-five excruciating minutes on the phone with the insurance company, I pay the fine with my last functioning credit card, gritting my teeth at the astronomical amount on the receipt. But my car is waiting for me in the lot, all mine again. For what it's worth. It looks a lot worse than I remember, but as long as it's running, I don't care.

Within another half hour, I'm leaving it at the curb across from the Shaws'. The house looks lifeless, all windows shrouded in curtains, but the two cars in the driveway tell me they're home. What I hadn't noticed the first time around is that their doorbell is a complicated system with an intercom speaker, a small glaring eye of a camera, and as far as I can tell, a motion detector. I ring and ring, to no avail. *Don't you ignore me, you lying bastard. Think you can just pretend I'm not there and I'll go away?* I knock, first lightly, then pound on the door, and before long, I hear hurrying steps.

Jacqueline Shaw looks frail, her skin nearly translucent without makeup. She blinks her red eyes in incomprehension, and the furious tirade I had at the tip of my tongue vanishes.

"Can I come in?" I bleat. I wouldn't be too surprised if she slammed the door in my face, but she only nods and steps aside.

With the lights turned down, the house has the feel of a funeral home after hours. It looks like a layer of dust has settled over everything, muting the colors. I notice the pictures are missing from the walls, leaving behind barely noticeable dark rectangles.

"Is everything all right?" Jacqueline asks, although from the looks of it, I'm the one who should be wondering. Her face is getting so thin that shadows draw chasms beneath her already pointy cheekbones.

Everything is not all right, as a matter of fact. But before I can say anything, I hear the crash of a slammed door and thundering steps coming from upstairs. The next moment, Tom Shaw appears in the doorway. He hardly looks better than Jacqueline—the stress must be taking a toll on him too. But while I feel a sort of fledgling sympathy for Jacqueline, the sight of his rumpled T-shirt and under-eye bags only fills me with fury.

When he sees me, his shoulders slump. "Jesus. Lainey, it's you."

Who did he expect exactly? Olivia to show up on the doorstep?

He runs his hands over his face. "Anything... anything new? If there's something... if you remembered anything, you should call Detective Ortiz first thing."

"I didn't remember anything," I say. Anxiety uncoils

beneath my ribs and turns to rage. "But perhaps you might."

Jacqueline takes a step closer. Tom gives me a look of exasperation. "What—"

"Lynden Jakes," I snarl.

In the background, Jacqueline makes a strangled sound. Shaw's eyes narrow, and the storm grows closer.

"I already spoke about this to Detective Ortiz," he says levelly. "And I'm not going to repeat myself to you. Not to mention that this isn't any of your business and you shouldn't have known about it in the first place."

"Well, too late for that." I scowl.

"This is a private matter," he cuts in. "Of my family. And my daughter." He emphasizes *my*, spitting out each syllable in an angry staccato.

"So you decided it wasn't important enough to bring up." My mouth twists. I'm starting to feel nauseous and know the tide of energy can't possibly last. I'll crash, and soon.

Jacqueline inches toward me, holding out her hands. "Lainey . . ."

Shaw gives her a withering look.

"What if it really was him? What if he—what if . . ."

"He didn't," Shaw explodes. "He didn't touch her, okay? That's why we had to settle without letting it get to the police. We got him to resign, because I couldn't very well just leave it as it was, could I? Word would get out; everyone would know about my daughter. And she was only eight. Can't you try to understand?"

"What is there to understand?"

"The Marquez woman, the one who testified." He rubs his eyes. "She told the truth."

My legs feel weak. I can sense the crash coming on, and there's nothing I can do to stop it.

"But Olivia . . . she told you and Jacqueline—"

"Olivia," he says, bitterly spitting out every syllable, "pretty much admitted everything to us. She did what they said she did. She didn't mean anything bad by it. She must have seen it on the Internet or something, you know how it is—the parental controls can't ever catch it all. And Olivia, she was always like that. Acting out on impulse. Just did whatever she felt like. Uncontrollable." He heaves a sigh. "What the hell were we supposed to do, huh?"

I don't know. Have a serious talk with your daughter? Get her help, maybe. But I decide to keep my mouth shut, which is for the best because I don't trust myself to speak. Something horrible and profane would come out if I opened my mouth.

"I don't know what I expected." Shaw's voice is tired, like the outburst consumed the last of his energy. "Jacqueline didn't know her history, but I did. I hate to admit it, and I despise myself for thinking it, but after that incident, I began to wonder."

"To wonder if you got a lemon," I say. Right now I don't hate anyone in the world more than I hate this man. I want to punch him and knock that look off his face, along with some of his teeth.

"Come on, Lainey. Put yourself in my place. Wouldn't you?"

"Tom," Jacqueline says, her voice plaintive.

"Would I blame an eight-year-old girl for something her father did before she was even born?"

He groans. For a while, he just paces without saying another word.

"Shit." He covers his face with his hands. "Shit, shit. Just listen to me. I don't know what the fuck I'm saying."

I stand in the center of the room, fists clenched—although he doesn't know this because my sleeves have fallen over my hands. I'm nothing but a storm cloud of heartbeat and pumping blood and anger.

"Lainey." Jacqueline reaches out to touch my arm. She must remember our first encounter, because she stops herself, her manicured hand hovering inches above my lint-covered sleeve. "I'm so sorry. He's just—" She draws a breath. "We loved Olivia. We did. More than—"

More than I could have. Yeah, I know that.

"More than anything," Jacqueline finishes softly. Only then I notice that for the first time, she spoke in the past tense.

*　　*　　*

"You should go home," Tom Shaw says dryly. He puts a protective arm around his wife, who looks like she's about to start full-on crying.

Like it's my damn fault. I silently shake my head.

"You really should. Or I might have to take measures to make you."

The threat passes between us, nearly tangible. He has all the power in this situation, and he's making it known.

And me . . . I'm the same I've always been. I'm no one, powerless. All I can do is watch from the sidelines, unable to change a damn thing.

Jacqueline says her husband's name in a whisper, but loud enough so I hear the tension in it.

"Do you want me to call someone?" she asks, and it takes me a moment to realize she's talking to me. I shake my head. "You don't look well enough to drive," she says, her voice still kind, but with a steely note.

"Jackie," Tom Shaw speaks up.

"I'm not kicking her out in this state," she says. Talking about me in the third person like I'm not standing right here. I clench my fists.

"She shows up here, threatening you—and you—"

"She wasn't threatening anybody. Look at her, for God's sake. She's as devastated as we are . . ."

"I'll go," I snap, putting them out of their misery.

"Out of the question," Jacqueline says.

"I'll call Detective Ortiz," says Tom Shaw. "Let him sort it out."

"No." The word escapes from me before I can stop it. "You. You said I could just come by anytime I wanted." This one is for Jacqueline, who avoids my gaze to the best of her ability.

"Can I speak with you?" her husband asks. "In the living room."

They leave me alone, Tom closing the door, softly but with a firm clink as the handle turns. I wait a heartbeat and press myself against the cool, smooth polished paneling but can't make out a single sound. This house doesn't have plywood walls like a motel or like my old apartment building.

I know I don't have long, so I decide to look around. I race to Jacqueline's purse that sits carelessly on an end table, next to a vase of calla lilies, or maybe they're orchids—who knows? But when I brush my fingertip against a soft white petal, it's definitely real. My fingernail leaves a translucent bruise, and a delicate scent wafts into my face. Real and fresh. How can they think of changing the flowers at a time like this? Or maybe they have help who do these things, automatically, and they just forgot to cancel.

Throwing cautious glances at the door, I pick up the purse and slide open the zipper. This purse alone, if I could get it to a pawnshop, could keep me in rent and pills for a month: soft, cream-colored leather, with a discreet designer logo etched in gold on the inside lining. The matching wallet is at the bottom, and, overcoming a brief flash of contrition, I open it. There are half a dozen gold and black credit cards, which aren't much use to me right now, and no cash. Of course not. Why would someone like Jacqueline carry cash around?

I glance at the door once more, but whatever they're

still talking about, it's keeping them busy. So I turn my attention back to the wallet. Hoping to find some money, I unzip the other compartment, and my breath catches.

There's a photo in the clear plastic insert, a smaller replica of the family portrait on the wall of the Shaws' house: Tom, Jacqueline, and Olivia against a generic background. I peer closer and realize the photo isn't identical—it's clearly from the same set, but different. This one was no doubt discarded as imperfect, except Jacqueline decided to keep it for whatever reason. Tom and Jacqueline stare with determined, cheerful gazes into the uncertain future, but Olivia looks slightly away, beyond the invisible frame. She's not smiling; her bow-shaped lips are pressed together, thin and serious—and when I bring the picture closer to my eyes, I see just how much she looks like me. Not just her features, but her expression is the same one I see every time I accidentally glimpse myself in a reflective surface, before I can compose my face into a blank, pleasing look.

A strange feeling spreads through my chest, hot yet hollow, and my mind grows fuzzy around the edges like I washed down painkillers with a too-big gulp of liquor. I'm about to close the wallet and put it back when I spy the edge of another photo tucked underneath the first one. I catch the edge with my fingernails and tug it out.

This one couldn't be more different from the formal family photo that was hiding it. A candid shot, a touch overexposed, it was probably taken with a phone camera and printed. It shows Olivia—the mess of curls is hard to confuse with anyone else—and a young woman, both grinning and holding out ice cream cones like trophies. Olivia looks younger, her hair shorter and her face round and chubby cheeked, no older than seven or eight. I peer closely at the young woman until the picture becomes grainy. She looks like Jacqueline, the same slant of the eyes and heart-shaped face—a younger, prettier version of Jacqueline.

I hear movement behind the door and hastily stuff the photo back in its place then throw the wallet into the purse. Even the hefty dose of medication in my system doesn't stop my heart from hammering, but with my luck, no one comes in. Turning my attention back to the purse, I retrieve Jacqueline's phone, which asks for a passcode. It takes me only a moment's hesitation, but I'm not too surprised when I get it on the first try: the code is Olivia's birthday.

Jacqueline is one of those meticulously organized people who has everyone's picture, phone number, and address typed up neatly next to their name, along with their birthday and other information she might need. I thumb through her contacts until I find the name Jacinta and copy the number and address into my own phone. I put Jacqueline's phone back where I found it and carefully close the zipper then hold my breath and listen.

Behind the heavy door, they're arguing. No amount of sound insulation can hide that fact, even though the words are too muffled for me to make out. But she's yelling and he's yelling back.

I throw one last glance around. I've had enough, and I have things to do.

So I leave them to it and slip out the front door, unseen and unheard.

In my car, I have to sit still for a while, wasting precious minutes until I'm in the right state to drive. It's the last thing I should be doing; I can't afford to get pulled over, although losing my license would be the least of my problems, with my history and all. But it's not like I have a choice.

Thankfully, the drive to Wedgwood is uneventful, and fifteen minutes later, I'm pulling up to a small but well-maintained bungalow at the address. Jacinta, it seems, still lives with her parents and, if I remember correctly from all the news sites and tabloids, goes to Seattle U for either psychology or sociology or some other middle class-girl major.

The house has that aggressively neat quality but blends in perfectly with the rest of the neighborhood. Two of the windows are lit, but as much as I crane my neck, I can't see a thing through the curtains. Two cars sit in the driveway, a silver coupe and one of those jewel-colored MINI Coopers—Jacinta's, I'm guessing. I glimpse a third one, a white SUV, under an awning behind the house. It looks . . . normal.

Maybe Sean is right and I do need help. I feel like I'm losing my mind.

I drive past but it seems I'm unable to press down on the brake pedal. A tremor travels from my core into my hands, and I keep driving until the house is gone from sight. Only then do I slow down and pull over.

What the hell am I doing? What if I show up on her doorstep and she calls the cops—rightfully so? I don't even know how much Jacqueline has told her about me. Besides, if the parents are home, I'm going to have to explain the situation to them, and I have no idea what I'd say.

I idle behind the wheel for a while then take out my phone and punch in her number. My pulse thrums in my ears, drowning out the ringing. God, I hope it's her cell phone and not the landline.

I picture her looking at the unfamiliar number on the display, hesitating, making up her mind. She answers after four or five rings, just as I'm starting to hope it'll go to voice mail and that will be that.

Her wary *Hello* in my ear takes me by surprise because I heard no click. Her voice sounds hoarse with the rust-edged notes of recent tears.

"Hi," I say. "You're—are you Jacinta? Jacinta Velasquez?"

A silence. "Yes. Who is this? Are you with the press?"

"No," I say hurriedly. "No. Jacqueline gave me your number." The lie springs to my lips, all natural and easy. "I don't know if she's told you about me..."

The rustle I first mistake for static is her sharp intake of breath. And in the leaden silence that follows, I realize, with a small jolt like an electric spark, that she knows exactly who I am. When she does speak, it's the wrong name, and I flinch with my whole body, glad she can't see me.

"It's Lainey now," I say carefully. She begins to apologize in a rush, and it sounds like she's about to start crying all over again—and I know, intuitively, that she'll buy anything I tell her at this point, and do whatever I ask. The power of guilt. I feel like a little shit for abusing it, even though my addict's sixth sense is supposed to make me impervious to shame. At least while the high lasts.

She agrees to meet me for a coffee in a few minutes. I park in front of the small twenty-four-hour coffee shop and hide in the bathroom until I see her come in, alone. She's hard to miss. Taller than Jacqueline, striking—although right now she looks about as put together as me. She must have dressed in a hurry, sweatshirt with university logo, sweatpants, and those sheepskin boots. Her dark hair hangs limply down the sides of her face. Looks like she hasn't washed it in a while, but I'm a fine one to judge.

When I emerge from the alcove by the washroom at last, I see my own thoughts mirrored on her face. I'm not what she expected—whatever that might have been. At this late hour, the coffee shop isn't crowded enough: only a few hipsters hiding behind the glowing Apple logos on the backs of their laptop screens and a single bored barista behind the counter. He doesn't seem to notice or care that we don't buy anything, which is just as well. A one-dollar coffee is about all

I can afford, and it doesn't look like this place serves those.

"Lainey," she says, as if trying the word out.

"Yeah."

I hope she doesn't start with the usual routine, *Oh my God, you cannot imagine how sorry I am for everything that's happened to you*, and so on. But her eyes, tired, rimmed with darkness, are shrewd. She gives a terse nod, and we sit down.

"What exactly did Jacqueline tell you?"

"Not much," I say carefully. Sooner or later it'll come to light that, not only did Jacqueline not tell me a thing, she certainly didn't give me this girl's phone number or address. "That you used to pick her up from school—"

"Three times a week," Jacinta interjects. "When my classes end early." She twists the worn-out hem of her sweatshirt. "The other two Jackie does herself. Did." She clears her throat and adds, I don't know why, "I've been doing it since high school. I always loved babysitting Oli. I practically lived at Jackie and Tom's."

Even when she's this disheveled, her big doe eyes make her beautiful. Jacqueline has the discipline to meticulously care for her appearance, but Jacinta is the one who got the natural beauty. It makes me wonder if there had ever been a rivalry. Does "Jackie" feel secure with this ingénue camping out at her house at all hours of the day?

Ugly thoughts, like a bad taste in my mouth. I cringe. Why is it that all I can think and feel is ugliness? Is it because of how my captor warped me? Was I just born like this? Did Val's prenatal drug use do something to my brain?

Jacinta misinterprets my silence. "I used to live at the dorm." She points apologetically at her sweatshirt. "I suspended my studies. When..." She swallows, and I don't need her to finish. What am I supposed to say to that? So sorry. I'm sure that, no matter what happens, your future is as bright as it's ever been?

Like it or not, but Jacinta, with her poreless skin and cute little car and college degree, is just another reminder of all the things I never got a chance to be. I could see Olivia being just like her in a few years.

Except now none of it will happen.

"What else did Jackie tell you?" she asks.

She may look like I dragged her out of bed, but her gaze is strangely sharp and aware. It sends a thrill down my spine, and suddenly I'm not so sure which one of us is supposed to be playing the other, extracting information under the guise of bonding in the face of tragedy. Well, she's in for a surprise. She may be majoring in psychology or whatever it is, but I have some experience she never imagined in her worst nightmares. I can handle her.

"I just wanted to ask you some things," I say.

"You can ask Jackie."

"I wanted to ask you. That's why I wanted to meet you, in person. I just wanted to talk. To someone else who...knew Olivia."

She sighs quietly. Her eyes soften, and her posture relaxes. It's barely there but I notice it. It's exactly what I do when the nurse at the hospital tells me I passed my drug test. When I know I'm off the hook.

"Do you remember anything weird that happened? Before Olivia disappeared."

Jacinta's brown eyes refocus at once. "Weird?"

"Unusual. Not just when you were picking up Olivia. Did anyone approach you?"

"In what way?" A frown creases her dark eyebrows.

"Just anyone approaching you, like a man? Trying to hit on you, something like that. Acting strange."

She gives a bitter laugh. "You have any idea how many times a week guys approach me and act strange?"

"I can imagine." I make myself smile, but she doesn't buy it. The mistrustful look doesn't leave her eyes.

"I mean, did you mention having to pick up Olivia? Mention anything about her at all."

"What exactly are you saying?"

"I'm not accusing you of anything. I just want to know. Anything you can remember..."

"You're trying to say I led him to her somehow." It's not a question.

"No!" I protest. Even though that's exactly what I'm suggesting. I'm starting to feel shaky, my emotions spiraling out of my control. "No, I—"

"Look, I already told everything to the police," she says. She gathers up her purse and cradles it to her chest, defensive. "If you need to know, why don't you ask that detective? What's his name—Ortiz."

The mention of Sean makes me flinch, and she notices. A look of cold composure returns to her face. She slides back her chair and starts to get up.

"Wait."

"I'm finished here."

I follow her to the door and outside, into the parking lot. I'd guessed correctly, the jewel-colored MINI is there, beeping when she pulls her keys from the pocket of her hoodie.

"Jacinta—"

"Look, Lainey." She makes an ugly emphasis on my name like it's a bad joke. "You think you're the only one who feels awful right now? You think you know what it's like for me? You think you can just call me up at random and then act like it was my fucking fault?"

"That's not—"

"You think you're the only one who wants to find her? Who wishes the cops could just do their fucking job?"

"Probably not." I manage to hold her furious gaze. "Maybe, if the cops were a little better at doing their fucking job, Olivia would still be home."

Her reaction is so strong it takes me by surprise. Her shoulders round, and she seems to shrink into herself like I punched her in the gut. Anger drains from her face, leaving behind nothing but exhaustion and the same look of vulnerability that I'm used to seeing in the mirror. "Shit," she says in a shaky voice. "Shit, I'm sorry."

Tears well up in the lower rims of her eyes, and she covers her face with her hands. I feel foolish. What am

I supposed to do, comfort her? So I just stand there and watch her sob her heart out, feeling at once vindicated and guilty for being vindicated.

"I'm sorry it happened to you," she says, once she's collected herself. Sniffling, she wipes her nose with the back of her hand. "I really am. And be sure I'd never, ever, let anything like that happen to Olivia." The cruelty in her gentle, melodious voice is striking. "So you can leave me alone now, okay?"

Without giving me time to answer, she climbs into the MINI, fumbles with the key longer than she has to—it seems her hands are shaking as badly as mine—and peels out of the parking lot with a screech of tires. I watch her numbly as the taillights of the car fade down the street. Her last words replay in my head, over and over, taking on new shadows and overtones of meaning.

Then I go back to my own car, climb in, close the doors. And scream.

CHAPTER TWENTY

When I finally turn the key in the ignition—which, thankfully, decides to work and the engine coughs to life—I'm still trembling. The car zigzags across the parking lot as I drive onto the street.

Next step is deciding where to go. Not to the hotel, not yet—I can't face the idea of sitting in that sterile room all alone, waiting for something to happen, for someone to deign to check up on me or give me an update, for Sean to remember I exist. So I drive in circles until my hands steady and my thoughts flow coherently.

I'm on the stretch of nearly empty service road on my way to the hotel when I notice I'm being followed.

Peering into the rearview mirror, I have to narrow my eyes to make sure I didn't imagine it. There's a car behind me, with headlights so dim they could be stray reflections of streetlamps in the glass. But when I look again, it's still there, and definitely still a car.

My first thought is Jacinta, but I dismiss it. I can't tell what kind of car it is by its height and the shape of the lights, but it's certainly not Jacinta's MINI Cooper. It looks like an SUV of some kind. And it's getting closer.

My hands grow sweaty on the steering wheel. In a knee-jerk response, I hit the gas pedal and speed up, well over the limit. In my shaky state, one wrong move, one missed turn, and this ride could be my last, but no matter how fast I go, the other car doesn't seem to fall behind. Instead, it gets closer. I hear—or I think I hear; I could be imagining things at this point—the engine rev as it steadily catches up to me.

Taking a huge risk, I glance away from the road. The car is in my blind spot, and when I look, the headlights flicker. On and off, on and off. Twice. I peer closer but can't see a damn thing through the tinted windows.

The lights flicker again. *Pull over.*

I can't be sure this isn't in my head. For all I know, I'm hallucinating the car itself. But one thing I know for sure in this moment—I'm not pulling over.

Crushing my foot onto the gas pedal, I grip the steering wheel and force my gaze away from the car, onto the empty stretch of road in front of me. There are no streetlights—only reflective signs that flash from the darkness as I whir by.

The driver of the other car hits the gas in turn. With a roar, the car levels with me, and I have no illusions: my prehistoric Neon will not hold up to a brand-new SUV. The car—it's either black or dark blue, this is all I can make out—could easily pass me, block the road, and cut off my escape, but for some reason, it doesn't.

I try to remember how far I am from my exit, the one that leads straight to the illuminated monolith of the hotel. Too bad I wasn't paying attention to any of the signs.

The car falls behind, but before I can allow myself a sigh of relief, it rams my Neon's rear bumper so hard that my head snaps back then forward and my forehead connects with the steering wheel. For an endless moment of terror, all I see in front of me are stars while the Neon careens ahead at nearly a hundred miles per hour, into nothingness.

I may be going crazy, but I sure as hell didn't imagine that. Gripping the steering wheel, I spin it as hard as I can and avoid driving off the road at the last millisecond. My tires give a pitiful screech as something clicks and clangs deep down in the car's mechanical bowels.

Behind me, the SUV follows, steady. I swear the dim headlights have a smug look to them.

Realizing there's only one thing left to do, I step on the brakes and pull up to the curb. I see the reflection of my lone brake light in the pitch-black windshield of the SUV as it slows down and pulls up behind me.

The engine of the Neon still running, I sink my fingernails into the worn plastic of the steering wheel. My foot taps a nervous tattoo, ready to hit the gas pedal. My gaze is glued to the rearview mirror, to the reflection of the SUV. My mirror cracked more than a year ago, and I never had it fixed, because even with a spiderweb of cracks, it was doing its job just fine, but right now, I'm cursing myself with every word I can think of. Sure, I couldn't spare the hundred bucks. What did I buy with them? Probably either makeup or dope.

So I sit and watch the car in the mirror, waiting.

Any moment now, he'll come out. He has to.

But as soon as the driver's side door starts to open, I lose it. My foot slams onto the gas pedal, and I peel away from the curb with a wail of tires. All I can think of is ahead, ahead, ahead, the exit that's already beckoning, so close. I know the car is already on my heels, and any second now its shiny, predatory bumper will rear-end my Neon and send me skittering off the road.

But I don't look in the rearview mirror. I just drive.

I take the curve of the exit at five times the legal speed and nearly go flying out of the driver's seat. The Neon careens into the vast, near-empty lot that separates me from the hotel. I twist the steering wheel, spin, and skid to a stop across two parking spaces. My heart hammers as I turn to look behind me.

There's no car. Like there never has been. I can't see a thing past the two lights at the entrance of the lot.

My shoulders cramp from gripping the steering wheel for dear life. I have to force my fingers to unbend and let go. Wincing, I feel around the bump under my hairline.

Definitely real.

Shouldn't I do something? Call someone?

And tell them what? Oh, there was a car. I think it was black, or maybe blue or dark gray, I'm not sure. Did you get the license plate? Oh, no, it was behind me the whole time.

I get out and circle my Neon. As if the busted front bumper wasn't enough, the back is now looking just as bad, but that will hardly surprise anyone. They're more likely to ask if I had been driving while impaired, and I don't want to answer that.

Shaky, I walk to the hotel. The woman at reception gives me a strange look, although at this point, it could be either my paranoia or the comedown from the pills. I make my way to my room, swipe my key card in the slot, and only then notice the stripe of light that escapes from behind the poorly insulated door frame.

My hand hovering above the handle, I freeze. I do remember with absolute certainty that I left the place pitch-black.

Not this too. Not my hotel room. Where will I go? How will I explain it to Sean? That thought scares me more than the idea of having no place to stay.

There's a creak behind the door, bedsprings, and soft steps growing closer and closer. I only have time to take a couple of shaky steps back when the door opens.

At once, I recognize the broad-shouldered silhouette against the dimly lit room. It's Sean.

CHAPTER TWENTY-ONE

I start to bleat something, but he mutely gestures for me to come inside, and I obey.

"I just spoke with Jacqueline. She's not angry at you, although her husband sure is. In fact, I'm not even going to repeat what he said to me, because I don't think it'll do anyone any good."

"Are you . . ."

"Am I what?"

"Angry at me."

He sighs. "Laine . . ."

"Please," I say. "Don't. Whatever you're about to say, don't."

"What do you think I was about to say?"

"Many things. The usual things. Just let me try to explain."

"What is there to explain?"

"It's Jacinta," I say, stumbling over my own words. But I can tell his patience drains away with every second, and I have so much to tell him. "Jacinta, the sister. Olivia's aunt." I flinch at the phrase. "She's not telling everything. I don't know what it is, but . . ."

He shakes his head. "Let me deal with Jacinta, okay?"

"What's that supposed to mean? Do you—"

Do you know something, I almost say, but he cuts me off. "It's supposed to mean it's my job to figure these things out. And it's a lot easier getting people to talk when someone doesn't sneak behind my back to try to confront them."

I need to sit down, but there's nowhere else to sit but the bed, so that's what I do. Now he's looming over me, and I don't like it.

"I know it's because you care. And I didn't want to say it, but your attempts at vigilantism, or whatever this is, they could actually harm Olivia instead of helping her. Do you understand me?"

I feel like I've been punched. I screw my eyes shut, so I only feel the bed creak and tilt as he sits down next to me. Not right by my side; there's a respectable two feet of distance between us, and I'm afraid to look again.

"I didn't mean to screw up," I say. "I'm sorry."

"When I first brought you here, remember, you said you weren't a bad person?"

Do I ever. "I don't really blame you if you don't believe that anymore."

"I think the person who doesn't believe it is you. That's the problem."

The pain coiled in my chest chokes off my air. How can he see through all my layers, all my defenses, right through my skull into the coils of my brain, see the things I can't see myself? How can he know me better than I do?

"My life ended in that basement, Sean. It's just that my body forgot to die for some reason. And I'm walking around, a body without a soul, waiting for someone to come along and pull the plug on me."

He doesn't speak. He reaches out and puts his hand on mine. I wish he didn't because his touch makes me melt inside.

"If you really didn't have a soul, you wouldn't have cared about Olivia. You wouldn't have chosen to help me."

Wouldn't I? Was it really for Olivia or just a selfish, deep-seated hope—hope for answers, for the real reason I'm still alive? Or was it all for Sean? Because I would have done anything he told me to.

"You're better than you think you are. You're brave. You're strong. You have a good heart."

"Much good it does me."

"You can't live without a heart."

"Some people manage." My smile feels like razors. He knows who I mean.

"They're the ones who aren't really living. They think they are, but they're dead inside. And every time they make you think like this, they win. Don't let them."

I stare at the floor. "Maybe I'm just waiting to become one of them. I feel hollow. All the time. I—" I'm this close to telling him about the pills, but I stop myself.

"That's not true. You deserve good things. Beautiful things." He reaches out and brushes away a stubborn corkscrew lock of hair that keeps tumbling into my eyes. "All the beautiful things in the world."

We kiss. In his defense, it's all me, from the start. I'm the one who leans forward. It feels like I'm leaping off a cliff when I touch my lips to his, but when he puts his hands on my waist and kisses me back, suddenly I'm no longer leaping—I unfurl my wings and fly.

I'm only half-aware of my hands tearing away his layers, first his coat then fumbling at the collar of his shirt, trembling as my fingers undo the buttons. I shrug out of my jacket, letting it drop to the floor. No need for the pills stashed in the pockets—a minute ago I was crashing but now I'm flying high all over again. Soaring. Maybe it's the only thing that keeps my head above water right now, keeps me from plummeting back into reality and understanding. It's the only way my hands and my lips can continue doing what they're doing without questioning.

I pull him down with me, down onto the mattress with its tangle of sheets while I finally pry his shirt off and let my palms roam his hot skin, the muscular expanse of his abs and his chest. My lips brush along his collarbone, and I feel him shudder.

"Laine." A hot whisper in my ear. I have to bite my

lip to keep in a moan, I want him this bad. "Laine, please."

Anything you want. I'm yours. I was always yours.

But his next words scorch me. "Not...not like this. Not here. Laine, stop."

He pulls away, and I slam back into my body. It's like someone flipped a switch, turned off the heady buzz, and all that I have left is shame and bitterness and what feels like a bottomless smoking crater in the dead center of my chest.

Sean kneels in front of me, a look of anguish on his face. "We shouldn't be doing this."

"I want to be doing this," I say stubbornly, fighting the tears that build in the back of my throat.

"You're upset. You had a rough day."

"Are you saying I don't have the capacity to decide what I do and don't want? Is that it?"

"I never said that."

"Then if you don't want me, just say so. Make it quick. No need to let me down easy."

He collapses onto the mattress and rubs his eyes with the heels of his hands. "God, is that what you think? That I don't want you? You think it's the only possible reason?"

"What other reason can there be?" Overcome with self-consciousness, I pull on the hem of my shirt, smoothing it down. The memory of his hands still burns on my skin.

"Many. For one, I'm an authority figure. I'm more than ten years older than you. That doesn't bother you?"

"No. I've been in love with you since I first saw you, and I was thirteen."

This is probably the most honest thing that's ever passed my lips. Seeing him flinch like I slapped him—like my one moment of truth was an insult—hurts on a level beyond the physical.

"This is wrong. This is wrong in too many ways to count," he says.

"I don't care. I want you. You're the only man I ever wanted."

I reach to his belt buckle.

He doesn't stop me.

So we collapse. We jump off the cliff into nothingness, and I can't tell if we're soaring or plummeting to our deaths.

And right now it doesn't matter.

※　※　※

I can't look him in the eye afterward. I'm afraid of what I'll see. I'm afraid we'll have to have the conversation about how we shouldn't have done that, how it can never happen again, and so on. And after that he'll sit up, put his clothes back on, and leave.

I can't stand the thought of him leaving. So I just curl up next to him, basking in his warmth. He stretches out and throws his arm over me.

"I never even asked," I murmur. "Is there anyone?"

For a few seconds he doesn't move, and I wonder if

I'd actually dared say these words out loud. Then he stirs and rolls over to face me. His body is powerful; his presence fills the double bed, the room itself. It makes me feel like we're inside a dollhouse, and we're the only part that isn't pretend. "No one," he says. "Not like that, anyway."

I think of the female voice answering his phone, and my thoughts must be plain on my face, because he pulls me close. "There have been, in the past, but nothing has worked out."

So was that a one-night stand? One with a particularly lacking sense of boundaries? Is that what we are?

But before any of my questions can slip out and ruin the moment, he speaks. "What about you?"

"Are you kidding?"

"Come on. There must have been someone. Some guy?"

Shit. I remember the cramped office at the police station, me answering questions into the other officer's phone recorder. And he knows all this; of course he does—he must have listened to that disaster of a conversation dozens of times.

"No one," I say flatly.

He pulls me closer, but I don't know if I can take any more. Instead of comforting, I find the heat of his body stifling, his weight on me too much. It squeezes my ribs so tightly that they seem to bend, like wishbones about to snap. I wiggle out of his grip. He makes a muffled sound of surprise but doesn't hold me back. I lock myself in the bathroom and put the tap on full blast while I retrieve a tranquilizer from my stash. This should keep me down and dreamless for a couple of hours. I gulp it down then crouch against the side of the bathtub, knees pulled up to my chest, waiting for it to start kicking in.

Resting my forehead on my knees, I close my eyes, the cold, hard porcelain against my back my only tie to reality, the lingering soreness between my legs the only indication that it was real. It was different in my daydreams. Isn't it always?

I turn off the water and peek out the door; I can see his form under the thin hotel blanket that only covers him from the waist down. The expanse of his back is stark against the pale-green sheets, and my heart starts to hammer. It really did happen.

He seems to be asleep when I carefully slip under the blanket. In any event, he doesn't try to cuddle me; he barely moves at all.

My thought is that I'll never be able to fall asleep next to him, but the pill is stronger. My eyes close, and my mind slows to a sluggish crawl before gently fading to black.

Sometime during the night, I wake up, disoriented and confused, struggling to make sense of the unfamiliar surroundings. The hotel room's electronic alarm clock reads three fifteen a.m., its red glow the only source of light in the room. I'm tucked comfortably under the bleach-stiff sheets, bundled up like a small child. Sean is still there, asleep next to me. His face looks smoother, softer in his sleep.

That's when another source of light flares up, and I realize what woke me. On the rickety hotel desk, I see the dark bundle of Sean's coat, and next to it, his phone buzzes to life in a brief flash.

Holding my breath, I sit up as carefully as I can, but I can't keep the mattress from creaking as I swing my legs over the edge. It takes forever to extricate myself from the sheet and blanket, and in the meantime, the phone flashes and buzzes twice. Each time, I freeze and watch him, unblinking, expecting him to snap awake any moment and then the chance will be gone. But he doesn't. He probably hasn't slept in days, not for more than an hour or two at a time. Once the phone goes silent again, I hear his even, deep breathing and imagine what it would be like to fall asleep next to him every night.

Finally, I walk barefoot from the bed to the desk. Thanks to the tacky wall-to-wall carpeting, my steps are muffled and soft. I pick up the phone, throwing a glance at Sean one last time, but he's fast asleep.

The dim light of the phone still makes me squint as I press the button on top and look at the lock screen. There they are, a string of texts, all from the same number, no name. Call me. Now. We need to talk. Call me! over and over, frantic.

The last one says simply, Call me or I'll call HER.

CHAPTER TWENTY-TWO

In the morning, he's gone. The only reminders are his scent, lingering in the bleachy smell of the hotel sheets, and the number I copied into my phone.

I try to tell myself that Sean never noticed me looking, that he was asleep throughout. But something tells me otherwise.

He doesn't call once, and I can't bring myself to call him.

I don't leave the room much at all. Or the bed. Except for a trip to the drugstore to get my last refill of sleeping pills, and I burn through the whole thing, a month's supply gone in one week. The moment it wears off, I pop another one and drift back into the gray.

It's reliable stuff. You don't feel rested, more like you're waking up from a coma, but at least it means you can go right back to sleep. And at least the coma is dreamless.

I know I need to get out of this room. I need to go back to my apartment. I need a new job or at least to beg Dom to give me back my old one.

I might need to suck his dick for that. Another girl told me he has three piercings. I wonder how much Oxy I'd need to get through that.

For now, it's probably better that I haven't touched the stuff in the last week. I have my checkup and shrink appointment on Monday, and I can't afford to fail my pee-in-a-cup test right now—I can't. Although being locked up in a place with padded walls doesn't sound so bad anymore.

The morning of, I can't even pop an Adderall and have to content myself with awful coffee from the hotel room's drip coffeemaker to power me through the day. I think of getting an energy drink from the vending machine downstairs, but I have to manage my money. How pathetic is that?

I guzzle my coffee, trying not to taste it. Hoping it'll keep me on my feet through the test and the hour-long talk with Dr. Rowland.

By the time I get in my car and drive, it's becoming doubtful.

The hospital is a squat building that almost disappears in the flat, gray landscape, especially on a rainy day like today—or three hundred Seattle days a year, really. If I don't pay attention, I could easily miss my lone exit in the middle of nowhere and end up in some deserted industrial district.

From the outside, the building looks like there are no windows, but they're just all facing inward—into a courtyard as gray as everything else. They keep sticking potted trees around the perimeter but the trees keep dying. Not enough light, or too many negative vibes or something. The lower-floor windows still have bars on them, even though the whole courtyard thing is designed so that we can see daylight but can't escape.

I walk to the second floor where a grim-looking nurse gives me my plastic container and points me to the bathroom. She follows me with a gaze that could burn a hole in my back—but she does that with everyone.

She used to watch me pee: leave it to an addict to try and smuggle in someone else's urine in a flask. But now they don't bother anymore.

I wish I could say it never crossed my mind, but something deep inside me just withers at the idea of disappointing Dr. Rowland. Maybe it's a leftover child's instinct since she's the closest to a mother figure I've ever had. Whether I admit it or not, a part of me looks forward to seeing Dr. Rowland, so I just keep clean the week ahead. I can manage this much . . . for now.

It's this part of the bimonthly ritual that I hate, the cup, the scuffed bathroom stall reeking of sanitizer and piss. The humiliation of filling out the health questionnaire with questions about whether or not I used intravenous drugs or had unprotected sex in the last x

weeks. The nurse's porcine little eyes watching me from under her low brow bone with that look that plainly says don't complain, you did this to yourself.

I want to blow up in her face sometimes. Throw the fucking cup and the clipboard with the questions. Tell her that I didn't do this to myself, I wasn't the one who stole me, who broke me. She probably doesn't know, or give a fuck.

I walk up to the third floor. Here, there are no big red signs reading NO ALCOHOL OR ILLICIT SUBSTANCES BEYOND THIS POINT, no methadone pickup schedules. There are prints of paintings on the walls. Potted plants, wilting, yellowing around the edges, but still.

I knock on the office door and go in. Dr. Rowland gets up to greet me and shakes my hand without squeamishness, as if she's not afraid I'll give her some deadly junkie-whore disease just by looking at her. She gestures at the armchair across from her desk that creaks when I lower myself into it.

Dr. Elise Rowland is a small, plump woman with light-brown skin and a mass of curls pulled into an eternal bun atop her head. She wears a white coat over her normal clothes as this place requires, but she has a thing for brooches—there's always a new one, some kind of jeweled insect. Big ruby spider, butterfly in all colors of the rainbow, ladybug, bee. Today is a deviation: a tiny blue-bird studded with rhinestones.

"Lainey," she says as she takes her place and opens my file where the results of my test are printed up. I carefully watch her expression for a frown or a twitch, something that might give away that the results are not what she hoped for. But her face is unreadable. She looks up, closes the folder. "How are you doing?"

"Okay." I'm always doing okay. Usually it's a lie, and usually she lets me get away with it. But today, she heaves a sigh, and I know it's not going to be so easy.

"You know I've only been trying to help you," she says. "This whole time. I hoped you might trust me a little by now."

I sit up in alarm, trying to figure out what she could possibly know and how. Shit. How long does it take for Adderall to leave your system?

"I know what's been going on, Lainey." There's no threat in her voice, no judgment, nothing. That alarms me above all. My inner child, what's left of her, anxiously looks for notes of disappointment, but I don't even find that.

Mercifully, she cuts to the chase. "I got a call from a Detective Ortiz," she says. My insides clench at the very mention of the name, and I'm afraid I couldn't hide my reaction fast enough.

But lucky for me, she misinterprets it. "I know you were involved in the Olivia Shaw case."

The air goes out of my lungs in a whoosh of relief. "I was," I say, careful not to let my mask of indifference slip. "But I was cleared. As a suspect, I mean."

Her penetrating gaze won't let go of mine. "And what did you make of all this?"

"What was I supposed to make of all this?"

"Did it make you feel worse?"

What do you think?

"Did it make you want to do certain things?"

"It should all be in my tests."

She ignores my remark. "I want to know how you felt about it. Not what you did about it."

I give a shrug.

"You were totally indifferent?"

"It has nothing to do with me. She's someone else's now." Dr. Elise is one of the few people I feel bad lying to, but the other option is unthinkable right now.

"But what happened to her, it bears a certain similarity to what happened to you," she says softly. "You can't ignore that completely."

"We don't know what happened to her," I say. "No one does. Some people think she ran away."

"What do you think?"

"I have no idea."

"Did it bring back any flashbacks? Bad dreams?"

I shrug. "The Ambien is working. I need a new prescription, by the way. I ran out. I think I need more pills. Sometimes I wake up in the middle of the night and I can't go back to sleep, so I need to take a second one." I blurt it all out without pausing for a breath.

"We'll deal with that in a moment. When Detective Ortiz called me, he asked for all your information, but I refused, of course, for the sake of your patient confidentiality. They didn't have a warrant or any real reason to suspect you."

Gratitude fills my chest, scorching hot and tinged with guilt for all the deceptions, all the lies big and small I've told her over the years, all the fibs she let slide. For all her efforts that bore no fruit.

"Thank you," I say hoarsely. "They didn't have any reason to suspect me. I didn't even know she...she was the same girl. Until Sea—until Detective Ortiz told me." Blood rushes to my face, but if she noticed anything, she lets it go.

"So you don't care about her? Olivia Shaw. Not at all?"

"Not at all." The lie is so easy. Don't I ever get tired?

She waits patiently. I stare her down.

"Go on," I explode. "Ask me if I had considered this might be the same man. Yes, I fucking have, okay? But it wasn't my job to find him. Maybe you should address your complaints to the Seattle PD, who had better things to do."

I expect her to chastise me in that way she has, re-proachful without judging. But she keeps looking me straight in the eye. "I know. It was an awful injustice. All their efforts should have been directed at finding that man. Stopping him. But because of factors we're both well aware of, it didn't happen."

"I tried to help," I mutter through my teeth. My eyes burn. I need my pills, badly. "I tried to. I repeated my testimony, but I'd already told them everything I knew the first time, and it didn't change anything."

She waits while I collect myself. I don't reach out for the pastel box of tissues on her table. I refuse to be that cliché. Instead I smear the tears all over my cheeks with the back of my hand.

"I want to remember," I say. "I want to try to remember. Can't you help me? Hypnotize me or something?"

She tilts her head with a look of sympathy. "It's not a question of repressing, I'm afraid. You remember everything vividly. But—"

"It's just not enough," I finish for her. "Isn't there anything you can do?"

"I've tried hypnosis already," she says sadly. "It didn't yield anything new. You presented a fairly typical profile . . . Sorry. I don't mean to belittle what you went through."

I mutter that it's okay. "Wasn't there anything?"

She heaves a sigh. "Besides your surprisingly vehement feelings of loathing toward . . . toward your pregnancy, no."

"Surprisingly?" I gulp. "Is it really so surprising?"

"Many other young women have found themselves in your situation before. They regarded the child as their one bright spot. Some called it their salvation."

I grit my teeth. I start to notice I'm doing it on purpose.

"You don't think you'd make a good mother?"

"Why do you ask me that? I thought you were supposed to help."

"So no."

I could never bring myself to tell her the truth: I just never knew; they didn't give me a chance to find out. They took her away and didn't even let me look at her. I think I might have loved her, might even have forgiven her if only they'd let me take just one look—but I was lost to anesthesia, far under. They came in like thieves and left before I woke up. By then it was too late to object and too painful to question, and no one in their right mind could argue with the fact that it was best for her, this nameless little girl. Especially not me. All I could do was try to mute it, forget it, put it out of my mind the only way I knew how.

"Obviously," I snarl. "Next question? Please?"

"Why do you think that is?"

I have no answer, not a truthful one anyway.

"What I think is that it stems from your experience of your own mother. Before and after the kidnapping."

My mother. My mother who bought me dollar-store toys on good days and who pawned the electronics on bad days. My mother whom I only saw at the hospital once after I was found—because she got her ass imprisoned for yet another drug offense. Surprise, surprise.

I think of our last encounter, and in spite of myself, the corner of my mouth curls. "My mother was stupid, junkie trash," I snap. Like mother, like daughter, rings a sarcastic echo in my head.

"What do you remember of her? From before?"

"What I just told you."

Dr. Elise shakes her head. "That also struck me. A

child, any child—and you were still a child back then, Lainey, no matter what you or anyone else says—will always call for her mother. Always, no matter what, no matter how awful the mother might be."

I want to tell her that the child in me died in screaming agony on the basement floor. But something about her words compels me to listen without interrupting.

"And you never called for her. Not once. Not in your sleep, not when you were alone. You never so much as asked about her. Like you never had a mother at all."

That was pretty close to the truth, and Dr. Elise knows it too.

"I'm not a monster," I say, holding her gaze. "Just because my mother was. Just because I have no maternal feelings toward my rapist's child."

"I never said you were a monster."

"You think I'm abnormal. You just said so."

"We all deal with trauma in our own way. The mind is a smart thing. It does all it can to make sure all the bad things are locked away where they can't hurt us so we can go on functioning."

"If you think this is me compartmentalizing..." Anger locks my throat. I squeeze my hands into fists.

"That's not what I said."

I glower at her, but she weathers my hate-filled glare like a stoic. Deep down I feel bad about all the shitty, mean things I have ever said to her, about every time I blew up at her when she was trying to help me. Even now I feel awful inside.

But I still can't help it. "I think our time is up soon."

"I can prolong the appointment if you need to talk more," she says neutrally.

I pretend I haven't heard. "How about that Ambien?"

"Maybe we can lower the dose. You should be trying to sleep naturally."

"I don't want to sleep naturally."

"And I'm loath to prescribe more sleeping pills to someone with your history." Her voice is steel.

"But..."

"You could try natural supplements. I can write you a prescription for melatonin..."

I push my chair back, leap up. "We're done."

"Lainey."

"I'll see you in two months," I say with a saccharine smile. I know she has the power to have me locked up again, but I see on her face that she won't. Because she believes in me, believes I can get through this and live a normal life and be a functioning member of society.

Stupid of her.

I storm out without a good-bye.

CHAPTER TWENTY-THREE

Keeping an eye on the arrow of the gas meter as it leans dangerously to the left, I drive off the exit ramp and turn in the opposite direction from the hotel.

As daylight thins and fades from pale-gray to carbon, the streets I drive down turn dirtier. Graffiti covers the walls, garbage everywhere. It's not quite as bad as I remember. In the last decade, there's been much over-hyped urban redevelopment, as the white guys on the news called it. Between the projects and neglected, dilapidated homes, glossy boxes of condos have sprung up like brick-and-glass mushrooms. Buy up now; this area is about to be booming. Smart investment for a savvy young professional.

Back then, it was just an investment for a savvy young

drug addict. For which my mom, Valerie Santos, certainly qualified.

As soon as the first echoes of recognition start to go off in my mind, anxiety creeps up, crackling in my fingertips like static. The corner store where I used to shoplift candy bars when I was eight or nine comes into view, still there, still kickin', same Sharpie-drawn sign in the window. Well, not the same sign but still hand drawn—boasting CIGARETTES WINE BEER LOTTERY. Valerie sent me here for peanut butter, milk cartons, and puffy, cotton-like loaves of plastic-wrapped bread when she wasn't up for shopping for groceries. After a while, the guy behind the counter started to recognize me and would sell me smokes, "for Val only, little lady." I remember being so damn proud of myself and sneaking a cigarette or two knowing Val wouldn't notice the pack was open. None of it seemed abnormal to me. The few other kids I knew lived the same way.

Circling the block, dreading the moment the old house floats into view, I start to wonder. My fingertips dance out a nervous tattoo on the steering wheel. I don't remember a damn thing about the actual day I was taken—this much I've repeated to everyone a million times. But now, after everything, thoughts creep into my head that Dr. Rowland wouldn't approve of. I remember her words vividly, and I've read enough about trauma-induced selective amnesia online. What exactly is my mind trying to protect me from? What could be so horrifying and traumatic that I chose to just blank it out—while the ensuing three years are crystal clear, every week, every day and minute?

The answer nags at me from the perimeters of my mind: I could have gone with him of my own free will. It can't have taken that much to tempt someone like me, like the girl I was back then. He wouldn't have had to promise me the stars; anything would have seemed better than living with Val. I could have gone with him for a chocolate bar, a pack of gum.

My foot slams onto the brakes before I realize what I'm doing. Luckily, the street is half-empty. My head snaps forward, not enough to give me whiplash, but nonetheless, I probably should have put my seat belt on. I pull over, rest my forehead on the steering wheel, and focus on my breathing, waiting out the oncoming panic attack. You can't think like this, Dr. Rowland would say. You weren't to blame for what he did to you. Or for anything. You were innocent.

She clearly never met a kid from my neighborhood.

Once I trust myself not to hyperventilate, I leave the car by the curb and walk in the direction I came from, to the convenience store. Hesitating, I push the door open. The chime that clangs over my head, disharmonious like broken glass, sends a tremor of memory racing up my spine.

It's a different guy behind the counter now. Of course it is. Did I really expect to find everything preserved as I remember it, some fucked-up time capsule? He gives me the side-eye as I browse the lone aisle. Doesn't want anyone shoplifting. To appease him, I buy a pack of smokes, even though I still have some left.

He makes my handful of change disappear and gives me a fleeting but sharp once-over.

"Hey, *chica*," he pipes up as I'm already at the door, bracing myself for another clang of the chime, "do I know you from somewhere?"

"No," I say too quickly and without turning around. "I'm not from around here."

"Sure, sure, I've seen you before," he goes on. My gaze darts sideways at the magazine stand under the counter. Huge black letters yell from a headline: SHAW ADOPTION DRAMA—THE ANSWER TO THE SHOCKING DISAPPEARANCE?

Air rushes into my lungs, burning. The chime gives a sad clink when I slam the door and flee.

Way to go, Laine. Way to go.

I know I need to save up my pills, so I content myself with a smoke, which isn't nearly enough. It only makes my hands shake more, and my heartbeat picks up at a desperate rhythm.

Having learned my lesson, I pull the hood of my sweatshirt over my head. With my baggy pants and my oversize man's pleather jacket, my hair and most of my face obscured, you can't tell I'm a girl at all, which can only work in my favor in these parts. My knife is still with Sean, and I'm defenseless.

The idea that I might get hurt or killed because he took my knife away fills me with bitter vindictiveness.

How sorry he'd be, I think as I peer through the shadows in search of unknown assailants.

The walk to my old house takes less time than I thought. It floats out of the descending shadows, sneaking up on me. One moment I was just walking down the street, and the next, there it is.

It's not a shock, exactly, but not a happy homecoming either. I don't know what I expected—maybe for it to be sold, so now there would be a happy family living there, two-point-five kids and a little yappy dog, a colorful plastic slide and swing set in the tall grass of the Kleenex-sized front yard. No such luck. It's abandoned. Not the only house on the street with windows boarded up, but it seems to be in the most advanced state of disrepair. The cheap white boards that cover the walls and façade have fallen away in places, and the rest have turned a yellowish, grayish color. Plywood-covered windows stare at me blindly, reminding me of my poor apartment I can never come back to.

There used to be a chain-link fence that reached up to my waist, but it's rusted through and pieces are missing. I don't even have to step over it to get into the yard. Tall grass rustles as I advance through it, crushing the dead stems under my boots, pushing them out of the way. They whip my hands and face, and I hit back with twice the violence.

Memories resurface as I circle the house. I know there's another door in the back, and that's where I'm headed.

The glass insert in the door is cracked and so coated with dust and cobwebs that it's nearly opaque. Two criss-crossed boards were once nailed over the door, but one has been pried away and the other is so rotten it's falling to pieces, crumbling under my fingertips. When I turn the door handle, it obeys with surprising ease and barely a squeak of rust. It doesn't take much effort to duck under the board and slip into the house.

It would be pitch-black if not for the massive hole in the roof, but the last of daylight is ebbing away, so I have to light my way with my cell phone. Naturally, the moment I turn it on, the empty battery alert starts to flash. I groan, but I don't intend to stay here for too long anyway.

This part is the kitchen, long and narrow, with an arched doorway leading into the main room. There's no hall—the front door opens right into the living room. Even back when I was a kid, the insulation always came unglued and icy breezes speared the place. Now long stripes of fading light fall from the door across the dirty floor.

There's a thin plaster wall separating the living room from my bedroom, which is the size of a closet and windowless. The doors are gone, and empty doorways are like gaping mouths, dark and forbidding. Beneath my boots, broken glass and the expected used syringes crunch softly—it doesn't even gross me out. The place smells like you'd imagine an abandoned house to smell, of human debris.

I don't know why I came here. What was I looking for? Did I think my memory would magically come back, a lightbulb going off in my brain like in a cartoon? Wouldn't that be convenient.

It does come back, but not like a lightbulb—more like a trickle. Mostly useless, random things. I remember the vomit color of the couch and the angle of the TV facing away from the door. Valerie's walls were painted a strange, deep red, mine a cloying pink—a rare attempt at decoration on her part, long before I could remember. I assume there was a time even Valerie gave a shit. At some point, I had one of those child's four-poster beds, before I outgrew it at seven or eight. There was no money to replace it, so I slept on a mattress on the floor ever since.

Something pulls me, some unhealthy need to see it with my own eyes. Not that there's anything left to see— all hints of furniture and appliances are long gone. But I take a step toward the dark rectangle of the door on the right, then another step, and then my legs are carrying me of their own free will.

Claustrophobia-inducing walls close in on me. When I raise my phone, I see humidity-stained paint with black flowers of mold creeping down from the ceiling, but the memory of the original color still lurks underneath.

I turn around and shine the phone light into the corners, one after another. The room is empty, and something about it is odd—I can't put my finger on it at first, but it nags at me until I get it. There's no trash here. Not like the rest of the place anyway. There are still dust and cobwebs and paint chips but no broken glass or condom wrappers.

When I turn to leave, the phone light snatches something out of the darkness, just the corner of an object. I spin around, and the phone nearly flies out of my hand.

There are rocks. A small pile of rocks and crumbled pieces of brick arranged in a square shape, and in the middle I see something rusted and metallic, bright-blue paint still clinging amidst dark spots of corrosion.

With the toe of my boot, I turn it over and stumble away until my back hits the wall. The phone slips from my hand this time and clatters to the floor in a halo of diffused light. I press my back into the chipping paint, unable to peel my gaze away from the object.

It's a doll, a child's doll on a toy bed. Its glass eyes glint dimly in the weak light.

I don't know how long it takes me to come out of my stupor. I slide to the floor, crawl toward my phone, and pick it up. My hands are shaking so much that frightening shadows dance on the walls, shadows that look alive.

Holding my breath, I examine the shrine—that's what it is, no other word for it. A bed, a doll, four walls. There are even stumps of candles. The doll looks like something you'd find in the bins at Goodwill, but when I lean closer, I realize the doll's peeling limbs have been painted brown over generic beige white. The hair has been slathered in something black and flaking. And her eyes are the wrong color, light gray, startling and bright against the dark paint.

The skin is too dark to be Olivia, but the eyes—the eyes aren't mine. A shiver runs down my spine like needles under my skin. I can't bring myself to touch the thing.

There's one of those plastic toy plates with dark flecks in the center, its contents spilled next to it: three cigarette butts. I grasp one between forefinger and thumb and hold it up, illuminating it with my phone.

It's fresh. Marked by humidity, already cold for some time, but the filter is still bright orange, unfaded. The end is crushed with a faint indent of teeth. I look at it and look at it, and things refuse to add up in my head until I see the thin stripe lining the filter. My brand.

I drop it like it suddenly burst into flame and wipe my hand on my jeans. My head spins when I scramble to my feet.

I should call Sean. The thought surfaces in my mind like an old habit, and I feel a cowardly rush at the idea that I have something for him, something real, finally. I scroll through my contacts, dial the number, and press my phone to my ear. Without the light of the screen, the darkness is near total, and I blink into it while the line takes forever to connect.

Then it goes straight to voice mail.

I curse and end the call, realizing too late that I really, really should have left a message. I try to take a photo, but the screen informs me smugly that I don't have enough battery left to use the camera function. No choice but to call him again. I mash the pad of my thumb into the Call button and wait, but the call drops without ever connecting.

There's a sound at the edge of my hearing, a sound I wouldn't have noticed if I hadn't been holding my breath. A soft scrape that cuts short almost as soon as I become aware of it. I freeze and hold up my phone, directing the light at the empty door frame.

The house responds with silence.

A part of me wants to think it's just the house in its normal process of falling apart, boards creaking as they rot, beams groaning as they get closer and closer to collapse. Crumbling plaster and bloated plywood falling away in pieces. Maybe it's nothing more than my nerves, and who could blame them? But that's the same part of me who, for all I know, followed a complete stranger without putting up a fight. The new me, the person who came out on the other side of hell ten years ago, knows better.

As I inch toward the door, I'm aware of the creak of floorboards under every step, and I'm not kidding myself. The other person is aware of it too. My breathing is like a gale in the silence, and all my attempts to control it fail miserably.

I advance into empty, pitch-black space. The hole in the ceiling no longer sheds any light—it's dark outside, and there have never been lights on this street. Without my phone, the darkness farther than a few inches from my face is so impenetrable it might as well be a solid entity.

An irresistible urge to yell scratches in the back of my throat. To shriek, to shatter the silence and hear the echo of my voice bounce off the walls and ceiling—to prove, to myself and whoever else is in here, that I exist, that I'm real. At the same time, the little-girl me silently begs to awaken from this like from a bad dream. Back at my apartment, or at the hotel, or anywhere.

I turn on my phone again, but the screen dims, the red empty battery icon flashes, steady like a heartbeat, and suddenly I know what to do. Please, only let the battery last just a moment longer. I desperately paw at the screen until I get to my contacts and thumb the number I copied from Sean's phone.

The screen goes dark, and my heart nearly stops, but then it brightens again. *Dialing*.

A moment later—a moment that fits the whole of eternity—a sharp, metallic ring erupts from the darkness, only a few feet away.

I hear the hiss of an inhale as the shadows move. The call cuts off to nothing, the phone flashes one last time, and the screen powers down.

I'm in the dark.

All my instincts scream at me to run. Out of sheer despair, or maybe because I know I'm shit out of options, I obey. After all these years, I still know the house pretty much by heart, and it kicks in like a reflex. I dart across the room to the doorway leading to the kitchen, to the back door, to salvation.

Just as I pass through the doorway, something brushes against me, something soft, fabric swiping across my face, my shoulder, my arm. A shriek escapes from my tightly clenched jaws as I stumble back, then trip over my own feet and go sprawling. The rustle is so close that I expect it to sweep over me any moment like a big predatory bird. I roll over and kick out at the darkness with both feet, as hard as I can.

My soles connect with something. There's a hiss of a breath being drawn through clenched teeth, a soft thud as whoever it is hits the wall. I strain my eyes but all I see are shadows stirring. Without waiting for my assailant to recover, I scramble to get up and make for the door.

It swings open without resistance. As I scamper out over the one remaining board, I half expect someone to grab my legs from behind, to pull me, kicking and screaming, back into the dank darkness of the house.

But there's no one. When I glance over my shoulder, all I see is a half-open door into nothingness. My animal instinct, honed for many days and weeks and months, takes over. I turn around and, like the scared rabbit that I am, I run.

CHAPTER TWENTY-FOUR

I run until my legs and my lungs are on fire, not caring that I'm headed in the wrong direction, away from my car. A new emotion rises from the pit of my stomach, choking the breath out of me, and even when I stop and double over, hands on the tops of my thighs, I can't recover. Instead, my ears ring at a tinny high pitch, the world begins to spin, and my thoughts refuse to fall into order.

I examine my dead phone like it holds all the answers, but there isn't even enough battery power to call 911. As soon as my breathing is somewhat near normal, I turn around.

The sight of my car, sitting at the curb where I left it, is enough to make me cry with relief. Once I'm in the driver's seat, I crack the window open, drum my fin-

gers on the steering wheel, and tear open the brand-new
pack of cigarettes in my pocket, grateful now for having
bought it. I light one and take a drag, but it only makes
me shake more, so I throw it out onto the damp pavement and roll the window back up. For the first time, I
realize I have nowhere to go and no one to ask for help.
It occurs to me to go to the Shaws', but after last time,
they'll slam the door in my face and they'll be right. I'd
sooner sleep on a bench than go to Natalia's, not after
that travesty of an interview. And I realize I can't go back
to the hotel anymore. Not to stay anyway. It's no longer
safe.

It hadn't been safe from the start. Sean betrayed me—
I know this for sure now.

I really thought I'd be angrier. Or maybe devastated.
Or something. I thought I'd want to scream and throw
things or drug myself into oblivion. But sometime in the
last fifteen minutes, a part of me accepted this as normal, a confirmation of what I've already known for a
long time. I'm all alone. No human being can be trusted.
Along with a new realization: if there's anything that can
still be done for Olivia, I'll have to do it myself.

The first thing I do is pull over at a gas station and
fill up the tank, silently praying my credit card can take
it. When *approved* flashes on the screen, I exhale with
relief.

Inside the station, it's bright and empty. My gaze wan-
ders the display of chips and candy, the fridge filled with
energy drinks.

"Ma'am, is everything okay?" I look up, only now noticing there's an actual human being behind the counter. His skinny neck sticks out of his bright-blue uniform polo, and his forehead is peppered with small red blemishes. He can't be out of high school yet.

"Yeah, everything is fine," I mutter. Here it comes—he's going to either hit on me or worse. Nervously, I check the exit routes. There are cameras overlooking every inch of the place, blinking in corners.

"Are you sure you're okay to drive?"

What the hell does he want from me? "I'm fine," I snap, and then look up and glimpse myself in the mirrored one-way window near the counter. My hair is a mess, strands like antennae escaping from my messy ponytail, and there's a smudge of dirt on my forehead. When I look down, twigs and cobwebs cling to my shirt and jacket, and there's a rip in the shoulder. I don't even remember it ripping. Did I snag it in the house somewhere?

"Do you want me to call . . . somebody?"

At last I clue in that he doesn't mean ill. I release a deep breath. "Actually, if I could buy a charger"—I hold up my phone—"for one of these."

He looks uncertain but turns around and examines the impulse items displayed over the counter: single-pack condoms, aspirin, batteries, headphones. "Here," he says and slides a generic-brand charger across the counter. He waits while I eye it with wariness. "It's on the house," he says with a shaky laugh. "I mean, it's on me."

I don't remember thanking him, but I hope I did.

My next stop is a fast-food restaurant tacked on at the end of a strip mall. All the other windows are either dark or covered with metal shutters and padlocked, or just boarded up. The fast-food place is the only beacon of life. Through the windows, I see that a few tables are busy, even though my car is one of only three in the parking lot. I go in and get a Diet Coke I won't drink, because it's the cheapest item on the menu and I don't want the staff harassing me. Then I find a table near a power outlet where I plug the charger. As soon as my phone is working again, I ignore the missed calls, the texts, the messages, and open the browser. I can't deal with Sean right now. I can't listen to him lying to me again, pretending that he cares, that all of this is about something else.

Even though the free Wi-Fi is barely alive, within minutes I'm on a page that will trace any phone number, be it cell or residential, and deliver an address within twenty-four hours—for the small and manageable fee of $19.99. I can't help but wonder if, despite all logic, my prepaid phone is also in some database somewhere, my information available to anyone with intent and a working credit card. A couple more impatient taps at the screen, and it's done. All I can do is wait.

I know people describe a craving as your veins itching, but I don't think I've ever truly felt it until now. My head is humming, the usual symptoms of anxiety spilling over to the realm of the physical. First my hands go clammy. Then I start to shiver despite the fact that I'm sweating. When I take off my jacket, my T-shirt has crescents of damp under my arms, and dizziness settles in the space right behind my forehead. Usually, nausea comes next, no matter that I can't remember the last time I ate. In my jacket pockets, I still have a few pills stashed away under the lining, but I'm not going to take anything. I want to be awake for this. I have to be.

After two hours, the number search still hasn't returned anything—if there's anything to return, I remind myself as I refresh my e-mail for the millionth time. The place empties out. The girls behind the counter start to give me those looks.

I end up sleeping in my car, parked at the end of the empty lot. There's no way to get comfortable in a reclining car seat that hasn't reclined in about a decade, and suddenly, my legs and elbows and hip bones are everywhere, all angles and no flesh, and no matter how I twist myself, an arm or a foot keeps falling asleep before I have a chance to. Gnashing my teeth, I take my last anxiety pill, trying not to think of the rest of my stash in the hotel room, not to imagine a cleaning woman finding it and pocketing it. Or worse, Sean discovering it when he inevitably comes over with his key and turns the place upside down looking for me.

But tomorrow it will no longer matter, I tell myself. Maybe I should stay up, watch the sunrise that could very well be my last, but I barely have time to finish the thought when exhaustion and the chemical buzz of my meds pull me under.

Tomorrow, I'm going to find him. I'm going to find Olivia and set us both free, if it kills me, at last.

CHAPTER TWENTY-FIVE

The morning is dizzying and gray, my mouth tastes like ashes, and my head pounds with a dull pain. I only turn on my phone long enough to check my e-mail. The address associated with the cell phone number came in, and I groan inwardly when I see where it is: a small town about a hundred miles from Seattle. Right here, so close. Close enough to drive a skinny thirteen-year-old girl in the trunk of a car, leave her on the side of the road, and make it back before dinner. And then resume your life like nothing happened.

Well, that's not going to work this time.

The chirping of my phone, once, twice, three times as more missed calls and message alerts come in, pulls me out of my thoughts. Sean's name and number, over and over again, and all I have to do is tap my fingertip to hear his voice again.

He will probably yell at me or, worse yet, do that false-kindness thing. I picture that empathy filling his deep-brown eyes, as if to say, *Look at me, I really get you, I know what you're going through, now do exactly as I say*. I can't and I won't. I'm done stumbling blindly along with what everyone tells me. It never got me anywhere, and now it won't help Olivia.

Before I set out on the two-hour drive, I go back inside the fast-food place and make myself eat something, unable to shake the eerie feeling of it all. My last meal could very well be a squished, greasy breakfast sandwich and hash browns. So that's that.

I get a giant coffee, too hot to drink right now, and put it in the cup holder, wishing I had something more effective to keep me focused. My hands slip all over the steering wheel as I pull out of the parking lot.

Maybe I should call someone, just to let them know where I'm going, but who am I going to call? Sugar, maybe? Yeah, I'm sure he'll shed a few tears at the loss of his best customer. The thought makes me chuckle grimly as I take a sip of scalding coffee, taking a certain enjoyment in the way it burns the roof of my mouth. I can't stop poking and prodding it with my tongue until the skin peels, and then it's like I have a mouthful of needles.

However, as I leave the city limits, a kind of calm comes over me. My breathing steadies, the tremor leaves my muscles, and my last shreds of hesitation give way to steely resolve. That's how I felt the second time I was trying to kill myself, the time I was sure I'd succeed, with no one to interrupt me, my method as sure as anything I could afford. The first time I OD'd, but my Craigslist roommate came back from her shift at the grocery store early and called an ambulance. Two weeks later, when I returned from my obligatory stint in the psych ward, I found the locks changed. The second time I was on my own, but I tied my belt to a ceiling lamp that fell out, leaving me there, wheezing and clawing at the painful welt on my throat amidst crumbs of plaster and paint dust with a busted, bloody knee and twisted ankle, humiliated and helpless. To make matters worse, it cost me my security deposit on the crappy apartment. But at least no one found out, because I never told anyone.

Oh right. I told Sean. Well, fuck. Soon enough it's not going to matter anyway.

I still have more than half a tank of gas, but I stop at a gas station right outside Huntington, Washington, my destination. Just so I can buy an energy drink and throw a glance at the security camera above the counter. There. One last proof of where I was if—when—things go wrong.

The town of Huntington—yup, like the disease—is one of those little places lost in the middle of the map, no charm, no attractions, not even of the kooky variety. No biggest plastic ice cream cone in North America, nothing like that. It's pancake flat, ringed by factories and car dealerships and sparse woodlands that look yellow, unhealthy like collapsing lungs choked in Japanese knotweed.

Only when I'm circling the narrow, convoluted streets of the town core do I wonder just what I'm going to do. I don't have a weapon, nothing to defend myself—or attack. But if I'm not going to confront him, then what?

For now, I just focus on finding the address. My only GPS is in my phone, and I don't want to turn it on just yet. Not until I absolutely have to. But as I drive down a street that runs parallel to the shabby-looking main street, tragically misnamed "boulevard," something catches my eye. First, it's in the corner of my vision, like a glitch, but when I glance a second time, the information travels through my nerves and jolts my muscles, making me slam down on the brakes. The car behind me honks furiously, and in the rearview mirror, I see the driver flip me off. I don't bother to return the favor, swerving sharply to stop at the curb.

It's the name on a storefront in bold burgundy and yellow letters: Lyons Car Parts and Repair. The logo is a rudimentary rendition of a roaring lion's head in the same colors. It looks like something someone hastily put together in Photoshop, but it's flashy enough to work for this place.

I double-check the address I scribbled on my fast-food receipt. P. Lyons, 334 Woodland Drive, Huntington, WA.

I get out, slam the door, and assess my poor battered Neon in a glance. The bumper is still misshapen from its encounter with the dark SUV, the only reminder that it all really happened. Worse comes to worst, I'm going to pretend I need that dent fixed.

When I go inside Lyons Car Parts and Repair, a chime dings above the door, and the clerk looks up. He's young and cute in that all-American way, blue eyes and biceps, with a hint of a tribal tattoo peeking from under the sleeve of his dark-navy T-shirt—to give that hint of bad boy that drives small-town girls wild. There's an appliqué of the lion logo right over his well-toned pectoral. "Can I help you?"

"I—I'd like to speak to the owner, please."

I don't know what I said wrong, but his expression shifts so fast that it feels like the shop itself gets a little darker. Those pearly teeth of his vanish, a cloud pulled over the sun.

"He's not in."

"I can wait."

"I don't think it'll do any good."

The heavy look in his deep-set eyes chills me deep to my bone marrow, and I try not to think about what it means.

"Well, I really need to talk to him."

"Not going to happen, sweetheart. And why don't you turn around and go right back where you came from, huh? No one here is going to talk to you."

"What . . ."

"You're press, aren't you? What, the *Herald*? Or some tabloid? Pete warned me you might show up eventually, and I know exactly what to say to the likes of you. You can forget about it. Turn around if you know what's good for you."

"I'm not press," I snarl. But he's already coming out from behind the counter, and I don't like where this is headed. So I turn around and push past the door, the chime giving a pathetic little ding.

The street I'm looking for isn't very far away. A few blocks off the main street, I see the sign, Woodland Drive. The address is almost at the end, a little bungalow that blends in so well with the rest of the houses that I almost drive past. There's one of those mailboxes out front, with the house number painted on it.

My mind races around in confused circles. The whole street is quaintly cute, white picket fences, American flags, and neat flower beds with little bursts of green plants poking through the dark earth. Porches are shrouded in mosquito nets, barbecues rusting under tarp covers. One or two have swings in the front yard or those plastic slides in bright colors. When I was a kid, it was the kind of street I always wanted to live on, naïve and idealistic as only a kid can be. If it looks pretty on the outside, it must be storybook perfect on the inside.

As I drive up to the house, I peer at every last little detail, every tree and fence post and slant of roof, searching frantically in the recesses of my memory. Any moment, I expect the trill of familiarity to go off, recognition awakening deep in my subconscious, but my confusion only grows.

The house is well taken care of, painted forest green with a tile roof. I have to double-check on my crumpled receipt to be sure: 334. No mistake.

Understanding sets in before I can fully admit it. Whatever it is, it's not what I thought. It can't be.

And then they run out into the front yard, yelping and shrieking with delight as they fight over a brightly colored ball before one of them takes hold of it and takes a shot at a basketball ring mounted above the garage door. He misses by a mile, and the other boy hoots.

My heart hammers, and I dig my fingernails into the steering wheel. Two boys, their sandy-blond hair cropped neat. They can't be much older than Olivia from the looks of it. They're dressed well, in new jackets fit for this still-chilly weather and clean sneakers that probably won't stay clean for long.

I squeeze my eyes shut, but the boys don't disappear when I open them again. Confusion turns to frustration, as if there's something I need to grasp but it keeps slipping out of my reach. The other boy takes a shot at the ring. The ball dances around the edge and by some miracle falls in, resulting in a burst of uproarious joy from both.

I'm still struggling to make sense of what I'm seeing when the front door opens and a figure appears in the doorway. I thought my first instinct would be to hit the gas pedal, but instead, I just sit there, paralyzed with doubt. The man walks down the paved path to the front gate, opening it with a two-note creak of hinges. He peers at me from under his prominent brow bone, mistrustful and hesitant. He's dressed in a navy jacket with the lion logo on the left side, and I can tell he's fit in spite of the substantial beer belly the jacket can't quite hide; he holds himself like that. His hair is salt and pepper leaning heavily toward salt, but it's thick and full. He looks like he hasn't shaved for a few days, his beard starkly darker than his hair.

My breath escapes in a long sigh, leaving me lightheaded. He raps on the window of my car.

"Hey," he says, his voice muffled by the glass but deep, powerful. "Hey!" He raps again, more insistent. Finally, I snap out of it and roll the window down just a crack.

"I thought you might show up eventually," he says. There's no malice in his tone or his words, but I'm still afraid to look him in the face, staring instead at the dashboard. "Lainey. It's Lainey now, right?"

I give a terse nod.

"Why don't you come in? We have a lot to talk about."

CHAPTER TWENTY-SIX

I walk as if in a fog, unable to shake the feeling of being trapped in a parallel universe where everything looks real but will crumble to dust under my fingertips as soon as I touch it. This place couldn't be any more different from the Shaws' house: small spaces, low ceilings, wood paneling that covers pretty much everything, quaint seventies furniture in tones of orange, yellow, and brown—but all maintained in meticulous order and cleanliness. There isn't a speck of dirt anywhere, which has to be a feat, considering the two boys outside. They gave me weird looks as I went into the house, but the man told them to keep shooting hoops for a while longer, and he'd call them for lunch. I wonder if they're supposed to be in school but don't dare ask.

Peter Lyons makes coffee, instant coffee of the kind

that tastes like grit and smells like cigarette ash, and I don't remember him asking me if I wanted any.

"We can talk like adults," he's saying. I watch his lips move, wondering if I'd just made a spectacular mistake. "I only learned about it myself two weeks ago, so I'm still trying to cope."

"About what?"

His frown deepens. Just like Sean, he has these leonine twin lines between his eyebrows, only his are far more pronounced.

"Isn't that why you came here? I figured you'd track us down eventually. If not through the press, then by yourself." He gives a barely perceptible shudder. "We haven't seen them here yet, but I imagine we will any day now."

"Yeah," I find myself saying. "They ambushed me, and..."

"I saw that. In that tabloid. Not that I read that sort of thing. I just—"

I get it. At least he's not going for any of the usual pronouncements, *So sorry this happened to you*, and so on. He doesn't look like the type for empty words.

"Look, I just want you to know that I had no idea. She never told me. If she had, I don't think I would have let her do what she did. I don't think I could have. I..." He rubs his eyes with the heels of his hands. He has neatly cut fingernails, but telltale black stripes still run along the edges. Machine oil stains have caked into the cracks on his knuckles and his palms, practically tattooed there so not even a wire brush gets them out. "Jesus, just to think about it. And I don't care what people say about me if this is in the press. I just don't want them taking it out on the boys, you know? They didn't do anything."

He looks at me like he expects a reaction, reassurances. All I can offer him is a blank stare. My thoughts are moving slowly like molasses.

"I know how this must be pretty overwhelming. But they are your half brothers, technically." He gives a shake of his head. "Not technically. They are."

"How old are they?"

"Gary is ten and a half, and Pete Junior just turned twelve." He gives a warm chuckle. "I let them skip school today. It may not show by looking at them, but they're pretty upset, about their mom and all." His shrug is weirdly apologetic.

"What," I finally burst out, "are you talking about?"

My mind is faster than my words, and by the time he looks up with an expression of dawning shock, I've already figured it out.

"You really don't—oh, Jesus." He covers his face with his hands then gets ahold of himself. "I didn't count on being the one to tell you this. Valerie. Her name is Sarah now...Anyway, your mother. She remarried...Shit, that's right—she lied about that too. I found out. I did a background check, after everything came out."

"She was never married," I say. "At least as far as I know."

"No, she wasn't," he says, shaking his head as if still in disbelief.

And that's when it all comes together.

*   *   *

"Is she . . . is she here?"

He shakes his head. "We had a fight. After the police showed up and she had to tell me everything. Even if she hadn't left of her own free will, I think I would have kicked her out of the house."

I can't say I blame him.

"She's not answering her phone. She hasn't in days. I left her message after message."

"Yeah. The phone number I tracked down to this place. That's hers, right?"

He nods, that incredulous look frozen to his features. "For some reason, I keep paying the bill."

We stay quiet for a few moments—for exactly three-quarters of a minute, if you count the loud ticks of the clock above the kitchen table. It has a pattern of leaves on it, and there's a tasseled lampshade on the ceiling lamp. I wonder who decorated the house. Not Valerie. I don't see her doing that. Maybe he inherited it and everything stayed the same way his own parents left it?

"When you were found," he says, "she went down to Seattle. It was right after Gary was born. I don't remember what story she told me. It only took a day. Then she was back, back to normal, like nothing happened. Except for . . . " He shakes his head. "You're not drinking your coffee?"

I throw a nauseous glance at the cup in front of me, but he goes on.

"As I learned two weeks ago, in that time, she signed you over to the state."

I've figured as much.

"If only I had known. But..." He trails off. "Did she even come see you at the hospital?"

"No. I guess she just wanted to move on."

He gives me a wary look, verging on suspicion. I wipe my palms on my pants then fold my hands in front of me on the table, like a good girl. All the things not being said swirl slowly in the air that separates us, heavy as lead. Neither of us speaks for another couple of minutes. Two minutes and twenty-six seconds, according to the ticking clock.

"Can I meet them?" I ask hoarsely.

He blinks, like he doesn't know what I'm talking about, and before he even speaks—carefully, weighing each word, in that gentle tone of an orderly at the psych ward right before they stick a needle in you—I guess what the answer is going to be.

"I don't think it's such a good idea."

I nod like I understand.

"I don't want to explain everything to them. Yet. They're just kids, and that's pretty shocking, pretty rough." He stumbles over his words, avoiding my gaze, and I know it's not about them. Kids, unlike what most people think, know and understand more than they get credit for, and they can take a lot and bounce back. At least for the time being, like ingesting a slow-acting poison. But it's not about the two boys whose names are already slipping out of my mental grasp, joining the masses of all the other people who have, at some point, almost been a part of my life before they left or I pushed them away. It's about him. And me. It's me he doesn't want his sons to see.

Mechanically, I get up, self-conscious of my small body that somehow still feels unwieldy in the cluttered space.

"Do you know where she is? Right now?"

I read in his expression that no, he doesn't. He shakes his head, confirming it.

Has she told you why? I watch him expectantly, but he only returns a puzzled look and I realize I haven't spoken out loud. I ask the question.

"I'm the one who told her I didn't want to see her again," he says hesitantly. He doesn't understand what I meant: Why did she sign me over, cut me out of her life?

And I'm not going to get answers from him.

When I walk back to my car, down the paved path from the front door, the two boys are nowhere to be seen. I take the briefest of glances over my shoulder and have time to see the curtain move as a small ash-blond head dives below the windowpane. I try to shake the idea that this is the second and last time I'll see either of them—*my half brothers*, buzzes the thought in the back of my skull, wrapped in numbness and shock—and can't help but wonder what he'll tell them about me. If he tells them about me at all.

If they're lucky, they'll escape the worst of the media

storm. Her name isn't Valerie anymore. It's Sarah, Sarah Lyons, proper housewife of a garage owner, who probably—who knows?—went to church with him and the boys on Sundays and chatted with her neighbors over a glass of wine, or *just lemonade for me, please; it's bad for my stomach ulcer*. There's nothing to bring the vultures to their door. They're not part of this, not like I am anyway.

I can't yet consider the idea that Valerie had anything to do with Olivia's disappearance. I hold it in my mind but can't look at it too closely because I'm not sure what I'll do then—twist the steering wheel at an inopportune moment, maybe, and send the car flipping over into a ditch. Or break my newfound sobriety and just swallow down my entire stash, washing it down with three mini-bottles of vodka from the hotel bar.

When I pull into the parking lot hours later, the sun is setting, dusty-orange rays that skewer the car and bounce off the rearview mirrors. I've settled into a kind of numbness, not just mental but physical: my legs tingle from sitting for so long and my arms are aching from gripping the steering wheel. I half expect police cars and CSI or something to be crawling all over the place, but the hotel is calm, serene; the sunset flatters its ugly surroundings, and with that caramel sky spilled for miles above, it could almost pass for beautiful.

It's like I haven't left at all. No one pays attention to me as I make my way to my room at the end of the hall. It's been cleaned while I was gone; the stink of bleach wafts in the air underneath the overpowering smell of air freshener. My bed is neatly made, and the sheets are new. When I bury my face in the pillow, there's not a trace of the musky smell of me and Sean, all the creases in the sheets ironed out, all gone. It's probably better that way. I check the garbage can under the nightstand— empty. I wonder if the maid saw the condom there. She has probably seen much worse and didn't think twice about it.

Another thought crosses my mind, and I sit up in alarm, the bedcover crinkling. I'm not going to take any- thing, I promise myself, but as I cross the room and open the door to the tiny bathroom, my heart speeds up in anticipation, or maybe fear. But it's all where I left it, in the vitamin container.

I stand there for a few moments, contemplating, then put the container back and fill the small bathtub. The enamel is discolored but looks clean enough; in goes the complimentary strawberry-scented "shower and bath milk"—could they not think of a worse name?—and foam starts to form at the bottom of the tub.

As I strip down, my phone falls from the back pocket of my jeans and clatters to the tile. My heart jumps, and I dive to retrieve it. Somehow, it survived; the cracks on the screen are maybe a little thicker and snake a little far- ther than they used to, and a small arrow-shaped piece of glass has fallen out near the edge. But when I thumb the power button, the phone obediently flickers back on.

In that moment, I manage to forget why it was turned

off in the first place, and the avalanche of missed calls takes me by surprise, mostly from Sean's number, which I still can't bear to look at, but there are others too. Jacqueline Shaw's cell, a couple of times. Others I don't recognize.

And at the end of the list, scrolling to the bottom, I see a flurry of calls from the same number, all within a half hour, earlier this morning. Her number. Breathless, I call it before I can change my mind.

But when I press the phone to my ear, instead of ringing I hear a monotonous beep followed by an electronic voice telling me the number is no longer in service. The rush of water fills the tub almost to the brim now, and I turn off the tap. I have to listen to the message three or four times to be sure before I hang up.

The screen goes black, but less than a second later, it lights up again, buzzing and vibrating violently in the palm of my hand. With a sharp intake of breath, I thumb Accept, but it's not the number I just called. Forgetting to exhale, I stare at it, not daring to hang up but not daring to speak either.

"I know you're there." His voice is so loud he might as well be on speaker. "Talk to me. Where the hell have you been? Unless you prefer I send over a police cruiser, if that makes you more comfortable."

"Don't threaten me." Not the first words I had in mind for when I spoke to him again, but not the worst I could do either. "You can't arrest me. I haven't done anything wrong."

He exhales with a hiss and a curse word. "I was worried about you. The hotel desk told me you haven't been in since you left...yesterday afternoon. What do you think you're doing? Where did you sleep? Do I even want to know?"

"Do you pay them to spy on me too?" I snap.

"I was ready to send out a search party."

You should have thought about that before you decided to lie to me all along. At least that's what I want to say. Instead, what I blurt out is, "I went to see them, my mom's new family."

"I know." His voice has the beginnings of that growl in it. That velvety reassuring tone he has when he's trying to manipulate me is fraying at the edges. "Believe me, I know."

"You had someone follow me?"

"No. Peter Lyons phoned me after you left."

Oh.

"We're going to talk about this," he says. "I'm coming over."

"No, you're not. I'm going to check out."

"Don't be an idiot. You have nowhere to go," he says, like it's an obvious fact. And I can't argue, because he's right. My situation is even worse than he knows.

"Where is she? Where's Valerie? And don't tell me you don't know."

And then something unexpected, a silence. A heavy, tense silence that lasts for barely the space of a breath, but I feel it nonetheless.

"Did she contact you? Today, yesterday?"

"I thought you had everyone's phone records at your fingertips. Where is she? You're not going to keep hiding her from me. I'll find her anyway, and she'll answer my questions."

"Laine, I don't know where she is. I swear." I gulp, wary, trying to discern the notes of another manipulation, his dishonesty. "Not since last night."

"What's that supposed to mean?"

"She was at my place. But while I was away, she took all her things and left."

CHAPTER TWENTY-SEVEN

Where would you go if you were a relapsed addict with something to hide and lots of people to hide from? Even in a city like Seattle, there are only a handful of places.

A couple of years ago, right before I took the job at the club, I had no place to live for a week or so and no friends to stay with—well, at least no one I'd trust to watch me sleep every night. Short of homeless shelters, which are permanently over capacity and filled with the kind of people you also don't want to sleep in the same room with, I found myself with the last of my cash at a motel near the airport. The administration turned out to be a lot less exacting than the landlords at the apartment buildings I visited, who didn't think I'd make a trustworthy tenant. In fact, the short, hirsute man behind the counter told me that for a little extra cost I wouldn't have to present any ID at all. Not that it wasn't already clear to me what kind of place this was.

On the second day, the neon sign of Silver Bullet Gentlemen's Club, with its phallic blinking bullet logo, was becoming more than an annoyance that glared even through closed blinds. I still couldn't get an apartment without a giant deposit, and my deposit money wasn't exactly growing with forty bucks per night draining away into the pockets of the hotel manager. A girl lived two doors from me, and she told me she was in from out of town to work over the long weekend—and to bring some work with her after hours, since the room was already paid for and all. She got me in as a shooter girl because the long weekend required extra staff at the last second. There I met Natalia, who taught me the basics of tending bar. I had my deposit within a couple of weeks.

In spite of everything, I'd managed to sleep till noon, and by the time I get there, the club is already open for business. The sight of it makes my stomach twist, because there's no going back to my old job now. The sign has been on since eleven thirty for the lunch shift, and in the light of day, the dusty neons have a sad look to them. The whole place looks permanently coated in dust, the burgundy-colored sheet paneling covering the windows, the early nineties pinup photos behind plastic, the kitschy font advertising lap dances (the price has stayed the same since the late eighties—apparently, strip joints are the one place that's inflation-proof). I turn away from it and drive to the motel across the mostly empty parking lot.

It's one of the three or four similar places strewn across the concrete lots that stretch for miles, too close to the airport to build fancy overpriced condos, too close to the residential areas to build factories or refineries. Motels, a strip mall, and a smattering of semiabandoned buildings are scattered like LEGOs, squat and lonely. The door marked Administration is half-open, and some outdated pop music is playing on a scratchy radio station. There's a new person behind the counter, a woman, and she barely spares me a glance until I come up to her counter and ask about a Sarah Lyons. My mother is probably not using her name, but I figure it's worth a try. I figure wrong, because the woman doesn't even attempt to look at the humidity-bloated logbook in front of her before telling me there's no one by that name here.

With a sigh, I slip a bill across the counter. She lowers her plastic-wrapped sandwich without taking a bite.

"What'd you want with her?" she asks, pocketing the money.

"She's my mother," I say bluntly, eliciting a throaty chuckle from her. I groan inwardly and describe her, at least as well as I remember. The woman gives me a pitying look.

"She has a mark," I add. This part I remember clearly. "Here." I draw a short, broken line across my temple.

The woman gives me a peculiar look. The only sound

is the staticky Christina Aguilera song circa 2002 on the radio. "Where is she?" I ask. "It's important."

"Look, sweetie," the woman starts, but I'm not listening anymore. I storm out of the office, letting the door swing shut behind me.

"Valerie?" I yell. Where the fuck are you, Valerie? Come here so I can gouge your eyes out, you bitch. I storm past the identical motel doors, pounding on each as I go. "Valerie, I know you're here. Come out."

Behind the thin plywood doors, reluctant noises start to stir up, steps, muffled exclamations, impressive strings of swear words. A couple of doors open, faces peering out. But none of them are hers. I turn the corner around the U shape of the motel and only have time to glimpse a door shutting, slamming hard. Across from it is a car, and as soon as I see it, knowledge races through my veins like ice water.

It's out of place here. Too nice, even though it hasn't been washed in ages, a thick coating of mud and Seattle black dust clinging to the once-shiny paint. A large black SUV, dark windshield, with a dent in the front bumper.

Nausea and anger twist together in my guts. I cross the distance in a few bounds, raise my fist to pound on the motel door then, unexplainably, take the door handle instead. It turns without resistance.

The room is pitch-black in that first moment, and I hover on the threshold, expecting anything.

"Close the door," says her voice. I recognize it at once, the voice that answered Sean's phone. Except now it has that smoker's rasp in it again, like she's coming down from a weeklong bender. Like in the good old days.

I feel along the wall and flip the light switch. Only once the light of the ceiling lamp fills every corner of the small room do I shut the door behind me. I think about it and turn the lock. We're going to want to talk in private.

"Did you do it?" I ask. "Do you have her?"

Valerie shakes her head.

"Please don't lie. Why would you do that? You never wanted her. You never wanted me, come to think of it."

"I didn't do anything," she says. "Please, Ella, I'm a victim in all this just like you are."

"You have some nerve."

She gives a wry smile. The overhead light in the room is meant to be flattering, or at least to hide pockmarks and track marks, but I see that the mark on her temple is even more serious than I remember. It's a little canyon in her skin, which is smoother than it should be, considering her former lifestyle. I guess the last decade has been good to her. She's put on weight, but it suits her. She still has that wedge haircut with grown-out blond highlights. I notice with a certain amount of glee that the scar on her temple tugs the corner of her eye down just a little, throwing her face out of symmetry. So she actually looks like what she is.

"What did you tell your husband about it?" I ask.

"That I got mugged." The wry smile widens. "Hear me out, please."

"I wasn't talking about your face."

"And we're not going to talk about it. Just tell me one thing."

"You're not the one asking questions," I say, bristling.

"Just one thing, Ella. Once and for all. What do you remember?"

ELLA

She wakes up to a presence in her room but doesn't have the time to be frightened.

It's the smell that sets off a chain reaction in her memory, familiar and yet new: cigarettes, a sour note of bad breath, but now there are other smells to mask it. Soap, shampoo, perfume. A too-strong, synthetic smell of flowers floats over it all. She opens her eyes, at last, and sees where it's coming from, a large bouquet of carnations, and behind it, a familiar face emerges wearing a grin that frays at the edges. Valerie. *Mom.*

"Hi, baby. How are you doing?"

She busies herself pouring cloudy water into a mason jar and snipping the flower stems with a pair of scissors from her purse before plunking the blooms down into the container. She leaves the scissors lying next to the jar on the windowsill. All the while she talks, talks, talks, too much and too fast for Ella to follow.

The flowers are the kind that you buy in a subway tunnel or a gas station, carnations dyed purple, their petals already edged in decay, with white flecks of baby's breath and pointy green ferns, all wrapped in crinkly paper covered with red hearts.

"Listen, baby, there's no point trying to hide it from you: I'm going to jail. You won't see me for a while. You know what that means?" Her mother's voice drops to a scratchy whisper. "You'll be a ward of the state. You won't be able to keep her regardless."

It takes Ella a moment to understand, because this is the first time she learns that it's a "her." She watches expressions shift across her mother's face.

"And these are good people, Ella. Very good people. She'll be better off with them."

Ella closes her eyes, hoping against hope that the woman will be gone when she opens them again, just another half daydream conjured up by her feverish mind. But even with her eyelids closed tight, she feels her presence on the other side, hears the rustle as she shuffles from one foot to the other.

"Go on. Don't just lie there. Say something. Jesus."

Reluctant, Ella opens her eyes to meet her mother's demanding glare. She doesn't say anything; her head is as empty of words as a clear glass jar.

"You know what? Fine," the woman says in a low growl. "Nobody needs your agreement anyway. You're a minor, and you don't get a say. I only came here to tell you, not to ask you. And because I wanted to see you before I went away. I don't know when I'm getting out. Not that you care, by the look of it."

Ella dully wonders what she did to provoke the surge of anger that crackles underneath the woman's thin skin. She knows that when someone's angry, it's because of something she said or did or because she made a wrong move at a wrong time. So the solution is to stay still and silent, which is exactly what she does.

The woman runs her hands through her hair, which is a different color than Ella remembers. It used to be light brown, and now it's brittle blond, with wispy bangs over her eyes.

"Damn. Ella, I don't know what to say. It has to be like this, okay? I can't help it. There's nothing I can do. I'm signing the papers, and that's it. God knows you'll have enough to worry about besides this."

She leans forward, drowning Ella in the perfume-and-smoke smell that's familiar and unfamiliar at once. The scratchy wool of the scarf around her neck brushes Ella's face as she leans closer and affixes a sticky kiss on her hairline. Ella takes a deep breath, filling her lungs with the scent, then twists her neck to see the pair of dollar-store scissors with plastic handles still sitting on the windowsill next to the carnations.

All she has to do is reach.

CHAPTER TWENTY-EIGHT

"I can't do this." Valerie throws up her hands in exasperation. "Do you know what this thing already did to me? Why would I take her, for God's sake? She had wonderful parents."

"Has," I correct. "And believe me, I'd rather you had taken her, if it were up to me. But it isn't. And you were too strung out to even report me missing on time so..."

"And I'm sorry for that," she says, on autopilot. I get the feeling she's said these words a few too many times in the last week. "Believe me, if I could take it back, I would."

I imagine her showing up on Sean's doorstep with that pitiful expression, begging him to help her. Still, for the life of me, I don't know why he did. Nobody can be gullible enough to fall for this act.

"You do realize this is probably the same person, don't you?" I take a perverse pleasure in watching her cringe.

"Oh? And so you think it's somehow my fault?" She's speaking without force or conviction, like this is what she thinks she's expected to say. Something about her flat, resigned tone puts me on my guard. "Or better, that it wouldn't have happened if I'd—"

"If you didn't leave us both in the care of the state. Yeah."

She waves her hand dismissively. "Do you even hear yourself? That's complete bullshit."

"You'll say just about anything, won't you? As long as you don't have to take any responsibility for what you did. You think I don't know? Sean told me." The lie is seamless, and I know I hit something when what little color there is drains out of her face. I wait, not saying a word, and the thrum of my own heartbeat is so loud I'm afraid she'll hear it and know I'm bluffing. But the shadows fall away from her face, and her cheeks glisten with wet tear tracks. The church-mom look has become a grotesque mask.

"Then it can't have been the same person, okay?" she explodes. "You may have been my fault, but this wasn't. Can't have been. She was kidnapped. And you were—"

She stumbles over the last syllable and goes silent. "It had nothing to do with me."

I take a small step forward. "Valerie."

"You have any idea how hard it is?" When she looks

up, her eyes are bloodshot. "To try and get your shit together when you have a kid. Try getting a job when you
can't pay for a babysitter. No man ever sticks around."

"Yeah? Maybe your meth lesions had something to do
with that."

She cringes. "You fucked up my life, Ella."

"I fucked up your life? Are you serious?"

"Yeah. Without you around, I had a chance in hell to
pull myself together." Her face twists in a grimace. "I was
a different person back then. I just thought, about damn
time you were earning your keep."

The words hang in the air between us as I struggle to
understand. But my mind simply fails, coming up against
the insurmountable wall I've built, a wall behind which I
had to lock away everything that happened in the basement, everything that happened after. A wall that had
allowed me to stay sane, more or less. Until now.

"You have to understand," she half sobs. "I had a
problem, baby. A big problem. I wasn't myself when I
did it. It was the drugs talking. Try to understand."

And I try. I try my damn best. I try harder than I've
ever tried for anything in my whole miserable life. But I
just can't.

"What did you do, Valerie? What?" I'm supposed to
know, but I can't keep up the pretense. She stops sobbing like someone flipped a switch and lowers her chin.
"The juice box," she says in a soft, tinny voice.

"What?"

"The juice box. I gave you one. Every morning. It

was grape that day, I remember; the grape ones are the cheapest, so they were almost all grape."

My gaze is still riveted on her, but the world around me melts away. I see the blinding sun pouring through the bare, curtainless windows of the kitchen back at the house. My mouth fills with the taste of cheap synthetic grape that I think is the best thing in the world because I've never tasted the real thing.

"I ground up a pill and put it in through the hole for the straw. I hoped it was too sweet for you to notice anything."

A faint roar starts in the back of my mind. Steadily growing stronger. Closer.

"I never thought this would happen! He was supposed to bring you back. You wouldn't even remember anything."

I am rooted to the floor, unable to move. The roar gets stronger, deafening.

"I—they'd send me to jail forever, baby. It wouldn't do anyone any good if I was in jail for the rest of your life. I—"

I'm weightless. I leap at her, clawing, scratching. Screaming words I don't even understand, *I'll kill you you fucking bitch I'll kill you—*

She raises her hands to protect her face, so I sink my fingernails into the tender, wobbly flesh of her forearm, making her shriek. She trips and goes flying, crashing into a lamp that breaks. Pieces of glass and ceramic scatter all over the floor. But while I'm distracted, she rights herself and lunges at me with unexpected strength, hands wrapping around my throat, thumbs sinking into my neck. Deep. I lose my footing, and she's on top of me—I have time to glimpse her face, completely distorted, bloodshot eyes savage, filled with the primal preservation instinct that got her this far. She sinks her fingers into my hair, taking hold of the roots, and slams my temple into the floor, once, twice.

It feels like something bursts inside my skull, and all I can hear is the ringing in my ears as I lie there, struggling to breathe. I'm faintly aware of her hurried steps as she grabs something from the nightstand then frantically paces the room, looking around. As she steps over me, carelessly, like I am already a corpse, I try to make a grab for her ankle but I'm seeing double and my fingers curl around air.

For a moment, her shape blocks the light of the lamp. I can't see her face against the glare, only the flyaways around her head like a halo. I wonder if she's actually thinking about killing me—she could, right now, if she wanted to. She could have back then, pressed a pillow over my face, and it would have been done. Slit my throat with those same scissors, put them in my hand. They'd have believed it, and her secret would have been buried forever, along with me, and with Olivia.

But before I can finish the thought, her steps race to the door, which slams; a lock turns. I feel more than hear the vibrations through the floor as the SUV's powerful engine roars to life and tires screech against the concrete of the parking lot.

It takes me another couple of minutes to manage to sit

upright. My throat is bruising, and there's a bump near my hairline, the skin raw and scraped when I touch it, but I'll live.

Her purse is gone from the nightstand, her coat from the hook on the door. There's a cell phone charger curled like a black worm near the bed, empty. I amble to the bathroom, holding on to the walls so I don't fall over—oh shit, prints. I should be thinking about her prints, and mine, and not destroying evidence. Because everything suddenly is evidence, and it all means I'll have to call. Somebody. Right now.

I turn on the tap and gulp coppery motel water then wash my face. She had time to grab all her stuff from the sink, no soaps or lotions or hairbrush in sight.

I groan with relief when I realize I still have my phone, in my back pocket where I left it. My hands are shaking so much I couldn't dial a number even if I knew who to call, so I search through my jacket pockets, but all I find is an empty pack of cigarettes. Just as I'm about to toss it into the wastebasket near the bed, I notice a folded piece of paper tucked neatly inside the package.

I ease it out and unfold it. Stare at it, trying to place that neat handwriting, careful loops of ink, spelling out letters and numbers.

Call me if you need anything. Don't hesitate. Remember, I'm always on your side.

—*Jacqueline S.*

And a phone number.

I don't know how it got there. When did she slip it in?

My only other option is Sean. And I'm not calling him, not for anything.

So I punch the numbers into my phone. And I call Jacqueline Shaw.

CHAPTER TWENTY-NINE

Jacqueline bursts into the room twenty minutes later. She looks so out of place here, in her neat trousers and cashmere sweater, her low heels clacking softly on the floor. Her face is creased with worry.

She rushes over to me and crouches to my face level. Her small, warm hands brush the escaped strands of hair away from my forehead, smoothing them down. Tilting my face up, she peers into my eyes. "Lainey. What happened? Are you okay?"

I try to nod but she's still holding my chin. And I don't want to break her hold. "It's her. My—it's Valerie."

"What did that crazy bitch do to you?"

I wince. The word is so jarring and ugly coming from her.

"Okay," she murmurs. "Okay. Don't tell me if it's too

painful to talk about. Only if you want to tell me, all right?"

I force a nod. "I—I can tell you. She did it."

"What? Sweetheart, what did she do?"

And I tell her, in a tiny, childlike voice threatening to escalate into sobs any second. I tell her about the juice box.

For a very long moment, she's silent, her eyes wide with shock. Overhead, the motel clock ticks away the seconds. It's just me and Jacqueline, and the clock, and the words.

Jacqueline draws me close with surprising strength for such a small, delicate woman. She pulls me into a hug, holds me to her chest, and strokes my hair.

"You poor thing," she whispers as she cradles me close. "You poor, poor thing."

Little by little, my tears start, first just a mist clouding over my vision, then a torrent, a river, a flood. Jacqueline holds me close. My tears and snot soak into her cashmere-clad shoulder, and she doesn't seem to mind in the slightest. She keeps stroking my back, keeps whispering small words of comfort until I can't squeeze another drop of water out of my exhausted eyes.

"I'm so glad that you called me," she says softly. She sits up, takes a folded tissue out of her purse, and dabs it over my swollen eyelids. It's one of those makeup wipes, damp and cool and delicately perfumed. "I didn't think you would."

"I had no one else." My voice sounds like something broken.

"Well, you have me. Always. Don't forget that."

I sniffle, unable to come up with words to express my gratitude.

"Does Detective Ortiz know yet?"

At the mention of the name, I jolt. I think the tears are about to start anew any moment, but I guess my eyes really can't muster any more. "No," I manage to say.

She sighs patiently. "I know you can't think about that right now, but you have to tell him. You have to call him."

The thought makes me want to howl.

"Even if he hurt you, sweetheart, you have to call him. This is very important."

I look up at her, blinking my aching eyes. "What—how—"

Her expression softens. "I could see it, plainly. Written all over your face. You love him, don't you? And you have for a long time."

Suddenly I'm glad I have no more tears. "He's—he's not for me."

"You can't tell that to your heart. And you can't tell that to the little girl you used to be, can you?"

No. No I can't.

"I wish I could snap my fingers and give you everything you need, as long as it could make you happy and whole. But even if nothing ever happens with him, there will be others, trust me. You're a brave young woman who deserves good things. Who deserves to be loved, and who will be. Very, very much."

I can't talk. Can only breathe. Just barely.

"And right now, this is something he needs to know. As soon as possible. It could help him help Olivia. And it could help him help you too."

I'm not a courageous young woman who deserves happiness and love. Not by a long shot. And if she knew, if she only knew the half of it, she wouldn't be sitting here, patting my head and letting me snot all over her thousand-dollar sweater.

This much I know for a fact.

And I also know she's right. I have to call Sean.

"Do you want me to call him for you?" she offers softly. I nod.

"Okay. I'll do that. But first, we're going to take you home, all right?"

I don't argue. I follow her across the gray parking lot to her immaculate white BMW while she dials Scan's emergency number on her cell. I climb into the passenger seat, slam the door behind me, and curl up, hugging my knees to my chest.

I can only hear muffled echoes of her voice outside the car.

And when she gets in, pale as a ghost, and grips the steering wheel with bloodless fingers, I don't ask questions.

*　　*　　*

When we get to the hotel room—my hotel room, as much as I could ever call it mine—there are two police cars outside, parked near the entrance. My stomach drops, but Jacqueline is gripping my hand and I pass them without stumbling.

On a good-natured and clueless impulse, she gave me one of her anxiety pills, the good stuff, much better than the generic I pick up from the drugstore with my prescription or the crap of unknown origin I get from Sugar. I'm wrapped in a soft cocoon of mental fog, like silk and velvet in my veins. It's the only thing that's keeping me from freaking out as I crane my neck, looking for Sean. But when we get to the room, he's not there. It's probably better that way.

There's no place to sit in the room except on the bed, so that's where Jacqueline leaves me, propping me up with pillows like a doll. Then she launches into a flurry of activity, asking me if I want anything, then, ignoring my silence, getting a bottle of water from the minibar and starting the one-cup coffee machine. It sputters and spews that filter-coffee smell that only makes my stomach churn. Then she gets a first-aid kit somewhere—I can only guess where, because there wasn't one in the room—and gets to work on the scraped skin along my hairline. As she tilts my head, the collar of my hoodie, which I'd pulled as tight as I could around my neck, falls away and she sees the bruises on my neck, which must be nice and plum by now. To her credit, she only falters momentarily.

"Did she do that?" Jacqueline's tone is serious, empty of unnecessary emotion. I nod. "Bitch," she mutters.

"Did you know?" I say. My voice is getting hoarse because of the bruises.

"I'm sorry?" She pats ointment on the scrape on my forehead.

"Did you know. About her. Did Sean tell you?"

"No. He didn't tell me anything."

"But—I thought—"

She gives an uncharacteristically bitter chuckle. "They don't tell us everything about the investigation. They never do. Because even though we've been cleared for now, we're still technically suspects, you see." She shakes her head in disbelief. "Just like you."

"I'm not a—"

"That's what they want you to think. It's not personal; that's how these things work. They can't rule anything out."

"But you don't believe that," I say carefully. If she did, why is she here? Why is she doing all this?

"No. Of course not. Lainey..."

"And you. You and your husband—you didn't have anything to do with it, did you?"

She meets my gaze and lets go of a sigh. Her eyes flutter closed for a moment, her eyelids paper-thin and dark, shot through with needle-thin blue veins.

"I'm sorry; I know you didn't," I hurriedly add. "I just want to hear it from you."

She resumes dabbing at my hairline, but there's something mechanical about it now. "Don't be sorry. I read the papers, and the things on the Internet. I know people make these crazy theories, but there's not a sliver of truth to them, I swear. Lainey, look..."

Behind her, the door opens, and I know who it is before I see him. His steps, muffled by the carpeting, stop a few feet away from us.

Jacqueline gives a tiny jolt but regains control of herself and turns around. Her mouth is a thin line; her eyebrows furrow. No smiles this time, no polite "Detective Ortiz." "I don't think you should be here," she says flatly.

He pretty much ignores her. "I need to speak with Lainey."

"Don't you think you've done enough?"

"It's about her mother. And it won't wait."

I'm sitting right here, I want to scream, but I feel so hollow I might as well not exist.

"Shouldn't you be out looking for her instead?"

He heaves a sigh, nostrils flaring, an expression I've learned to recognize, and my insides twist with foreboding. "There's no more need for that. She's been found."

Jacqueline's mouth opens, but he doesn't give her time to speak. "I'm sorry; I didn't want to do this here. But Lainey, we found her car off the side of the highway outside town. She was in it, but it was too late. She had a gun. She killed herself."

CHAPTER THIRTY

Jacqueline is outside, talking to another officer. It's just me and Sean again.

"Are you okay?" he asks. It's the first stupid thing I've ever heard him say.

"Did you know?"

"About your mother's new family? Of course I did."

"You know what I'm talking about."

He doesn't answer right away, and the worst kind of suspicions start to creep into my mind.

"If I had known for sure, I wouldn't have waited. I'd have arrested her in a heartbeat," he says at last. "I was aware she knew something, of course. That's why I went along with the whole thing, let her stay. I would have gotten her to tell me eventually. But then you went looking for her, and she panicked."

"Oh, really? It's my fault now?"

"I never said that. I was going to gain her trust, or get her to slip up, or—"

"Gain her trust? Were you fucking her too? Jesus." I cover my face with my hands. I almost wish I were sober right now.

"No. I—"

"Can you please just not talk?"

"I hurt you. I'm sorry for that, but not for anything else."

"You saw me differently than anyone," I say into my hands. "You looked at me, and you saw me. Not Ella. Not me the victim, or some broken flower who can't go grocery shopping without having a mental breakdown. Not some walking time bomb on suicide watch. The real me."

"I do see you that way." He has the presence of mind not to touch me. I'm not sure what would happen if he did.

"My whole life I've been defined by other people, by what they did or didn't do to me. I just thought I could be myself for a change. I could want something and take it. Just this once. That's what it was all about, all right? I'm not in love with you or anything. I'm not going to kill myself over it, if that's what you're wondering. Just go and do your job—find Olivia. There's nothing more I can do. I'm finished."

"It's not that simple. You can't just decide you're finished."

"What more do you want from me?" I explode. "I've

answered all your questions. I've turned every dark corner of my soul inside out looking for some shred of suppressed memory that could help. I was sure it was my fault for not being able to remember, and it turns out everybody's been lying to me for years. For my own good."

I choke on a manic laugh and realize my cheeks are wet. Bewildered, I wipe the tears with the heels of my hands. "So, you know what? I'm finished. I'm going back to my apartment, and my life, while I still have one. It may not be your idea of a good life, but at least it's all mine."

He watches me for a few long moments, and I can't read his expression—it's become closed to me again. Or maybe it never was open. I had just imagined the whole thing because it was what I wanted to see. I guess I'll never know now.

"Is that what you want? To go back to that dump, to your so-called job at the strip club—"

"I'm a bartender," I snap.

"Well, at this rate, you won't be for long. Just keep numbing yourself to it all until it completely overtakes your life, or you just overdose. Whichever comes first, right?"

Silence rings hollow inside my head. "What?"

"You really think I'm an idiot?"

My gaze darts to the bathroom door. All I want is to race there and look in my hiding place, but I have a guess what I'll see there.

"There were police here. I didn't want you to get into more trouble than you're already in, so yeah, I went over every inch of the place before I let them in. Although on second thought, maybe I should have let them find your stash. It was quite impressive. I think there was enough in there for possession with intent to distribute, don't you think?"

"What did you do?" I whisper.

"Flushed it down the toilet. Old-school. Which is why you're here right now without handcuffs. You're welcome."

"That stuff was prescribed to me."

He ignores me. "I'm still offering you my help. I can check you into a center where they'll actually help you, not just lock you up. A place where you could kick this thing for good . . ."

"I don't want your help."

" . . . So you don't end up like your mother."

I want to hit him. I want to destroy him. The only thing that's stronger than my hatred for him right now is my love for him, but that can never exist. It has to be hidden away like something secret and shameful. Like me. Like my whole life.

So hatred it is. "Leave."

"You're going to destroy yourself."

"I think it's a little too late to worry about that." I hold his gaze with contempt.

"If that's what you believe." He shrugs and yanks up the zipper on his jacket. "If you think you have nothing to lose because you're already destroyed, then I can't help you."

"So what are you waiting for? Go."

And he does. He slams the door so hard that the door frame shakes. And I sit on the bed and squeeze the sheet to my chest, twisting it around in my hands.

I keep waiting for someone to come barging in, cops maybe, or Jacqueline, fussing over me, thinking she could understand me, making it only worse with all the misguided kindness and compassion. But minutes tick away and nothing happens, and when I tiptoe to the door, turn the handle, and peer out, the hallway is empty.

I'm all alone.

CHAPTER THIRTY-ONE

There are times when I'm sitting perfectly still, with a blank, safe look on my face like a good little lobotomy patient, and all the while I'm screaming inside my head. I've had lots of time to perfect it to an art form.

But in here, in this hotel room, I could scream my head off if I wanted to. I could kick and break and smash things—someone else is going to take care of it, someone else picks up the tab. Instead I sit on my bed, with a sheet crumpled in my lap, and shiver. And inside my head, I scream for what feels like hours.

Sometime near morning, I get up and start to pace until life returns to my arms and legs, and with it, understanding, and pain, and all the other stuff I always managed to cut myself off from, the stuff that stayed outside my safe, fuzzy chemical cocoon.

I race to the bathroom and check everywhere to be sure, throwing all my makeup tubes on the floor. Everything's gone. Fuck, I don't even have an aspirin.

The walls of the room move in on me, threatening to crush me. I can't stay in here another minute. I can't. I'll go crazy.

I go through every pocket, through my bag, but there are only a few dollar bills and my bank card to an empty account.

My hands shake when I get my phone. It takes me even longer to pull up Sugar's number.

He picks up on the third ring. "Princess."

"Hey." I'm mortified to admit it, but I go wobbly with relief when I hear his voice. My muscles quiver so much that the phone almost slips out of my sweaty hands.

"What can I do for you today?"

"I . . . I need a huge favor." I try to make my voice all sweet sounding, but it seems I forgot how. "Can you advance me some Oxy? I get paid next week. You know I'm good for it and you know where I live so . . ."

He stays silent for a moment, and my hope sinks. Terror clamps down on my heart. I'm sweating bullets, and I'm glad he can't tell over the phone.

"Hey, look, you're one of my fave clients. Sure, I can do it. How could I say no to Laine freaking Moreno?"

"Thank you." The air rushes out of my lungs with a whoosh. "Can you come down? Like, soon?" Like fifteen minutes ago.

"Hey, look, I don't do hotels anymore. Had a close call. Get your ass down here; I'll get you sorted out."

Hotels are his best source of business, so he's lying, and I know full well why, but that doesn't stop me. It takes a good forty-five minutes to get to Sugar's from where I am, so I should have just enough gas left. "Okay."

"Be alone though, right? No friends, no well-meaning acquaintances."

"Got it. You know me. Would I narc on you?"

"Ha-ha. Hilarious. Hurry up, Princess; I don't have all day."

I change my clothes in a fog. Oversize army pants, a T-shirt, a sweatshirt that's getting ripe, but I don't have anything else. I lace up my boots and tuck my phone into the right one.

Outside, it's the first real warm day of spring, and the sun is beating down from a flawless blue sky. For once, Seattle decides it's going to stop the rain. It sure has a funny sense of timing.

I'm drowning in my sweatshirt, and my back breaks out in sweat. Shielding my eyes from the sun, I wipe my forehead with the cuff of my sleeve. The couple of hotel patrons I come across give me odd sideways looks and step aside, not obviously but noticeably. Squeamish.

This is what I've become. Untouchable. The thought doesn't have any sting left anymore.

Sugar lives in an apartment at the top of a shitty slum building. I huff and puff up the stairs until I think I'm

going to pass out. My lungs burn, and my ears ring by
the time I get to the door.

I pound on it with both fists. He takes his sweet time,
and for a moment, I think the bastard forgot and took off
to do some more lucrative deal somewhere. I take out
my frustration on the door, kick it, try to punch it, but
after a couple of minutes, I hear shuffling steps inside
the apartment.

"It's me!" I yell.

"I can see that. What are you doing? You trying to
wake the whole neighborhood?"

"It's almost noon, Sugar. Normal people are at work."

"Oh yeah?" I hear him chuckle through the door.
"Since when are you the official spokesperson for normal people, huh?"

"Just open the door." A bit of desperation seeps into
my voice. And I'm sure he heard it, because he spends
two or three more agonizing minutes shuffling, fumbling, and sighing. Finally, the locks click one after
another, and the chain slides aside with a squeal. Sugar
takes his privacy seriously. Even for a drug dealer.

The door opens a crack, and he peeks out. He looks
like he just woke up. He's wearing nothing except discolored boxers that might once have been white—great,
one sight I could have done without. He still has the
eternal baseball hat perched on top of his head.

"Get in here," he says, and moves aside. I slip through
the crack in the door, doing my best not to brush up
against him. He makes it pretty difficult.

I've been in here maybe once before. It's worse than I remember, or maybe my standards went up from staying at that fancy hotel. Yeah, hah. It's a loft, with messy seams where the walls had been demolished, and it reeks of old tobacco and pot, like a giant ashtray. The main piece of furniture is a couch that's folded out right now, with a mess of sheets piled on top. Clothes and empty takeout containers are strewn everywhere. It's actually worse than my old place.

And this is the guy who claims he makes five Gs a week. Wonder what he does with it.

"So." Sugar claps his hands then stretches his arms over his head, giving me an eyeful of hairy armpits. "Spill. What's the sob story?"

"There's no sob story. I have a situation—that's all. Something I've been hoping you can help me with, and there's something in it for you too."

"Cut the crap, Laine."

I trail off. He puts his hands on his hips; his fading tattoo peeks through sparse chest hair.

"I talked to Dom the other night. They haven't seen you in weeks, but he did tell me, if I ever saw you, to let you know your ass is fired."

How did I not consider this? I clench my fists inside my sleeves. I need to think of something, some lie that will convince him to help me, but for once, I'm drawing a blank.

"Look, I get it. You're broke, you need your stuff, you're in a bad spot. You want me to do you a favor."

"Something like that."

His grin widens. "You really think you're worth that much, sweetie?"

In guise of an answer, I pull my hoodie over my head. Underneath, I only have a T-shirt, no bra. I remember that I'm not wearing anything to cover my scars and notice the way his nervous gaze flickers to my wrists. "How about, you've wanted to fuck me since the day we met? And you think I have no standards, but I actually do, so you're not getting another chance. So? Take it or leave it."

He gulps, and his tongue darts out from between his pale lips to nervously trace the top one before disappearing again, like an eel. "Come on," he says, feigning a sigh of resignation. My legs feel soft as I walk over to the foldout couch. He sits down, making the whole thing creak, and pats the sheet next to him. I follow suit.

But instead of reaching for me, he reaches for the nightstand. "We're going to have us a little party," he says as he extracts a couple of tabs of some pill I don't recognize and grinds them up on the top of the nightstand with the bottom of an empty glass. "Special occasion and all."

He does a line first, to show me he's not trying to poison me, probably, then gestures for me to do the same. I still have no idea what it is, but it's good. The tight knot in the center of my chest starts to unwind, and my head feels light in all the right ways. I let my eyes close and savor the initial rush. The couch creaks and tilts as he gets up.

"Drink?"

He must interpret my silence as a yes, because I hear him clang around, and when he comes back, I open my eyes to see him holding out a glass, waiting for me to take it.

"Oh. So you like that." He grins and clicks his glass to mine. It's hard liquor, and I down it in one gulp. "Whoa. Pace yourself."

I don't want to pace myself. I need help to get through this, although "this" becomes more and more fluid and less definable with every passing moment. It turns from an enormous, gut-wrenching ordeal to barely a blip on my mental radar.

I lean over to do one more line and can't seem to sit upright again. So I let myself rest, my face on his dank sheets. He stretches out next to me.

"So it didn't pan out, I take it?" His voice fades in and out.

"What didn't pan out?"

"The thing with your new boyfriend. Or I doubt he'd be okay with you being here, stoned out of your mind." He gives me a look. "Or he doesn't know?"

The knot in my chest tightens again, and I realize it never disappeared in the first place. I just stopped being aware of it. "There was no boyfriend. I told you."

He chuckles. "Don't freak out—I'm just messing with you. I know everything, and it's fine by me. No judgment. I'm the last person to judge anyone, right?"

"What are you talking about?"

When he says Olivia Shaw's name, I feel myself sinking, and the drugs only make it worse. I think I might throw up; the booze already burns the back of my throat. "How do you—"

"I watch the news, and I know how to use Google." He sits up, shaking his head. "And right now, you look like you could use a pick-me-up."

Numbly I watch as he makes a small baggie of coke appear, dips in the tip of his fingernail, snorts. Holds it out to me. I shake my head.

"You're about to pass out. Come on."

Coke is the absolute last thing I need. I tell him so. He shrugs and takes out another of these mystery pills and grinds it up into a fine powder.

From there on, everything swims in and out of a foggy state, and time is brief flashes of clarity followed by more fog. When I come to, the room is darker, and a horror movie flickers black and red on the flat-screen, lots and lots of Technicolor blood, carefully edited screams. It's nothing like reality, I find myself thinking. Real-life horror is quiet.

"What's that?" Sugar leans in, bathing me in his Jack Daniel's breath. I have forgotten he was there.

"I didn't say anything. Fuck off."

He slaps my ass playfully, and I realize I'm down to my underwear. I'm momentarily thrown into confusion and panic, but it subsides when he gives me a sip from his glass. Like a lover.

Next time I surface, the TV is dark, only our reflections dance on its screen like ghosts. I become aware of being fucked from behind, the wet slap of flesh. When I can't see him, it doesn't feel that bad. I don't feel much at all, but it's nice to be filled. I don't even notice when he comes with a shudder until he collapses next to me and grabs the back of my head, pushing me close to kiss me wetly on the mouth. I taste sweat and booze but don't pull away.

"I kind of always knew you'd be hot," he says. He can't catch his breath as he wipes more sweat from his eyes with the corner of a sheet. "But damn. We need to do this again sometime."

"There won't be a sometime," I say. It's funny, not feeling my lips move. "It's the last time. Tomorrow I'm starting a new life."

"Wow. You're breaking my heart."

"All the more reason to enjoy it while it lasts."

He gives a loud, shrill laugh, like fingernails on glass, and my skin prickles with gooseflesh even though it's boiling in here and my sweat hasn't yet cooled. I climb on top of him, straddling his skinny thighs, and try to guide his still-soft cock inside me. He rolls me over onto the damp sheets, facedown.

"So this new life," he's saying, "are you absolutely sure? Do you need a place to stay in the meantime? 'Cause I'm available, and at this rate, you won't even need to pay rent." He nudges my legs apart with his knee, but his halfhearted erection can't last longer than a couple of thrusts. "It's not exactly chic, I know, but it could use a woman's touch." A laugh bubbles out of him at his own joke. "And it's safe, with all these locks. Not as easy to break into as your old place. I was thinking of getting a security system installed, and ... " He trails off with a huff, the head of his dick poking me in the thigh.

I feel like I've been plunged headfirst into ice-cold water. Instinctively I squeeze my legs closed just as he manages to find his target, and push myself up from the couch. "What—did you just say?"

"Your old place was broken into, right? That's why you had to leave." I glimpse his confused face before he rolls me over again. I'm breathing in the stale stench of his sheets, aware of it more acutely than before.

"I didn't tell you that," I mumble, but my tongue won't obey. And it wasn't on the news. Or on the Internet. Was it?

"Someone at the club told me. Relax, babe. Everything's fine. Do you want more—"

I do want more, and he obliges. He was right—everything is fine again, and the contours of my body begin to gently dissolve. That last line hit hard—and the more I try to fight it, the faster it pulls me under, like one of those Chinese finger traps. When I lift my face out of the sheets, Sugar isn't around anymore, and not too far off, I hear the shower running. I'd only closed my eyes for a moment, hadn't I?

I can't think about it right now. I can't think about anything.

I want only emptiness, dark and silent.

I want nothing at all.

CHAPTER THIRTY-TWO

When I wake up, my mind is quiet, filled only with the dull throb of pain. My throat is dry; each breath is an effort, inhale, exhale, inhale again.

I'm shrouded in darkness, soft as velvet. As my vision starts to adjust, I gradually make out my surroundings. I feel the stab of panic when I realize I'm lying on a hospital bed and the steady beep at the edge of my hearing is a heart-rate monitor.

I try to prop myself up on my elbow only to hear a strange clang. The sound reverberates in my bones, and a sinking sense of foreboding fills my core. The tug on my wrist is painfully familiar, a sharp bite into the tender flesh of my scar, and I already know what I'll see when my gaze travels to my right hand. The handcuffs gleam dully, locking my wrist to the metal bar on the side of the hospital bed. I tug and pull, clink, clink.

Someone moves at the edge of my vision. I look up in a panic, and relief floods me when I realize it's Sean, getting up from a chair at the other end of the room.

He can make it stop, pleads a tiny voice in the back of my mind. He can take off these cuffs; I just have to ask nicely. He can't say no. He knows about me, what it's like for me. He understands. He'll take them off. I'll beg if I have to.

Memories come flooding back. Sugar's apartment, the plastic baggie of coke, the ground-up pills, three or four or God knows how many I snorted.

My mouth tastes bitter. And I remember the rest.

Shame and self-loathing fill my chest until I think my rib cage might burst, my ribs snapping like twigs. It all spills out in ugly tears, in sobs that shake me to the core. I squeeze my eyes shut so I can't see the look on Sean's face.

I don't know how long I cry like this. It's a wonder I can make tears at all, there's so little water left in my body. All the while I'm painfully aware of his presence by my side, not moving or speaking. I wish with all my soul he'd reach out and touch me, hold my hand, brush my hair off my forehead.

But then again . . . I don't blame him if he doesn't want to touch me.

"I'm so sorry," I choke out. "I'm so sorry. I didn't mean for it to happen." I hate my own words sooner than I can get them out. They ring so hollow but I can't seem to stop myself. "I'll go to rehab. I'll do whatever you want. Just—"

"Laine," Sean says softly. There's no anger in his voice, no disgust or hatred. That makes it even worse...if it could be any worse.

"Just get this thing off me." The cuffs give another feeble clink against the metal bar. "Please?"

"You really have no idea what's going on, do you?"

I can't stop it—my face screws up like a child's, except there are no more tears left. All that comes out are dry sobs that sound like heaving, which isn't far from the truth, because I feel like I might throw up any second.

"You OD'd. And you're lucky that your dealer isn't a total scumbag and had the presence of mind to call an ambulance rather than just dump you somewhere."

I sit up, tugging on the cuffs. "Sean..."

"Please stop. You're just making it worse."

The door opens, and three more people come in. The ceiling light flickers on, slicing across my eyes, and when I can see again, two people in cop uniforms are standing at a short distance. Next to them, a nurse glances anxiously from them to me and back.

"What's going on?"

"I can't believe it," Sean mutters, not to me, not to them, but not really to himself either. "I can't believe I trusted you."

The very same words I was two seconds away from hurling at him.

The other two officers come closer, surrounding me. I feel like I'm shrinking inside my hospital gown, Alice about to tumble down the rabbit hole. "Sean, what's happening?"

"I mean it. Keep your mouth shut. Everything you say can be used against you. And will be."

One of the other two starts to speak, and all words bleed together into a crimson river. He rattles off term after meaningless term, and I can't make sense of any of it except for certain words that pierce through the cloud of fog in my head. You are under arrest. Possession . . . distribution . . . involvement in the disappearance of Olivia Shaw.

This cannot be happening.

I have to still be dreaming. Maybe I'm in a coma or something and this is just in my head, like in the movies. God, I need my pills. All these thoughts crowd inside my mind, and I feel a bizarre urge to giggle. I'm about to wake up any moment, right? They can't mean it. The very idea is crazy. Involvement in the disappearance . . .

Sean puts a stack of folded clothes at the foot of the bed.

I have to wake up.

Without a word, without a backward glance, he walks out the door, leaving me alone with the two other officers. My gaze slides across their faces, searching for a response, a reaction of any kind—but there's none; they stand there like marble statues. When I try to meet the nurse's eye, she avoids looking at my face.

They all think I'm some kind of . . .

They all think I'm guilty.

The words replay over and over in my head as they walk me down the hall to the indoor lot where a car is waiting. The ride takes barely a few minutes before we pull up to the station. One of them unceremoniously tugs the hood of my sweatshirt over my face, and seconds later, when the flashbulbs start exploding in my eyes, I understand why. They drag me to the door through the clamor of voices and all I can see are the toes of my boots: left, right, left, right.

Then there's quiet.

*　　*　　*

The vents are too strong in the interrogation room, it's freezing, and it smells like a mix of cleaner and stale air. I haven't been able to stop crying. The briny streaks down my face have solidified, and I feel them every time I blink.

I'm alone. I don't know what I'm supposed to do. What do they do on TV? Ask for a lawyer or something. I can't pay for one. And so far no one has been asking me any questions. No one has said so much as a word to me.

The door opens eventually, and Sean comes in. I almost don't recognize him because the look on his face, everything about him, has shifted. With him is a woman in a dark-blue suit, dark hair and lined face—

she reminds me of Jacqueline, but harsher, metal to Jacqueline's porcelain. She introduces herself, Sergeant Detective this and that. But my gaze is riveted to Sean the whole time, and only him.

I feel just like I did ten years ago. Thrown from one prison into another, people with judgment in their eyes asking me questions I just don't have answers for.

Sean sits down while the woman remains standing. For a while, he just looks at me then slides something across the table, stopping halfway. The flat silver object sits between us in mute accusation.

My mind still can't put it together when he speaks up. "Does this belong to you, Lainey?"

My laptop. My stolen laptop that was taken out of my apartment. There isn't enough air in this room.

"I don't have to answer," I say. At least I have this much self-awareness. He glances at the woman. She returns the look then nods and leaves us alone.

"It's just us, Lainey. If you want me to help you, you have to tell me the truth. Is this your computer?"

"I should have a lawyer." My voice crackles with hoarseness.

He slams his palms down onto the table. "You have a lot of nerve."

"I know my rights." I think I'm about to cry again. He's the first person to meet my eye in this place. How can he do this to me? Now? After . . .

After I screwed up the one good thing life ever gave me. After I let him down in more ways than I can count.

"Is this yours or isn't it? I'm trying to help you here. You know I am. Dammit."

"How . . . Where did you get it?"

"It doesn't matter where I got it. Answer the question or I can't do a thing for you."

I shake my head. "I haven't done anything wrong."

This is a lie. I've long ago lost count of all the things I've done wrong—lashing out at the press conference, confronting Jacinta . . . Everything I've done has just made things worse, but goddammit, I didn't mean to. I was only trying to help.

He breathes in and takes out a folder that he slams down next to the laptop.

"Here. Have a look at what we found on your hard drive." He gives a strange, forced chuckle. "Except you know this already, don't you?"

I take the folder with my fingertips and open the cover.

It feels like I'm drowning from the inside. That first glance and I understand everything.

A strangled gasp escapes from me as I stare down at the pictures. Grainy printouts, but it's more than enough: girls, naked girls. Some look young, some very young.

"There are over a hundred folders," Sean's voice says from the periphery of my mind. "All of them full of photos."

He doesn't need to say anything more. It was only a matter of time before my laptop surfaced, because who-ever had broken into my apartment had found exactly what he was looking for. And he set the perfect trap, but the rest I did myself. By acting stupid and irresponsible, by stubbornly refusing to trust the people who tried to help me—just like I've always done. By making myself look guilty from the start.

I'd played into my kidnapper's hands. Again.

"This isn't mine," I say. Like it matters what I tell him. What else could I possibly say anyway? Isn't that what all the guilty people say? And I'm sure he's heard more creative excuses before.

"There are pictures," he says in a steely tone, "that could be of Olivia Shaw."

I didn't think there was anything worse he could say, but there it is. I think I might be sick.

"We are still figuring it out. So if there's anything you want to tell me, now is a damn good time."

"This isn't mine," I repeat, obstinate.

But they'll say it is. I've read about this sort of thing many times—victims of abuse turning abuser and the cycle goes on. And I certainly didn't act like any sane person from the start.

"Your dealer... insisted you gave it to him in exchange for your fix."

"That's not true." No, of course it isn't—the sad truth is, I didn't even have that to give him, so I decided to give him something else. I've never wanted to die more than I do right now.

"He also said you told him you were going to skip town."

"I never said that. I . . . "

"Is this your laptop?"

"Yes." I gulp. "But the pictures aren't mine."

He rubs his temples, such an achingly familiar gesture. "I rooted for you this whole time," he says, his voice strangely level. "I was always on your side. You stupid bitch."

The words don't hurt anymore, and I barely wince. All I want is to tell him the truth, at least as far as I know it, as far as I remember it. "Wait. My apartment got burglarized. A couple weeks ago. They took my laptop, and other things." I stumble over the words. "Sugar did. It had to be him. He knew, and I hadn't told him. I . . . " Even as I stammer, I'm no longer sure. How much did I tell him, exactly? I can't remember. The whole day fades in and out, more blackouts than reliable memories.

"And you didn't call the police because . . . ?"

"Because no one would have done anything!" My voice trembles. "There's a break-in in my neighborhood every other day. And I'm not white enough or rich enough for anyone to give a fuck."

"You should have told me. Why didn't you?"

I should have, like I should have told him a lot of things. I remember dialing his number, the woman's voice picking up—Valerie's voice, I know now. And like the idiot I am, I changed my mind. When I tell him, the look in his eyes verges on sadness.

"Do you have anyone who can corroborate that? Did you tell anyone else?"

"Natalia. My friend, the one I went to stay with."

"The stripper."

"Bartender."

"Whatever. I already tried to contact her, and it turns out, no one's seen her in about three days. She missed work without warning; her phone goes to voice mail. No one has any idea where she is." I flinch away from his glare. "You wouldn't happen to know, would you?"

I have a guess, a good one, and once again it's all my fault. What a shocker.

"I can't do anything for you anymore. You realize that."

I do—what I still don't understand is how he ever thought he could do something for me in the first place. But the words seem to fly off my lips. "You have to believe me. Someone took my laptop and put all these...things...in it." I glare at the folder, and its image blurs with the tears that fill my eyes. "You can't really think that I—"

"It doesn't matter what I think."

"But you do believe me." I'm practically pleading.

"Convincing a judge to believe you is another matter."

I lower my forehead onto my hands. The handcuffs give a soft clink, and I realize, as if for the first time, that there's nothing to hide the scars. "Do you hate me now?"

"No. I don't hate you. I just feel sorry for you."

I can't utter another word.

"I'm sorry that you let him win. Your kidnapper. Sorry you let him turn you into this."

Fighting dizziness, I sit up straight. "I didn't let him win. I didn't let him turn me into anything! I was ten years old, for fuck's sake. Don't you dare imply that I—"

The tears spill out and flow down my cheeks. I shut my eyes in a vain attempt to stop them.

He starts to talk, telling me how they'll set my bail soon, get me a public defender and this and that. His voice blurs. No matter how much I try to refocus on it, I can't. His face seems to smudge too, its lines losing their familiar precision until I can't even tell who I'm looking at.

Everything blacks out. Things are happening, but I'm aware of them on a superficial level, like a TV show I'm only half watching. My consciousness is fading as I retreat inside myself, let my eyes become glass and my skin a hard, brittle shell.

I don't have the strength to fight it anymore.

CHAPTER THIRTY-THREE

One of the girls from the photos comes to me at night, all wide brown eyes and coltish legs. She looks maybe fourteen, and her breasts are small, underdeveloped little things like mine, her stomach a flat plane between protruding hip bones. I want to know how she ended up on that photo that ended up on my laptop, but I can't speak. I don't have a physical presence; when I look down, I can't see my own hands or body. I'm ethereal. One gust of wind and I vanish.

I want to know who she's smiling at on the other side of the camera. If he ever got his ass thrown in jail like he deserves.

The world is full of people who think I deserve it too.

The other girls follow, all kinds of girls, an endless parade of limbs and expanses of skin. Sometimes they wear the faces of the girls on all the missing posters from the last decade. Sometimes I peer closely enough and recognize myself, mole here, scar there. Sometimes I suspect they may wear Olivia's skin, but I'm afraid to look in case it's true.

How would I look into her eyes?

A part of me is putting together theories. Maybe they're right. Maybe I did it all and just forgot it—wiped it from my memory like I did with the day I was stolen. Maybe I did download all these photos in a surge of late-night delirium. Frantic, I think back to all the places in my memory that are worn thin from doing pills or getting drunk and all the other ways I tried to forget I existed. And my laptop—did I take it from my apartment? Did I really give it to Sugar at some point and forgot about it?

Maybe I've cracked completely. I've always known it was only a matter of time. I reach out to all these girls that swarm me like ghosts, begging them to tell me the truth, but just like me, they don't have voices. Their voices, I know on some deep level, were stripped away from them, staying forever on the other side of the camera.

A clang jolts me out of my thin sleep, and I sit up, pushing away the narrow cot. My back aches something horrible, and I barely feel the side of my face.

There's an unfamiliar cop and the woman I saw earlier. She wears different clothes, so it must be the next day. How much time passed? How long was I out?

Behind them, Sean walks in, and in spite of everything, my heart starts to race.

The woman starts to say something but I can't seem to understand the words, like I've forgotten the language overnight.

"Come on," Sean says. It takes me a few more moments to figure out what he wants. All I can gather is that they're letting me go.

Shaky, I get up and sway when he hands me my jacket, neatly rolled up and folded. I don't even remember when I saw it last or where I left it—at Sugar's, at the hotel? It's heavy as a rock, pulling me toward the floor. He's standing right there but he won't help me—he waits while I steady myself against the wall.

"What..." My voice works on the third try.

"Someone posted your bail," he says dryly. He must read the question in my gaze, because he adds, "Anonymously."

"The pictures," I choke out. I only need to know one thing—were any of them Olivia? And until I know the answer, I'm not going anywhere.

"We couldn't identify if any of them were Olivia or not. You're still being charged with possession of juvenile pornography. Not to mention the controlled substances."

Just as I shakily make my way to the door under the watchful eyes of the woman and the cop, he leans in closer. His whisper rustles in my ear. "He's out there. Be careful."

I barely have time to comprehend the words before he's gone. And then I'm outside, a little bewildered, blinded by the fading light of day—or is it dawn? Can't tell until the orange sun moves one way or the other. I should get the hell out of here before they change their minds, or before whoever posted the massive bail for me decides to take it back, but instead I linger. I shrug into my jacket, and its worn pleather settles over my shoulders, its familiar weight and smell cradling me. I pat down my pockets, hoping against hope to find my pack of cigarettes—there it is, with my lighter next to it—and at the bottom of the pocket, inside the lining, another heavy oblong-shaped object.

In utter disbelief, I plunge my hand through the lining, tearing the seam. No, not here. I start to jog and sprint for several blocks, the wind whipping the sweat out of my hair. Only when I can't run anymore do I let myself stop and pull my hand out of my pocket.

I'm looking at my knife, just as I last saw it. The blade flies out without a sound as soon as I flick it, shiny and sharp. I glimpse the slightly distorted reflection of my shadow-ringed right eye before I flip it closed.

He gave it back, trills the thought in the back of my mind. It must mean he believes me, or why would he do it? I recall his words, not without a shiver: be careful.

But all that matters is that he knows it wasn't me.

It's exactly what I needed. Now I can let go.

I have nowhere to stay. My apartment? Out of the question, even if my landlord hasn't put all my stuff out on the curb yet. No more hotel. And I've run out of people who are willing to put up with me. I've alienated everyone I could. Even the thing I had with Sean, no matter how brief, how messed up—no matter that he was never mine to begin with—I still somehow managed to fuck it up. I couldn't do a thing to get Olivia back. I can only hope I didn't make things worse, didn't indirectly cause something irreparable. And my court date isn't going anywhere. I have few doubts; no matter what Sean can or can't prove about my laptop, I'm getting locked up someplace without windows.

All I can do is keep walking. I barely know where I am but I know exactly where I'm headed. I've been heading for it my whole life. What's surprising is how long it took to get there.

* * *

There's a bridge across Lake Union called Aurora. A fence lines it but it never stopped anyone—and it won't stop me. All I have to do is climb over, let go, and gravity will do its work.

I don't know how long it'll take me to get to the bridge, and I don't care if I have to walk all night. It's raining—but then again, when is it not fucking raining in this place?—and I start to shiver, my chin tucked into the collar of my jacket.

My kidnapper should have been the one to kill me, but he didn't, and I'll never know why. It's time I finish what he started. As I walk along the empty highway, I take out my phone and turn it back on. There's still one bar of battery left. I should call Sean, tell him how sorry I am about this whole mess. He probably won't pick up, and I don't see why he should. And later, when he learns the news, he'll only feel guilty about it.

But if I'm gone, maybe it'll be easier for him. He won't have to think about me anymore, or worry about me or torment himself about things that are out of his control. I owe him this much.

I put the phone away and keep walking. Rain soaks through my clothes, and they cling to my skin, heavy and cold, leeching my life energy. I drag my boots like a punishment, and they seem to grow heavier with every step.

The phone in my pocket erupts with ringing, making me jump. My heart springs back to life, hammering against my matchstick ribs in a desperate frenzy. I want it to be Sean so badly that, when I see an unfamiliar number, I almost drop the phone into the puddle at my feet. The call goes to voice mail, and I let out a sigh of relief but just as soon it starts to ring again.

God, what do they want from me?

I bring the phone to my ear, intent on telling whoever it is to just forget about it, it's over, please call back never.

But on the other end, I hear a slightly muffled woman's voice. "Lainey?"

"Who is this?" I frown. The voice is familiar but I can't

quite make it out through the static and the rustle of rain.

"Lainey," she sighs. "Thank God I got ahold of you. It's me, Jacqueline."

"Hi," I say on autopilot. "This isn't really a good time."

"I know what happened. I'm so glad they let you go."

Mutely, I blink away the rain.

"I know you have no place to stay, so I'm coming to pick you up."

"You really don't have to," I say carefully. She can't not know why I got arrested. That I'm actually a suspect in her daughter's disappearance.

"We're staying at our summerhouse to get away from the reporters. I'll take you straight to it; just tell me where you are."

I shake my head then realize she can't see me. "No."

"Don't be stupid." The urgency in her voice alarms me—I can hear it through the background noise.

"You don't really want me there," I choke out. I can't bring myself to tell her the truth.

"Yes, we do. I do. I need you to come over here, as soon as possible. Please." A sigh. "It's about Olivia."

I stop so abruptly that I nearly trip over the soaked hems of my pants. "What about her?"

"There's something I need to tell you."

"Then tell me."

"I don't think we should be discussing it on the phone."

"Did you—did you call Sean? I mean, Detective Ortiz."

It's hard to say his name. Its syllables get stuck in my throat.

"We're trying. But at the precinct, they told us he's not available and he's not answering his personal cell. I don't know what to do." She sounds like she's this close to tears. "Can you just tell me where you are? Please?"

I listen to her ragged breathing through the hum of the rain.

Before I can change my mind, I tell her and hang up.

*   *   *

The car pulls up to the curb, brake lights flaring. It's Jacqueline's white BMW, and I race toward it only to skid to a halt when I see the silhouette at the wheel.

Tom Shaw rolls down the window. "Get in. Come on—hurry."

"Where's Jacqueline?"

His gaze grows somber. "She wasn't well enough to drive. Now please, before you catch pneumonia in this rain and die."

Wouldn't that be the easy way out? Reluctantly, I open the door on the passenger side and get in. My clothes drip murky rainwater all over the seat.

"Good. It wouldn't be very nice of you to refuse, since I'm the one who posted your bail."

I'm too astonished to speak when he takes off into the curtain of rain.

The summer residence is less than an hour outside the

city limits. The trees on the sides of the highway become taller and the road itself more deserted. Shaw doesn't speak, and it's better that way. I have no idea what I'd say to him. I don't know where I'd even start.

"Jacqueline is sure you're innocent," he says as he takes an exit ramp. The road gives way to a narrower street, then another and another. We're going in zigzags. Here and there, I glimpse luxury homes through the trees. At this time of year, they stand empty and dark.

What about you? I almost ask.

"This thing has been really hard on her," he says by way of explanation. "I can't really blame her if she's starting to lose her head."

And there I have it, my answer. "You really think I'd do something like that?"

He gives an infuriating shrug.

The last lane is the longest, a stretch of unpaved gravel road that dwindles to nothing between the trees. The house itself rises out of the evergreens, one of those modern constructions where the entire front is made of glass. Only one light is on inside, gleaming like a dull star through the branches.

"I had this place built for Olivia, you know," he says, and his voice cracks, skipping over her name. "Right after we adopted her. I was thinking a lake house, but Jackie didn't want to. Too afraid Olivia might drown." He shakes his head, chuckling bitterly. "What a joke, right?"

I'm stricken speechless.

"All for her, so she could have the best of everything. Do you know what it's like to love someone? Really love them, not just in words."

We get out, and he starts toward the house without glancing over his shoulder to see if I'm following. The rain has slowed down, and the silence is deafening. I've never been outside the city before, I realize. I've never been in a place this quiet. No hum of cars, no distant sirens. It's almost quiet enough to be eerie. Just steps and the whisper of rain...

"When it's not cloudy, you can see all the stars," Shaw says as he unlocks the front door. I follow him in. "I regret now that we never really spent time here. Olivia hated it, said it was boring. She always wanted to go back to the city after only a day or two."

I attempt to speak again, but he cuts me off. "Kids these days, right? You give them everything, and they just ask for more."

He turns on the light, and it fills the space with a warm glow. It's lovely with a large, open living room, an arched doorway into a long hall, and a winding staircase that leads to a second level. Everything is done in warm-toned polished wood, like you'd expect in a place like this. It smells dusty, a bit damp—unlived in.

"Jacqueline," I speak up. My voice echoes uncannily. "She said she had to tell me something when she called. She said it was about Olivia."

Tom's face falls. He rubs his eyes and pinches the bridge of his nose, and my heart drops.

"There's nothing to tell. There weren't any new developments, sadly. She just knew it would sway you when nothing else did."

The bad feeling that's been coiled in my chest for a while rears its head. "Is she okay?"

"Not exactly," he says, his gaze heavy. "You see, she's had problems in the past. She was stable most of the time, but then, with Olivia's disappearance, it went downhill fast. She had to start taking medication again."

"Medication?" I choke out. I think of the elegant, coiffed, tiny woman who held me in her arms like I was her own daughter. Nothing makes sense.

"She's been having episodes. But I wanted so badly to keep it low profile. There's been so much press around us already, and if this got out, you can imagine. Vultures."

I stare at him blankly, still uncomprehending.

"They'd go as far as accusing her of kidnapping her own daughter," he says, not so much to me as at me. "Call her crazy. A pillhead. So I would really appreciate if you kept what I just told you to yourself, okay?"

I'm not sure what exactly he expects me to do with the information. Sell it to a paparazzo?

"I know you two grew close."

I can hardly call it growing close. She came to pick me up once, when I had no one else to call. "No," I say.

"I'm so sorry. I can only imagine how hard this must be for you, even without my wife adding to it."

I'm shivering again. He heaves a sigh.

"Ugh. I completely forgot. I'm rambling on, and you're freezing. Let me get you something to change into."

He shows me to the bathroom while I try to keep my teeth from clattering too violently. I notice that all the pictures have been taken off the walls here too. Poor Jacqueline.

Once the door is closed and I've made sure the latch is turned, I towel off my hair and change into an enormous, fluffy bathrobe, one of Jacqueline's. I wring out my socks and leave them on the edge of the bathtub, next to the disgusting wet pile of jeans and sweatshirt, and then wriggle my bare feet into the cold, damp leather confines of my boots. Taking my phone and knife from my ruined jacket's pocket, I put my phone in one boot and slide my knife into the other, snug against my calf.

Outside, Tom Shaw waits for me with a tumbler in each hand, filled halfway with something amber and aromatic. "I figured you could use something to warm up."

The smell alone is enough to warm my clenched, frozen insides, but I shake my head. "No. I don't. Thanks."

"I know you're not a teetotaler. And we both deserve this."

His smile is a touch too tense. He doesn't like to be told no. Suddenly I feel hyperaware of the fact that I'm wearing his wife's bathrobe and underneath I'm completely naked except for my underwear.

He takes a swig of the amber liquor. I only take a tiny sip, but it burns all the way down, making me sputter.

"What's wrong with her?" I blurt. "With Jacqueline."

He looks surprised for a moment then collects himself. "I just told you. Please be discreet..."

"What do you mean, she has episodes? You didn't tell me anything."

"No offense, but I don't feel comfortable discussing this with you."

"And if she's sick, I can talk about it with her, in person," I say. "I won't bother her for long. I just want to make sure she's all right."

"She took her medication, and she's asleep."

"You pumped her full of meds." It's not a question. "That's your solution to everything. When someone doesn't behave the way you want them to, give them a pill."

"I'm really not interested in your opinion," he says coldly.

"Then why did you bring me here? Just take me back. Drop me somewhere on the side of a highway."

He looks at me for a few long moments, his face unreadable. Then he shakes his head. "Fine," he says. "Fine. If you insist. You can see her—she's fast asleep, so just try not to disturb her."

I follow him down the hall, to the door at the very end.

"You know what I regret?" he says as he holds the door open just a crack. All I can see over his shoulder is darkness. "I regret getting you involved in this to begin with. I was hoping you could be at least marginally useful in helping me find my daughter. All you did was screw up things with my wife."

I bite back the scathing words at the tip of my tongue.

"And you know what else I regret? Having adopted her. It was stupid of me to hope she'd turn out different. I mean, just look at her mother."

"You—" My hands curl into fists. I start to say something, but at that moment, he swings the door open, its dark maw gaping, and sidesteps me. Before I can realize what's happening, he gives me a shove in the back, hard enough to knock me off-balance. Darkness rushes toward me and I topple into emptiness until a flight of stairs breaks my fall. Pain lances my arm, my shoulder, my ribs, but my scream dies in my throat. I tumble for what feels like an eternity, my hip, my side, my head connecting with sharp edges until finally I sprawl on the floor.

Everything reels before my vision as I struggle to press myself up with my arms. My whole body hurts, and the ringing in my ears rises in pitch, drowning out everything. As my eyes start to get used to the dark, I make out another figure, crouched by the wall, terrified. When I try to speak or scream, my voice won't obey me, and my lips grow numb, followed by everything else.

Thunder rumbles above my head, growing nearer and nearer, and I squeeze my eyes shut. And then a kick in my bruised ribs, a kick that knocks the air out of my lungs. Pain shoots up my spine to explode between my ears. The bitter bile of the alcohol I'd just drunk wells up in my throat, scorching everything in its way, and sputters out of my mouth and nose. Everything is on fire; my eyes water as I retch and retch until my stomach is empty and shriveled. As soon as I stop, another kick sends me flying onto my side. The sour reek of vomit fills my nostrils.

Through all that hell, I hear Tom Shaw speak somewhere far above.

"Enough playing around. Time to get talking. Tell me—where did you hide her? Where did you hide my daughter, you cunt?"

And that's when I recognize the voice.

CHAPTER THIRTY-FOUR

I roll over onto my hands and knees, but the room won't stop spinning. Every breath is a fight. Through my blurring vision, I recognize the figure crouched next to the wall: Jacqueline. She's hugging her knees, and her eyes are dark and enormous in her pale face.

She murmurs something, and at first I can't understand what she's saying. "I'm so sorry," she sobs, her hand clasped over her mouth. I notice that her other wrist is cuffed to a heater. "I'm so sorry, Lainey. He—he held a gun to my head."

My mind fractures. All the pieces of my short, miserable life spin in front of my eyes, finally—for the first time—falling into place.

Another wave of dizziness sweeps over me. My arms

tremble, my elbows give out, and I topple forward. My cheekbone hits the floor, and I choke on a cry of pain.

He grabs my shoulder in a vise grip and flips me over onto my back. A little more bile bubbles at my lips. You sick bastard, I try to say, but all that comes out is a hoarse rasp.

"Where is she?" he yells. Spittle flies from his lips. "I know you two bitches hid her somewhere. Well, one of you is going to talk!"

Underneath the sheer terror, underneath the flood of memories I struggled for ten years to forget, underneath the realization that I probably won't leave this room alive, relief fills my chest, manic and giddy. He doesn't have her. The monster doesn't have Olivia; he doesn't know where she is.

And he won't. I'll do everything I can to make sure of that, even if it costs me my life. This is the only thing I've ever been 100 percent sure of.

I turn my head, and Jacqueline's terrified face swims into view. "Leave her alone," she rasps. "She had nothing to do with this."

"Nothing to do with it? She's the one who started this whole mess."

His face is twisted with rage, his eyes bulging. He's completely out of his mind, so utterly lost in his delusions, convinced of his absolute right, that he can't hear how insane he sounds.

He leans over me, and deep down, a part of me withers in terror. He grabs my shoulders and pulls me up.

My head lolls, I can barely feel my face, and my arms and legs begin to tingle.

He gives me a shake. "Answer me, you good-for-nothing junkie bitch."

I want to spit in his face, tell him to go fuck himself, but my mouth refuses to form the words. His face blurs and turns into a leather mask. Primal terror shrieks within me, but when I blink, it turns back into Tom Shaw.

He collects himself, an easy smile floating on his lips. "At least the tranquilizer I gave you seems to be working. It was hard to find. I wanted one that would keep you awake and aware of everything, but unable to do anything about it. And by the time it wears off, trust me— you'll be ready to talk to me."

He lets go, and I crumble like a puppet with its strings cut. Pain shoots through my ankle and up my leg when it twists under me. An animal-like moan escapes from my lips.

He crouches over me, yanking away the robe. Icy, damp air hits my skin, making it crawl. He's straddling me, his weight pins me to the floor, crushing my rib cage, squeezing the air out of my lungs drop by drop.

Out of sheer instinct, the old but resilient instinct of a frightened little girl, I withdraw inside myself, as far as possible into my frail body, into the deepest recesses of my mind. But I'm not screaming. Instead, a cold resolve fills me, even as I struggle to draw a breath.

Even when he grinds on top of me. Even when he

leans close and I hear as much as feel his wet breath on the side of my face. He pants into my ear, and images flash before my eyes: Dark. Cold. Basement floor, rough under my naked body, abrading my skin. The bite of rope on my wrists and ankles.

I push the images away, but they crowd back in, every moment of those months resurrected from the depths of memory. He gropes for my breast, squeezes and twists my nipple. In my head, I cry out.

"You know, you're still attractive," he whispers into my ear. "You've still got it. A little old for me, but you still look like a child. I could manage one last time for you. What do you think?"

I sputter and choke. By my sides, my hands are working. I'm squeezing my fingers into a fist, a quarter of an inch at a time. They feel like lifeless, unwieldy sausages, but I force them. Little by little, my fingertips start to tingle. I clench my fists, relishing the pain of my nails cutting into my palms.

He starts to fumble with his trousers. I hear the clink of a belt buckle, then the hiss of a zipper, and when his image fades from my vision, I realize I've managed to close my eyes.

I force them open, force myself to look into his face. My tongue feels thick in my mouth, numb, and it takes me several tries to get the words out. "You won't find her."

He stops fumbling, and for a moment, his face comes into sharp focus. His smile widens, showing off those perfect teeth. "Oh, I will. Whether you tell me or not. I will find her, and then it'll only be worse for you."

"You're going to kill me anyway," I say. It feels like I'm talking through a mouthful of cotton.

"I should have killed you back then. Saved myself all the trouble."

My eyes burn, and I can't breathe, but this time it has nothing to do with the drug, nothing to do with him slowly crushing the life out of me. I don't realize I'm speaking until I hear the croak of my voice. "Why?"

"Why? Why didn't I kill you? Why indeed. I don't know. You were pregnant with my child." He shrugs again and sits up, wiping the sweat from his forehead. His face has gone blotchy.

And that's when it clicks in my head. The last piece of the puzzle that is my life falls into place, and the big picture is so sad and pathetic, so simple, a three-year-old could have figured it out. I can't believe it took me ten years, ten fucking years for it to finally download.

My life had meant nothing to him. I was less than an animal. He would have killed me like one steps on a bug, with little thought and even less remorse. The only thing that mattered to him was an agglomeration of cells buried in my flat child's stomach, cells that were part him. Those cells made the difference between my life and death. Let her go or kill her, strangle her, smother her, or slit her throat?

But those little cells mattered. So he decided to let me go and take my child when she was born.

I turn my head and see Jacqueline cowering at the edge of my vision, pressing herself into the wall. And I finally get the rest of it.

"Don't tell him," I say, and my voice cuts through, loud and clear. "Don't tell him a goddamn thing. He can't get his hands on her—he can't, okay?"

I only catch a glimpse of her face, twisted in terror, before his fist connects with my cheekbone. My head snaps to the side, and my vision explodes with black motes against blinding white.

The weight lifts off me, and for a brief moment, I can draw air into my lungs. Not nearly long enough. Next thing I know, his boot connects with my side, and pain lances my entire being. I curl up into a ball on the floor, blind, deaf, senseless.

When my head starts to clear, I hear his steps thundering away, finally away from me. I pry my right eye open; the left is swelling shut. He's leaning over Jacqueline, and she starts to scream her head off. He grabs her arm; the handcuff jangles against the pipe of the heater.

A tiny voice deep down is screaming at me to do something, but my limbs won't obey, my muscles weak and useless. I roll over and fumble with my boot. My fingers are still numb but I tug out the laces with all the agility I can muster.

Jacqueline is still screaming. I hear the dull thwack of fist against flesh and shudder with my whole body. *Don't look up. Don't look. It won't help her.*

I finally ease my phone out, clutching it with clumsy hands. It's running out of battery, but there's enough.

There has to be.

Please let there be enough.

Jacqueline lets out a shriek that slices across my eardrums, and I can't help it. My head snaps up, and my gaze meets hers. Her eyes are filled with pain and terror, locked on me. On the phone in my hands.

I only have time to give a frantic shake of my head. Look away, please look away, don't let on.

I'm too late. He spins around, zeroing in on the phone. I mash the Emergency Call button but don't have time to see if it works.

He's upon me in the blink of an eye, kicking the phone out of my hand. It goes flying, crashes into the wall, and skitters across the floor, far out of reach.

The next kick catches the side of my head, and the world explodes.

I can't see. I hear nothing but the deafening ringing in my ears, and my mouth fills with blood that drips down my throat, choking me. For a moment, I'm sure he broke something crucial, driven a shard of skull into my brain, and this is just agony.

Then the cold floor hits my cheek. I slowly come back to my body, panting for air, spitting blood, but before the pain can fade, he's pulling me up. I cough blood all over his face. He's yelling something, but I can't make out the words, bitch, cunt, stupid whore, something like that. He shakes me.

At the edge of my hearing, his voice is calm now. Deadly. "You wanted to die so badly? Well, you're about to get your wish."

He throws me against the wall, and more pain explodes in the back of my head, in my side. A cracked rib?

Through red fog, I see him reach behind his waist and come back with a gun. Its black eye points at me, level with my face.

In the background, Jacqueline screams at the top of her lungs, and for just a moment, he falters. He half turns, his gaze slipping from me to her—

I don't know where I find the stamina to move. I kick out with all the strength I can muster, slamming my boot into his shin.

The gunshot explodes inches away from my ear. He howls, falters, pinwheeling his arms, and topples backward. His head smacks against the concrete with a sickening thwack, and the gun flies out of his hand and clatters to the floor.

My right ear is filled with high-pitched ringing, and something wet runs down the side of my jaw. Disoriented, I slide to the floor and reach into my other boot where I find the smooth handle of my knife.

Just as he starts to scramble up, I flick the knife open and lunge for him. I'm still weak from the drug that I've ingested, but he's hurt too. Blood gushes from a cut at his hairline, streaming down his face and flooding his eyes.

He swings at me and misses. His eyes widen when I loom over him.

My wish? "I changed my mind, asshole. I'm not going to die. I'm going to kill you, and I'll dance on your grave."

And I drive the knife in, just above his collarbone where the veins are.

At first I'm terrified—did I stab hard enough, was the blade sharp enough? What if I screwed up, blew my only chance? But when I pull the knife out with a sickening sucking sound, red wells up, so much red, pulsing out in little bursts like a fountain. More of it in the corners of his mouth, turning to red foam. His hands scratch at the floor uselessly until he presses his palm over the wound, but it's not enough to staunch the flood.

Jacqueline is still screaming.

I push myself up to my feet, looking around for my phone until I see it, or what's left of it. I can't use it to call anyone anymore. I have to get out of here. I have to get upstairs. I have to call for help.

He flails, trying to crawl, and grabs for my ankle with his free hand. But even in my drugged-out, pained state, I sidestep him with ease. A steep stairwell leads up, back into the house. I start to climb but can't keep going after two steps. I get on my hands and knees, like an animal or a child, and crawl up. Toward the dark rectangle of the door.

Jacqueline's screams fill my ears.

I want to yell at her that I'm going to get help, that

I'm not leaving her down here, but I don't have the strength to speak. The inside of my cheek is swelling up quickly. I feel around with my tongue where he chipped my teeth. My nose might be broken too, because I can't breathe and all I smell is blood.

Only a little distance left to the door. I'm almost there.

The gun blast explodes at the same time as an unseen force slams me forward. My face connects with the stairs, and my vision explodes with red. What—

I can't see out of one eye. My cheekbone feels like it is cracked in two, and another, persistent ache is working its way into my shoulder blade. Like a bee sting.

The stinging spreads. Turns into fire. Something hot and sticky runs down my back. Oh fuck.

It drips down my legs. I look down and see shiny black drops on the stairs, almost invisible against the dark paint. I want to raise my hand, to feel my back, but it won't move. My arm hangs at my side, a limp piece of meat. And the numbness is spreading.

I turn and glimpse him crawling forward in a pool of blood. He's clutching the gun, but it slips from his fingers with a clatter. He grabs for it, pulls it toward him, but doesn't quite make it. His hand goes limp, twitches, then stops moving.

I turn back to the door. Only two, three steps away, and I realize I'll never get there. My eyes burn with the tears I won't get to cry.

Jacqueline is still screaming, but now it's not just that

inhuman wailing sound; it's words. A word. My name, over and over and over like a stuck record.

I want to tell her I'm okay. I want to tell her that he's dead, that it's over. But when I open my mouth, only a rasp comes out. So I do the only thing I can. I push myself forward and up. Forward and up.

One step. Two. I press against the floor with my good arm, and my jaws open in a silent howl of pain. Forward and up.

I reach for the door, push myself up, and manage to get on my knees and feel along the rough wooden surface until I find the handle. I turn it, and it swings open with the smooth whisper of oiled hinges.

The light of the hallway is enough to blind me, and I collapse onto the carpet, the softest, most comfortable thing in the world. All I want is to stay here, curl up, and rest. Maybe even close my eyes. But I can't, not yet; there are things I have to do. I need to find the phone. Where's the phone?

I crawl on my hands and knees, ignoring the pain that shoots through my arm with every movement. The door. The front door.

Tears pour from my one good eye and drip down my face, mingling with the blood.

The front door.

In the windows, lights flashing. Blue and red. Blue and red. I know what they mean, but I can't remember. My mind hurts.

The front door. It's not locked. He thought no one

would bother us. I get it open and topple onto the porch.

It's raining in a thick, solid wall of water that whispers against my skin, washing off the blood and tears and grime.

And, lying sprawled at the door of my kidnapper, of the father of my child, I start to laugh. I won't make it out of here. I spent the last ten years looking for death, and just when I stopped looking, death found me.

But at least *she* will be okay. She is a little girl and she has a name, Olivia. Why have I never thought of her like that? Olivia will be okay. Olivia is hidden someplace safe, and she'll be fine.

I barely hear the steps through the rain. Steps hurrying down the neat gravel path, splashing through the puddles. A shadow falls over me, blocking out the red-blue lights.

The shadow has a face. It's a face I know well. I've thought about this face on many lonely nights, nights of pain and despair and hopelessness, when it was my only ray of light to lead me out.

Maybe he's here to take me to heaven or hell or wherever the fuck I belong.

He's saying my name. His hands are brushing my hair out of my face, the blood, the rainwater, and he won't stop saying it, "Laine, Laine, Laine. Please. Stay with me. Please, Laine. Please don't go."

I don't care if I go or not. There are three things I need to say to him first. I can't go until I do.

First, I love you. You're a manipulative bastard, but I love you anyway. It's stronger than me.

Second, it's Ella. It's Ella fucking Santos. I may not like it, but I'm not dying with a fake name. No way.

And the third one is, I'm sorry.

But I don't have time to say any of these things. Darkness pulls me in, wraps me in a cocoon of painless bliss, swallows me up.

And I am no more.

CHAPTER THIRTY-FIVE

I wake up.

Not in heaven or in hell. I'm still not convinced I believe in that stuff. There's heaven and hell on earth in abundance—I should know; I'm intimately familiar with them both.

And this isn't it. This is a hospital. I stay in that hospital for many weeks.

It's not like the other hospitals I've been in. Here I have my own room with a big window with no bars, and a view of a garden that I discovered when I was well enough to get out of bed. A little garden with lilacs and a fountain in the middle. The lilacs are blooming right now. If I get the nurse to open the window, the aroma wafts into the room, and it's almost enough to mask the stink of disinfectant and medicine.

Almost. This is a hospital, after all. No matter how private or fancy or expensive.

Besides the daily physiotherapy that's supposed to make my left arm work normally again, I'm doing addiction therapy. I shit you not—that's what they call rehab here.

When I got well enough to understand, they told me what I was like when they brought me in. Besides my injuries, I was severely dehydrated, and my vital organs were this close to failing because of all the drugs. And Tom Shaw didn't do this to me; I did it to myself. I'd be lying if I said it wasn't sobering.

It occurred to me that maybe, just maybe, I *was* tarnished. But not by what Tom Shaw did to me, now or thirteen years ago—by what I did to myself over these ten years. I thought finding my captor would redeem me, but I was wrong. The only person who could make me shine again was me.

I haven't seen Sean. Not since that night, since the blood and the rain and the red-blue lights. He hasn't visited. Just like ten years ago. I can't blame him.

Jacqueline, however, comes to see me every day. She's unofficially adopted me, I think. She brings me treats that the hospital won't allow, Twizzlers and soda, and romance novels that I pretend to read out of politeness. It's Jacqueline who's paying for the whole thing, for the fancy private clinic, for the "addiction therapists" who treat me with kid gloves.

Sean had made Sugar crack and admit I didn't give him

the laptop—a man did, a man who closely met the description of Tom Shaw. Without wasting another minute, he sent cop cars to the Shaws' residence, and when he realized they were gone, he rushed to their summerhouse.

Olivia was safe this whole time, hidden away with Jacqueline's mother. Jacinta was the one who helped Olivia get away. Before Olivia was born, when Jacinta was her age, Tom Shaw abused her too. When Jacqueline told Jacinta she suspected he was molesting Olivia, Jacinta broke down and told her everything. They put together the plan.

Jacqueline didn't dare publicly accuse Tom. She was afraid of what he'd do to her and to her daughter and sister. She never guessed, she told me, crying, that it would turn out like this.

I will never know now exactly how much my mother knew, whether she merely had her suspicions or whether she recognized Tom Shaw. Just like I will never know the real reason she pulled the trigger—was she genuinely sorry for what she'd done or simply afraid of the consequences?

I'm trying to think it was the former. It's something I need to learn to believe.

A week or so after I got transferred to the rehab—sorry, addiction therapy—facilities, Jacqueline brought Olivia to visit. I wasn't exactly brimming with enthusiasm at the idea, but it went okay. The moment she walked in, with a lost and somewhat bewildered look on her face, I knew it was going to be okay.

Jacqueline hadn't told her who exactly I was yet, hadn't explained the whole sordid story to her—that's a lot for a little girl to understand, and she'd already been through enough. But her mother won't be able to shelter her from it forever. Too much has already been leaked to the press, so much that Jacqueline is considering moving someplace quiet for a couple of years. Until Olivia is old enough to understand.

I looked into her serious, pale-gray eyes and knew that her life wasn't going to be easy. Her father was a monster, her biological mother his victim. He'd already done things to her no child should have to endure. For all the private schools and nannies and toys, for all the things money can buy, her childhood was not what it should have been.

And knowing it, I looked her in the eyes and finally stopped resenting her—after all these years. I know it's selfish, I know it's shitty of me, but what can I do? I'm just a normal person, and like most people, I'm flawed. If nothing else, my "addiction therapy" finally ingrained that into my stubborn head. But that day, for the first time, I didn't regret giving birth to her. Not even a little bit.

Olivia looked at me silently, her lips pressed together, surely puzzling things out in her head already. She isn't dumb, this much her teachers were right about. She ignored Jacqueline when she prompted her to come closer and say hi. She just stood there, at a cautious distance, and studied me with those mistrustful eyes.

I didn't know what to say to her until the end, when it was almost time to leave. I got up and crossed the distance between us.

The girl was going to be tall, I could already tell. I only had to lean down a bit to be at her eye level, and she didn't back away.

That's when I finally found my words. "Don't let anyone tell you that you're tarnished," I said. "Ever. Fuck what anyone thinks. You shine—you got that? You shine."

I can only hope that's enough to get her through everything that lies ahead.

*   *   *

I'm released in early July. Jacqueline is supposed to come get me at noon; in the meantime, I pack my meager belongings into a duffel bag with the hospital logo, one they gave me at reception. That's technically all I have to my name. Talk about starting fresh.

In the last weeks, I've developed a habit of getting up early. First because the nurses woke me, and later because I started to wake up by myself. So I spend the long hours of the morning hanging around the central garden, walking down narrow twisting paths among groves of lilacs. I sit on a bench across from the fountain, my legs curled up under me, and watch the water sparkle in the rare sunshine.

I'm almost going to miss this place. Almost.

Absorbed in the hypnotizing sound of water, I don't immediately hear the footfalls on the gravel behind me. At first I think it's one of the nurses and don't turn around. The steps stop a few feet behind me, but whoever it is doesn't speak.

Maybe it's just curiosity, or old instincts rearing their head, but I turn and glance over my shoulder, lowering my feet to the ground, ready to bolt just in case.

My heart soars, and a lump forms in my throat. Sean is standing behind the bench, just a few feet away. He squints in the sun, his hands in his pockets. He's wearing old jeans and a T-shirt, not his work clothes.

"What...are you doing here?" I stammer. "Jacqueline..."

"She'll show up when she said she would. I just wanted to see you first." He raises his eyebrows questioningly. I finally clue in and nod at the bench next to me, inviting him to sit—even though deep down, I'm not so sure it's a good idea. The thought of him being so close...You can't offer a former addict to sit next to a fix and expect her not to be tempted.

Maybe he understands that, because he stops a few steps away.

I feel my face flush. "I'm sorry," I murmur. "I was supposed to call you. For my...for my program. I'm supposed to apologize to everyone I've hurt."

His answer is a soft, sad chuckle. "You? You haven't hurt anyone. People have hurt you."

"Exactly. They made me understand it was just an excuse, my reason for being shitty to everyone and not being sorry."

"I haven't exactly been an angel either," he points out.

"You saved me. Twice."

"You saved yourself. I was just . . . there. I should have figured it out sooner. I should have called you. Warned you. It might never have happened."

"And we might never have caught him," I say. All these months later, talking about it still hurts. Every word echoes the pain in my head, in my back, in my arm. In every rib Shaw had cracked.

He sighs. "I don't know how to thank you. You have no idea."

"Then don't," I say. I think of Olivia's serious face. Of the tears in Jacqueline's eyes when I spoke to her. "Don't thank me. I don't want credit. For that or anything else."

"You have your life back now," he remarks.

"Yeah," I say grimly. "Not much of a life. I basically have to start from scratch."

"A lot of people would kill to be able to start from scratch."

I get up from the bench. Glancing down at my hands, I realize with a rush of self-consciousness that I'm not wearing long sleeves or armbands or bracelets. I haven't in weeks. And until now, I seemed to have forgotten about my scars altogether.

They're still there, of course, raised pink welts an inch thick circling my wrists. A lifetime souvenir of Tom Shaw, along with a ragged star-shaped scar on my left shoulder blade, a chipped tooth, ribs that ache when it rains, which means basically all the time...

I'm going to stop there. What's the use? Everyone has scars. Even if they're not on the outside.

When I glance up, he's looking at my wrists too. He lowers his chin, embarrassed. "Are you changing your name back to Ella Santos now?"

I shrug. "I don't know. To be honest, I'm kind of used to Laine."

The silence wears on. I listen to him breathe like it might give me some kind of clue to what he's thinking, what he's feeling.

"Are you...are you okay?" he finally asks. "Do you need help? You're released soon. Do you have a place to go?"

"Yes," I say quickly. "Jacqueline, she's arranged everything for me. For as long as I need it. Until I get back on my feet."

For a while, he's quiet. "Good," he finally says. "Good."

"You don't need to worry about me anymore," I say. My turn to be generous. My turn to let him go. He no longer has to save me. From here on, I'll save myself.

"I'll always worry about you," he says.

"Really?" I say, and my voice suddenly turns hoarse. "Then you could have visited."

"I did. For the first week and a half when you were unconscious, I came by every day and stayed for hours."

My heart clenches. It hurts so much I can't stand still.

I want to double over and weep. It hurts more than being shot. "No one told me," I whisper.

"Did you ask?"

No. I didn't; I just assumed, because of everything that happened between us. Because I always think the worst of people.

"And then I talked to Jacqueline every day. She still hates me, but she was understanding. She gave me updates. You were walking again, your arm was starting to move again. You went out into the garden by yourself. You were being moved to the other wing. Everything."

"You could have just shown up."

"I didn't think . . . I didn't think it would be good for you. I wanted to let you have your life."

"So why are you here now?"

His smile is full of sadness. "I wanted to ask you for forgiveness."

"You? You didn't do anything wrong."

"Yes, I did. And you know it. You have every right to hate me."

A sigh escapes through my clenched teeth, and I think I might start crying. "I don't hate you. I could never . . ."

"I fucked up your life."

"You saved it. And I'm not talking about the Shaws, or ten years ago."

"Does that mean you forgive me?"

"Of course I forgive you." The words well up at the tip of my tongue like blood in a cut, and I can't stop them. "You were my only light. For years."

"And you will have other lights now. Many of them."

"I hope so."

"You will. I promise."

This time, I know they're not just hollow words of comfort. He means them.

He starts to leave, and I watch him go, surprisingly calm. As he's about to turn a corner and vanish from sight, he turns around and gives a short wave of his hand. I wave back. The sun blinds me, and I can't see his face clearly, but I know he's smiling.

Thank you for being in my life. I can move on now. I'm free.

Nothing about this will be easy, but then again, nothing worth having ever is. I'm in an unfamiliar place, starting my life over in many ways. I have a family now, people who care about me, and it's more than I ever could have hoped for. So that's something. There are things I know I will still struggle with for a long time, maybe for the rest of my life. Certain scars just aren't going anywhere.

But right here, right now, in this moment, I am shining.

ACKNOWLEDGMENTS

First, thank you to my wonderful agent, Rachel Ekstrom, who took this book from slush pile to bookstore and who believed in me all along. Thank you also to Brita Lundberg and the team at Irene Goodman Literary Agency.

Thank you to everyone at Grand Central and especially to Alex Logan, my editor, for giving me a chance.

Books don't appear in a vacuum, so thanks also go to the people who were there for me throughout the lengthy process of writing, editing, querying, and everything in between: Margarita Montimore for listening to me rant, Maude Michaud and everyone at The Ladies for the encouragement and camaraderie (and wine), as well as Alana James, Nisha Sharma, Marie-Pierre, and Jessica—my A-Team. Thank you to Kim Graff and Lauren Spieller for the editorial input at the earliest stages. Thank you to Patrick, my love, for putting up with me during the many ups and downs of this process. Thank you to my creative-writing profs at Concordia—Trevor, Sina, Tess, and Mikhail—and to my other profs for not failing me at times when I neglected my course work in favor of this novel. Thanks to everyone in the creative-writing workshops. Finally, thank you to my parents and extended family—even if you never read a word I write, I'm cool with it. No, really.

Also by Nina Laurin

THE STARTER WIFE

Claire Westcott tries to be the perfect wife to Byron but fears she will never measure up to his ex, Colleen. After all, it's hard to compete with the dead.

Colleen disappeared eight years ago. Her body was never found but the police ruled it a suicide. So when Claire receives a phone call from a woman she believes is Colleen, it opens up a million terrifying questions.

Claire discovers the couple weren't as happy as they would have people believe. And now she's worried Byron hasn't been completely honest with her.

There are secrets in every marriage, but Claire is about to find out that sometimes those secrets are deadly.

Out now in paperback and ebook.

MULHOLLAND
BOOKS
HODDER

Also by Nina Laurin

WHAT MY SISTER KNEW

". . . currently wanted by the police. If you know anything about the suspect's whereabouts, please call . . ."

I look up at the TV screen, and my twin brother's face is splashed across it, life-size.

It's a shock that makes my breath catch. This is my brother as an adult, my brother who I last saw fifteen years ago after the fire that killed our parents, covered in soot, clutching a lighter in his hand, his knuckles stark white against the dirt and ash.

Everyone always said he'd grow up to be a heartbreaker. But his face has gone gaunt instead. The stubble on his cheeks and chin is patchy, and his eyes look dull and dark.

My first thought is that it's not him. Not my beautiful brother, the golden boy who everyone loved. Yet, deep down, I've always known this would eventually happen.

What did you do this time, Eli? What the hell did you do?

Coming soon in paperback and ebook.

MULHOLLAND
BOOKS
HODDER